From Pavlova to Pork Pies

From New Zealand to England looking
for love, laughs and the way home

Vicki Jeffels

Writer's Cat

Auckland New Zealand

pav@writerscat.com
Writer's Cat
www.writerscat.com

The extract from The Wasteland is used under the Gutenberg Project's license - http://www.gutenberg.org/files/1321/1321-h/1321-h.htm

Book Layout ©2015 BookDesignTemplates.com

Ordering Information:
Quantity sales. Special discounts are available on quantity purchases by corporations, associations, and others. For details, contact the 'Special Sales Department' at the address above.

From Pavlova to Pork Pies/ Vicki Jeffels. -- 1st ed.
ISBN 978-0-473-369354

Contents

Dedication

For Mark, Oliver, Hilary, and Felicity - all my gratitude for your support. For Mum, Dad, Kim, Ally and the cuzzies and for the family I chose for myself - my friends - thank-you for your encouragement
Love you all. Vx

Faith, hope, love, these three,

But the greatest of these, is love..

—13TH CHAPT. I. CORINTHIANS

CHAPTER I

RUNNING AWAY

'JUST AS LONG as you realise that's it.' Her mother's Australian accent is emphatic down the phone.

'It?' Meg asks.

'No man's going to want to take on another man's three children.'

End of story?

'I'm not going to Europe to find a man Mum. I'm going to look after Catherine's kids...and to see Europe finally... and to have a break...Anyway... I can't live my life through the kids. I can't become a nun.'

Is that it? Exit one wedding band, and enter one nun's habit? Throw yourself into a cell and take up cat-fur knitting? Megan wonders angrily.

When she first split from her husband, it hadn't been that hard to find admirers. She'd had all kinds of lascivious invitations from all sorts of men. Husbands, boyfriends of friends, even the sodding lawnmower man. But love? Maybe that was a completely different confidence trick. Maybe, that *was* it. Meg couldn't believe it.

She hadn't been careless or completely lacking in morals in the two years since she'd asked her husband to leave, she'd been choosy, but she had also been lonely and so she had partied and kissed and cuddled her sorrows away. She'd made just enough mistakes to be aware that finding another love could be difficult.

If not impossible.

There was hardly a queue forming to sweep a 38-year-old somewhat under-tall, mother of three, pet-owner of two, off her feet.

Mum's still talking.

Meg pulls a face and thanks God that video phones are not yet in general usage.

'...I just don't want you to be disappointed...'

'Ha! Disappointed! You said that 15 years ago!'

'Yes, well maybe you should have listened.'

Meg's cheeks burned.

'It wasn't all a gigantic mistake Mum. I did try hard to make it work...What about Alex, Sarah and Jayne? I wouldn't have had the kids without him...'

'Well yes, exactly. Wait a few years when they've left home and then you can find someone.'

'That's at least ten years away! Anyway, Mum, I'm going to Europe to have some time to myself, I'm not going on a man hunt!'

Or a Bear Hunt. Wishy washy, wishy washy.

'Right now, I don't want to go at all!' She sniffed a little.

'Oh listen, Meg, they will be OK. They'll have a good time. He's their father!'

Images of Darth Vader flashed across her mind.

'It'll do them good. Just don't think you're going to find the man of your dreams in Paris or something. I think you need to be a little more realistic than that!'

'Yes, Mum. Uh huh. I won't. I mean, I will... I will be more realistic than that.'

Yes, Mum, I get it. Too fat, too tired, too old, too many stretch marks, too many attachments. I know, I know.

She's still talking, oblivious to Meg's raised hackles.

'When I was in England it was very cold you know....'

'But it'll be summer Mum!'

'Yes it was summer then too and I still had to take a decent coat...'

Even Auckland, New Zealand was too cold for her Australian mother.

'Yes Mum, thanks. I'm sure I'll be OK... I'm quite tough...'

'You will be safe won't you, with all those terrorists running around...'

'Yes Mum I will. I won't get blown up by terrorists...'

'But they're everywhere. You can't just blindly wander about you know...'

'Yes Mum, I know. Yes. I know. Mum... I'd better go now...'

'Why don't you have a bath Meg? It will calm you down and might even help you sleep on the plane.'

She didn't have time for a bath. But then, if she didn't start breathing sometime soon she wouldn't make the plane.

'Yes Mum. That's a good idea.' (And a perfect break in the conversation) 'Love you. I'd better go now.'

'It's just, I do worry Meg,'

'I know Mum, I know...I'll go and have a bath. Bye.... love you...I will send you an email when I get there...bye...'

She called off.

'Arrrgh!'

Why do mothers do that?

Yes, OK you could say that from time to time, she hadn't really taken care of herself. She was exhausted and nervy. She knew she hadn't behaved terribly well. She'd been shipwrecked many a night down at the local The Pond in Mission Bay. At first it had been fun. Liberating even. As if someone had woken her up to living with a great big slap, and told her; 'Get on with it'. That she better get her arse into gear and have a life, before that life was over. But then, she had tired of it. It wasn't her. Dating, as a 38-year-old! Pah! Who needed the grief?

But that didn't mean that she deserved to be punished by a life of solitude. Did it?

Problem was that she'd married and settled down at 23-year-old and hadn't learnt the ropes of modern dating. Let alone online dating. She'd gone back out 'onto the market' as a 38-year-old ingénue and made some appalling hands-in-the-air mistakes. Then, over time, what had once been so hilarious and a little bit sexy, became humourless.

She was just another one of the used-up people put out in the recycling.

Free to good home, slightly used, vaguely broken, somewhat cynical but essentially a good woman...with pets, and kids and baggage...

She walked into the kitchen. The ceiling was perpetually wet around the range hood and it was now starting to crumble. The rain soaked through whenever there was a hard blow. Every time the Auckland storms came, she'd fret that they'd lose the roof. They had lost the back fence in a storm only last month. It had ended up on the neighbour's doorstep and poked half-way through his cat flap. He hadn't been very impressed, but she'd felt invincible fighting the elements in her white fluffy dressing gown, reclaiming the fence posts with rain dribbling down the back of her neck.

I am Survival Woman! Hear me roar. Though probably more likely, meow with intent.

She raised the bottle of merlot to refill her wine glass. Mood enhancer was often required after talks with Mum, especially this last night at home. This last night, before the big trip.

'This is my blood given for you.'

All those goblets of Christ's blood she'd slurped down over the years. In the Pentecostal church in the Dunedin of university days, it had been Ribena; thick and syrupy, like the service itself. The women dressed in smiles and pearls, each as fake as each other. The men in their skinny leather ties carrying their God-given authority like a patriarchal cape; flouncing about knocking demons and impertinent women off their pedestals. In the churches of Scotland and England that followed the Pentecostal quest, it had been the real McCoy, real wine. Claret perhaps? She'd often wondered if it would be rude to ask for a second serving.

She certainly could do with some right now. Passing the mirror above the fireplace her reflection stared back - a hollow exhausted stare. She should be spending the money on the house, or the kids, but she was spending it on running away. It was ridiculous. *She* was ridiculous.

What kind of woman runs away and leaves her children behind?

Gulping back rising panic, she sat down on the couch in front of the fire. It had been sneaky to get the gas fire installed before she'd given him the ultimatum to leave. But then when you're leaving your husband you do need to think things through. She'd been thinking them through for at least ten of those 16 married years.

Such a very long time to be unhappy.

The fire is deliciously warm. So this old backpacker is finally getting to London after 20 years of trying! *Oh God, will the kids be ok?*

'But he's their father Meg, for God's sake' Ally had said adamantly. Everyone had said it *adamantly*. Everyone except Mum, who'd said 'you'll never find another man'. The irritation engulfed her once again. She wasn't going to Europe to find a man. She was going to Europe to help Catherine with the kids and to get some distance between herself, her new life and this sad old shell of an old life.

Earlier that evening, standing at the top of the drive as her ex-husband unceremoniously placed the kids' bags into the boot of his silver BMW, seven-year-old Jayne had thrown herself into her arms clumsily thumping her back with her chewed Bearie.

'Mummy, I'm going to miss you.' She jutted out her lower lip.

'Aww, but you're going to have great fun with Dad! Won't she Alex?' Her eldest son grimaced a little in the dark cool June evening. He was so pale that even in the low light she could play dot-to-dot with his freckles.

'Yeah.' He wasn't convinced.

She couldn't watch the car snake down the driveway, instead she'd turned shaking and tearful, walked up the stairs, yelling behind her - so very cheerfully - 'bye'.

No one tells you that. They talk about love and marriage and raising kids. They never mention the bone-chilling vulnerability that comes when you realise that all of a sudden you are utterly dependent on this man, to bring home the bacon, to remain loyal for at least as long as it takes to raise your children.

What if I never come back? What if terrorists blow me up in the Underground, or hijack the plane? What if he kills the kids driving like a maniac on the Desert Road?

Knocking back the rest of the wine she dragged herself off to the bath. The wine hadn't worked, maybe Mum was right and a warm bubble bath would do the trick.

So, so tired and I haven't even started on the 30-hour plane trip! I haven't even begun my month away from my home, my kids, my pets and all the security I've cobbled together over the past two years. Bailey's come to check on me. The bath bubbles dot her black whiskers and she looks impossibly cute.

Meg is crying now, adding to the tub a ladle full of snotty, soupy despair.

'I don't want to go,' she's sobbing. 'I don't want to leave them.'

Reason has floated away on a burst bubble. Big strong woman no longer roaring, nor meowing, with or without intent.

It's too late now. In four hours' time, I will be on that plane flying to Australia and then to the other side of the world for a month.

She dips her head under the water, holding her breath.

In.

She can only hear the pinging of bubbles as they burst. She's not thinking, she's just there – suspended in time and space.

NO thinking.

Just breathing.

In.

The cold tap's dripping in time with her heart beats. It must be time to go now.

Out.

The gigantic bubble on her belly burst suddenly, white froth revealing the silvered stretchmarks underlining her belly-button. She'd told Jayne that she would be OK then too, that her belly-button was just taking a bit of a trip; that it would be cut out and moved just a bit further down her stomach. She'd been right mainly; she had been OK. In the end.

It was funny how at the same time she'd been so wrong, too. Until two years ago she'd always thought that it was the surgeon who was the god in charge, but experience had shown her that wasn't so. When an operation is about to begin everyone waits for the anaesthetist. Even the surgeon. Everyone waits until the one who is entrusted with ushering the breath through the void between life and death, is ready.

Everything had changed for her after her operation. Somewhere in the halls of limbo overcome by anaesthesia she had forgotten her way home. Oh yes, she'd come back to them, but she had changed. She asked him to leave four months later.

But she'd not forgotten the lesson. If only she could keep remembering how to breathe she would be fine.

In.

Out.

No heart flips, or white blood coursing through veins as taut as violin strings.

Just in and out.

And follow your breath, your heart, back home.

She dresses carefully, checks her luggage, passport, money and phone for the fourth time and then drags the trolley case down the stairs to the waiting taxi. As the taxi drives down St Heliers' hill and through the dark deserted streets of Glen Innes and out to the airport at Manukau she grants herself permission to feel a little excited.

I'm going to see Europe and England, and when I see the kids again, we'll all be in a better place. Maybe they'll learn to enjoy each other whilst I'm away? In fact, I'm really giving them a gift - some time to work out their relationship with their father without my interference.

She won't think of Jayne's tears.

She will banish the image of Bearie's chewed ears and beige fur – once a pristine Mothercare bear, now dirtied by seven-year-old love - from her mind. Alex had been matter of fact, his shoulders far too narrow to carry all that sadness, all that responsibility. Sarah had been as stoic as an Amazon. Ever her mother's daughter - fearless until you dig down or you confront her in the bathroom at 2am in the morning when the tidal wave of panic overwhelms.

'Just over there, mate, thanks.'

The taxi driver pulled the Toyota Camry with the velour covered seats into the loading bay outside the Departures Terminal by a sign for Singapore Airlines.

'How much?'

'That's $86.'

Bloody hell, that's a lot of money.

'Do you need a receipt?'

'Er, yes please. I guess I'll write it off for business expenses.'

Well Catherine's family are paying me to fly with the kids to England!

Not the typical income her marketing consultancy raised, but income nevertheless. When Catherine had contacted her out of the blue from Brisbane and asked her to chaperone the children to London all expenses paid, stupidly Meg had hesitated. But then she had reasoned that the trip would give her a chance to turn the corner and face the next step of her sudden single-dom – learning to live alone, to be the only one leading her little family. The one responsible for making the school lunches as well as taking out the rubbish bin.

She hated taking out the rubbish bin. He hated, hating taking out the rubbish bin. She should be stronger than that.

The driver handed over the receipt and leapt out to take her bag from the corporate cab's boot. She shouldn't have paid for a corporate cab, it was a self-indulgent hangover from when she'd lapped up Koru club travel, business class flights and hotel breakfasts. Back then, when she was someone.

'There you go love. Have a good flight eh! Give us a call when you come back and I'll meet you at the airport! When are you coming back?'

'Four weeks.'

I AM coming back. I am.

The airport forecourt is eerily quiet in the pre-dawn dark. A cool breeze laced with an agricultural smell – manure and mud - checks in with her through the automatic doors. If you listen carefully you can even hear the sound of cows mooing in the paddocks just past the airport rental car yards. There was barely even a queue as she waited to check-in.

She watches on as a man kisses goodbye his wife and baby. The woman is wearing a huge diamond ring on her wedding finger and the baby's red-cheeked giggles cut through the somnambulistic haze.

She turns her head away from the display of domestic bliss. They may as well have just cut her throat and left her bleeding on the carpet tiles.

My ring had never been that big, but it had been pretty, small but sparkly, until the day the diamond dislodged and swept down the bath plug-hole. Nine months later that's where my marriage went. Out with the waste water.

'Did you pack these bags yourself?' The Singapore Airlines girl asked conscientiously.

Seriously, if I hadn't done so, would I really say?

'Yes.'

'And are you carrying a parcel on behalf of anyone else?'

An AK47 and a packet of C4 under my woollen wrap. Really!

'No.'

The Singapore Girl checked her passport photo. Yes, there she was lifted from the page, standing in front of her. Dark eyes, dark long curly hair (naturally, not permed. She'd done that once in despair at a breakup. She always did weird things to her hair during breakups) a round face with a thick chin and a small rounded nose. Thankfully this time round her hair had remained pretty much unscathed. Her body though, well that was a different story.

Earlier this week she'd bumped into an old acquaintance from the kids' school and she'd commented on how much weight Meg had lost. 'You look great Meg, what's your secret? What have you been doing?'

'I left my husband' she'd drily informed her.

'Boarding will be at about 7:15. Have a good flight,' the Singapore Girl told her.

Meg lifted her head and walked down past the other check-ins, up the escalator and without looking behind her, passed through into the departure lounge.

Meg smiled a self-satisfied smile in the airport departure lounge, she was finally doing it again. Backpacking! Albeit not with a backpack this time, but with a purple polka dotted trolley case (won't miss that on the baggage carousel) and a red mohair wrap her best friend Ally had given her.

'All the women use them to snuggle up with at night on the plane', Ally had confided knowledgeably.

Ally travelled a great deal with Elliott - her businessman husband - and Meg had often found herself feeling jealous beyond reason as Ally jetted off to yet another fabulous destination whilst she struggled on with her little bloodless life. Going through the motions of respectability and common sense, attempting to ignore the muted pain of a beige life.

Now, it was her turn. Catherine's Mummy and Daddy had arrived in her life waving a magic wand that opened the door and now *she* could get out there to where life was happening.

What a relief to be travelling again, I thought I'd buried that brave adventurous part of myself under suits, and PR briefs and then nappies, packed lunches, bottles and vegemite sandwiches. Then ultimately midlife panic, stalled careers and guilt.

Now I'm back.

She lazily perused the airport shops until her boarding call came a couple of hours later signalling it was time. She walked confidently down the airway onto the plane, found her seat next to the window and after taking out contact lenses' case, glasses, a journal and a book she would never read, she carefully lifted the carry-on into the overhead locker.

As she did, her mind flashed back to the first business trip to Wellington and how her laptop had weighed so much she couldn't lift it above her head. Red-faced she'd had to ask another businessman to ease it into position for her.

She gently nudged her head into position in the space between the seat and the icy plastic glass of the airplane window. Carefully winding the scarf around her shoulders, she sniffed back the cold, leftover remorse and closed her eyes.

The plane steadily bounces along the tarmac before coming to a mechanical pregnant pause. The engines roar and in the cockpit the pilot is going through the motions of the pre-take-off checklist.

She chose to ignore the taunts in her head that take-off is statistically the most dangerous time in flight. She'd watched the safety programme. It is necessary to watch the safety schiz because that's the magic spell that keeps you from crashing.

I've believed that since I was five. If you should crash and not be able to find the exit because the cabin is full of smoke and you don't know to look for the row of lights that will lead you to the nearest exit, then you only have yourself to blame, after all.

The engines are roaring now and then the aircraft is storming down the runway, and with a thump it's airborne, climbing fast it settles into vertical suspension, neither up nor down, like all the king's horses and all the king's men.

When we're up we're up, and when we're down we're down, but when we're only half way up, we're neither up nor down. That's how my life is - neither up nor down, simply suspended. Perhaps when this journey is over and I'm back in NZ air space again, I will be at peace with myself and ready to settle down again at home, just me and the kids. Back home, with the flying pigs.

The plane starts to even out and the stewardess starts making her way along the aisle with the drinks trolley. The Singapore girls dress according to a universal style chart. The tidy up-do is this season's hairstyle and the girls' ages are indistinguishable under their Clarins' masks.

She'd wanted to be an air hostess when she was a child. She fancied a life of travel and adventure, looking hopelessly glamourous and having a well-stocked pantry of miniature liquors. Her father was horrified when he heard of her ambition – or rather lack of it.

'You know they're really just trolley dollies who pour the drinks,' he mocked.

She was sure there was more to it, but she didn't like to argue with him. After all, with the amount of travelling he did, surely he would know. She had travelled eventually, backpacking around Australia and up into Asia when she finished university and was in that space in the ellipsis in time between life chapters.

The seat belt sign extinguishes and Meg reaches over for the inflight magazine. She spends the next half an hour losing herself in an imaginary shopping spree, throwing Louis Vuitton luggage, Bobbi Brown cosmetics and a double pack of Bombay Sapphire into her wishful shopping cart.

'Would you like something to drink Madam?'

She ordered some Australian champagne and the Singapore girl doesn't bat an eyelid at her 8am drinking habits. Nor did she hear Meg ever so quietly toast herself.

All new beginnings need a little head wetting don't they?

She knocked back the Champagne. It was surprisingly good. She'd always enjoyed Champagne Breakfasts, even though it wasn't really Champagne, it was Sparkling Wine. But still. *For breakfast! Delicious.* For the next four weeks, it would be her turn and maybe she would try Champagne in France, for real.

Hah!

No man, no kids, no pets to care for, no-one to please, or appease. I could drink Champers for breakfast and coffee for dinner if I want.

And it would be wonderfully liberating. Not one other soul to compromise for, to quieten for, to care for. She would finally spend some time saving herself and so be it if the rest of the world went promptly to hell.

Hah! Nothing would stand in the way of her finding some perspective and the chance to make some life-defining changes. Well, once she'd delivered the terrible two of course. And with three kids she manages day in day out, weekend after weekend (quite well, thank you very much) on her own, how hard could it be to manage Catherine's two kids?

Chapter 2

Fly little birdies, fly!

THE FOUR-DAY STOPOVER in Brisbane to pick up the dynamic duo had been relatively uneventful. She'd finally started to relax; resigned herself to serving them tomato sauce at every meal (yes even breakfast) and even had a bit of fun watching *Big Brother* with them on TV. She was even looking forward to travelling on with them - Sophie and Jamie - to Europe. By the time they fronted up at the Singapore Airlines check-in counter at Brisbane Airport on their long-haul to Singapore and then to London, she had already negotiated the carriage of two stuffed toys.

'No you can't take both of them Sophie, there's no room.'

'But I can't leave them!' Sophie wailed.

'Ok, well, maybe you can take *one* of them, but two is overkill'.

'Are these yours, as well as the bag' the Singapore Girl asked Sophie at check-in.

'Yes, that's right' Meg confirmed. She didn't dare meet Sophie's eyes.

She was finally on holiday and on holidays the rules were relaxed. It was only right. Who cared whether you had tomato sauce on your eggs?

The first part of the trip long haul to London via Singapore was likewise fairly uneventful. The kids slept, watched TV and even drew a little. There was a minor fracas at Changi, but that was only to be expected when you were tired and the time zones were all wrong. By the time they had boarded the second flight headed to London they were all starting to flag. It didn't take long for them to succumb to sleep on the second, long flight, heading towards Europe.

She's floating in space and there's a dull white hum. She can feel a dull pressure on her eyelids, it's almost a tactile buzzing. As if her eyelids were themselves a buzzer. *How odd,* Meg tells herself. The humming's becoming louder and louder. She can just make out some kind of words, is it singing?

Who on earth could be singing as they buried her? Oh, it's him.

But why don't I have a coffin? I want to peel off the shroud and tell that insensitive sod to stop it. How dare he sing. I'm dead. Doesn't he want to cry instead?

Nup. He wants to sing. And then he leers over her.

From Pavlova to Pork Pies

'What kind of mother leaves their children for a month to flit around Europe?'

She wakes with a start and lifts the shawl tentatively off her face, opening her eyes to the cabin. She rubs her eyes and peels her tongue back off the roof of her mouth.

Good God what unholy hour is this?

God doesn't answer. Instead, He sends the Singapore Girl, who is as always, immaculately groomed.

Do they have a makeup suite on board? Complete with Hollywood mirrors, lights, makeup palettes and mascara ready to operate, at any time?

Meg catches her eye. 'Yes please.'

The cabin attendant hands over the pre-breakfast snack. Or is it lunch, or some type of airline made-up meal? Who needs to eat every three hours? Especially when they haven't moved for six.

It's cheese sandwiches, more intestinal glue to bond the bowels. Jamie the youngest is sitting next to her in the middle seat, humming loudly as he draws in his airplane supplied kids' kit pad.

Poor kid, it really is a long, long way when you're 39, it must be eternal when you're eight.

He is a cute looking kid, with long dark eyelashes and a cheeky grin that curls his face up and makes his freckles polka dance. He's one of those hyperactive types that bounces from thing to thing and is in perpetual motion. Undoubtedly smart, and with parents like Catherine and Dave you would hardly expect anything less, Meg swears that sometimes you could almost see his synapses snapping.

I'd was so chuffed when Catherine called saying 'you're the only friend I'd trust to travel with my kids'. I knew she thought I could manage because of Alex.

Alex had been like that, at eight, so impossibly smart, he was squarely on the annoying side of intelligent.

I can't think of Alex, and Sarah and Jayne right now. It hurts to think of them.

She puts her own children firmly at the back of her mind and looks over to 13-year-old Sophie and studies her sleeping face. She's not about to wake anytime soon. Thank God for that! She's so tall at just turned thirteen, it was easy to expect so much more from her than her years made capable. She's a little girl still, but with very long legs, and a teenage attitude that often prompted Meg to click her tongue in frustration. Sophie's head has settled in a crick-inducing position to the side of her head-rest, and her legs are bunched up underneath her. Her mouth is slightly open, as she struggles to breathe through her blocked nose. Thankfully, her cold hasn't made her ears hurt on the plane.

At least one of us is getting some sleep. Hardly surprising it's the teen who manages it.

She shoots out a panicky thought: How will her kids be when they all reached their teenage years?

Alex was the same age as Sophie, in fact that's how she'd met Catherine, all those years ago, when Alex had picked up a three-year-old girlfriend at the Ascot park in Brisbane. The cute three-year-old belonged to Catherine a fellow expat, a UK national sweating her way through her first Brisbane summer. They had all become firm friends and kept up the close relationship, albeit at a distance when Murray – at that time Meg's husband - got the boot from his job and Meg and the family had to return home with him to New Zealand.

Would her teens be OK, in the end?

Alex was relatively well behaved for a teen. Would it be different for the girls? Has Meg completely ruined their lives with fighting and divorce? Will they pierce their nipples, tattoo their bum cheeks and raise a small nation of feral children under her slack roof?

Couldn't I have hung on just a little bit longer until they'd left home before I'd blown our home life apart?

The cheese sandwich is a soft sponge she rolls around her mouth. There really is too much time to think on planes.

Down below, a crack of dawn is shining through the veil of darkness.

Towns in the 'stans are preparing themselves for yet another day. *It's night in New Zealand now and the kids are probably tucking in to Burger King on the waterfront at Mission Bay. They'll want to race across the road to the playground by the fountain and the beach and their father will limp along behind, annoyed at their youthful mobility.*

No more thinking about the kids until home. This is probably my only chance of experiencing England and Paris. I need to grab it. I can't ruin it by thinking about home and my kids and worrying myself stupid about how they are. Somehow, I need to detach from them so I can have some time to remember who I am. No more thinking about kids until I'm on the way back. Or at the very least, until we land in Heathrow.

She flicks on the flight path tracker on the screen at the back of the seat in front of her and is mesmerised by the aircraft's progress across the world.

The plane is still hushed, it's a suffocating hush that wedges cotton wool into her ears and barbed sponges down her throat. Breathing through the barbs she sucks in calm. In. Out. She's reached that point half-way across the world where tolerance runs out. *How much longer?*

In.

Out.

Down below through the pink edged clouds there's an expanse of water. *Could that be the Black Sea? Who knows?*

She closes her eyes and dozes.

Four more hours pass and whilst Jamie's mouth had finally closed, he is still misbehaving, this time kicking the back of the seat in front of him and then when that didn't raise attention he started poking the sleeping man in his ample sides. Meg pretends she didn't see.

Listen mister, they're not my kids. I cannot make them behave.

She can almost hear the guy with the sweaty pate muttering under his breath, no doubt calling her all sorts of body-parts (mainly genital) in the soft dark of the cabin. Jamie's fidgety kicking hasn't been all the time, as if it were on purpose – which it completely was – oh, no, it was intermittent. Like the stress tests they run on lab rats!

When he elicits no reaction and tires of that activity he starts making pretend airplane noises with his pencil.

The rest of the passengers have discontentedly curled their limbs around the grey velour of their seats in a vain attempt to snare sleep. The wise ones are plugged into headphones or ear plugs. The cabin is quiet, exhaling the lands Down Under and breathing in visions of Europe and the Old World. Everyone is at peace, and calm - all except two kids, who are in Meg's care. They are tired and grumpy, not at all sleepy and are relatively feral. And if they can't find sleep, well, no one else could be allowed that luxury either.

Meg pops in the ear plugs and longs to hang a sign that says:

These are not my kids. I am NOT the nanny'.

How much longer? Why can't they make decent coffee on planes? Why did the Concorde fail? And jet-packs? Could we ever do the long-haul in our very own private jet-pack? Imagine reaching out and grabbing at the clouds. That would be cool...

She wakes hard. She couldn't be certain but she has her suspicions that a poke with a pencil had something to do with it. She turns to check out the kids – Sophie is still asleep (lucky kid) and Jamie is innocently drawing.

'What are you drawing Jamie?'

'It's a cartoon of you. Sophie did it earlier and I'm colouring it in a bit.'

The image is of a frizzy haired woman with a super-hero cape. Her eyes are wide open and her mouth is a bright red semi-circled focal point. It's surprisingly good. Though she's not sure how accurate a likeness it is. Is her mouth really that big? The lines of the character are curved and cuddly and best of all the figure is smiling, though Meg confesses to herself she's quite possibly swearing on the inside.

'That's really good Jamie. Look here comes breakfast. Are you hungry?'

The breakfast carts are rattling down the back of the cabin now as the plane starts to bounce and shiver. Acrid coffee greases the air between the galley and the cabin seats. Even burnt coffee would be better than this polystyrene feeling in her mouth.

'No, I want the loo.'

'Can you wait just a little bit? It's hard getting down to the loo when they're serving breakfast. Can you hang on?'

'NO! I can't.' His eyes narrow and he pouts.

The man sitting in front of them turns around tut-tutting. She doesn't meet his eyes.

'Sshhh. Jamie! Ok, ok. Keep your hair on.'

She would have to wake Sophie to get him out.

She gently reaches across to touch the sleeping teen's shoulder and leans in towards her speaking in a soft, low voice.

'Sophie you need to wake up love, Jamie needs the loo.'

Sophie's face grimaces and she starts to whine.

'I'm sleeping. Leave me alone.'

'No really Soph, you have to get up, so he can slip out. Come on hun, it's breakfast time anyway.'

Jamie has already started to climb across his sister, who is sleeping in the aisle seat, and has plunged a foot into her side.

'OW! Jamie!'

'I want to go to the loo!' he wails.

The woman two rows up has turned to stare. Her eyes are arrowheads laced with Ricin.

'Sshhh. Come on Soph, come on you could probably do with the loo too.'

Blinking hard and grumbling loudly she releases her seatbelt and moves to the aisle. Meg follows smiling and apologising to all the passengers who are mentally wishing them a skydiving trip sans parachute.

'Sorry, excuse us. Kids! You know. Poor things they must be really tired. Sorry!' Meg keeps her head up, eyes straight ahead. Thank God she never has to see any of these people ever again!

When they reach the toilet cubicle, Sophie barges ahead leaving Jamie jigging with impatience at the locked door.

'I know. I know. Just hang on Jamie. She won't be long.'

It was an eternity. And just as Meg had assumed she would be replacing undies (hers, if not Jamie's) sometime soon, Sophie unlatched the door and moved aside for her red-faced little brother. In a flash he was out again and Meg took her turn before following the children back up the aisle.

The children walk like tired spiders through the narrow aisle until they find their row. Jamie sees his chance and pushes forward demanding the window seat, where Meg had previously been sitting. He is insistent. His eyes wide with exhaustion.

'I want the window seat' he whines, squeezing his face up and starting to stomp. 'I want it!' his whine becomes increasingly louder.

'But come on, you're the smallest Jamie, so you should be in the middle. You were in the middle before and it was OK.'

Meg tries to jolly him along, reminding herself that he's only eight. 'Let's just keep it as it was. Sophie has the aisle seat so she can get up and walk around, you have the middle one because you're the littlest and I'll take the window.'

Meg had long held the view that the window seat is the best seat in the row. In that seat you can fold the pillow up against the window and as long as you can reconcile your spine with sleeping at an 80-degree angle, you can actually get some sleep. At five foot one she knew that wasn't usually a problem. She knew too that she could always climb over the kids to get out to the loo, a small inconvenience compared with not having the window seat's space. There was of course also, that crème de la crème of the Pro's List - the ultimate prize – the first view of England. Something she'd been waiting for over twenty years to see.

'But I want it. I want it. I want it' Jamie said. He barged forward into the seat claiming it via occupancy. Meg reaches out and grabs his arm briskly and he bridles with anger.

'Owww. You're hurting me!'

'I am not. Sorry! Don't be silly. Everyone's looking. Shhh.'

For the love of God and everything holy please be quiet Jamie.

'You know what Jamie?'

People were staring. Meg flushed with embarrassment, and tried to tone down her voice.

Inside voice! Inside voice! Damn those years of Speech and Drama lessons and theatrical projection!

'I want, I want, I want. Someday you'll realise that in life you don't always get what you want'.

But you get what you need. Ba dum bash!

Jagger would be so proud.

Breakfast comes featuring an omelette that tastes like manna from heaven, and coffee that tastes like ashtrays. The cabin is humming with activity now and the daily ablutions have started. Queues are forming at the loos and somewhere a baby has started bawling for its morning feed. Sophie has gone straight back to sleep and Jamie has found something to amuse him on the entertainment system. Meg starts to write in her journal, a habit she's kept for over twenty years. Back then, her journal entries were about backpacking adventures around Thailand and Australia. Back then, she peppered long tear-stained entries with verses she had memorised in the Pentecostal church she'd attended during her teens.

Down below the cruising aircraft, Europe is waking to another overcast Summer's day and down in West Sussex Catherine has started the long drive up to Heathrow to meet her children's plane. Meg's eyes frighten sleep and she dozes lightly.

'That must be France, Jamie.'

Sophie's pointing it out past Meg's face. Sensing the finger in front of her nose, Meg wakes with a start. Drowsy and sleep-hungover she watches with them as green land turns into the grey waves of the Channel and sea quickly retrieves land once more.

Meg's glued to the window now. Excited, she joins in with the children's chatter.

Is that England? Is it? I'm not sure what I expect to see from up here. What is it that will look different from landing in New Zealand, Australia or America for that matter?

'Ladies and gentlemen, as you may have noticed we have started our descent. Could you please make sure that your seat is back up, your tray table folded away and that your safety belt is buckled. Take a moment to reacquaint yourself with the safety instructions and make a note of your nearest Exit. Cabin crew can you please start preparing the cabin for landing. Thank you.'

Down below, green fields, not unlike the fields of Waikato, are bordered by strips of dark green hedgerows. Every third or fourth field is coloured yellow – wheat or barley, or rapeseed? – and then there are glimpses of rivers cutting through the farmland.

Is this it? Is this the moment?

Meg's whole life has been shaped by the promise of one day going to England. As a child growing up in Fiji, her family had lived a sort of English colonial lifestyle; with a house-girl, a driver and gardener and childhood friends sent away from the colonies to boarding school in Hampshire or Berkshire. She'd devoured Enid Blyton's Famous Five series and Bednobs and Broomsticks and dreamt of places where kids tobogganed in the winter.

The North wind doth blow and we will have snow

Her Mum and Dad had even met Prince Charles and her Mum had learnt to curtsey and scoured Lautoka for fresh cream for the diplomatic High Tea. As an over-eager Brownie she had waved her New Zealand flag when The Queen came to visit Manukau City, and as a student she'd listened to the boastful stories of those who had already made their OE to London, with mounting envy. She'd studied Chaucer and Shakespeare and TS Eliot. She needed to see England. It was after all, her spiritual and artistic home.

Now, finally, this is it. With England at her feet, the plane starts to lower and seriously descend.

Down below, fields are making way for houses and streets and then the steel water of the Thames. Meg is amazed at how much detail she can see. She can see red double decker buses – like crimson ants - and rows and rows of brick houses. The landing gear grinds down into position and the aircraft starts to point downward despite there being no sign of a runway. Apparently, this aircraft is determined to land in the middle of an outer London suburb. Meg can't look any longer.

If we're going to slam into one of London's outer suburbs head-first, I'd prefer to do it with my eyes shut thanks.

Besides, there appears to be something in her eye.

'Ladies and Gentleman, welcome to London. The temperature is a cool 8 degrees Celsius. Local time is 0730 Greenwich Mean Time. We'll be pulling up outside Terminal Four in just a moment, just as soon as there's space for us. Please remain seated until we have reached the gateway and refrain from using your mobile phones until you are well inside the terminal buildings.'

Meg's inner monologue is screaming - *We're here! OMG I'm here, I'm here! Big Ben, the Tube, the land of Shakespeare and pints. I've finally made it to London, before I'm forty.*

It takes an age to de-board the plane. By the time they do so and have made their way along the moving footpaths (which Jamie runs along). Meg's own three children have grown up without her and graced her with grandchildren, and jet-packs have become as commonplace as flying buses.

Meg's first view of England out through the aircraft window, is of drizzle. Unrelenting drizzle. The second impression is formed by the longest customs' queue she has ever seen. The children march forward, unaccompanied, to the queue sign-posted *British and EU Citizens* whilst Meg limps along to the Others queue.

It's by far the slowest queue, as people from all the other nations line up for inspection. There are women with saris and men with turbans and at least a couple of loud Australians corralled in front of the row of desks. A grey-faced official is taking the time to question – at length – every single applicant. He doesn't crack a smile; it would break his face. Meg watches in horror as a young girl is asked to sit and wait to the side of the desks and is then escorted off to the little closed door room. The girl is crying as she follows resignedly behind the border official.

Meg shivers involuntarily. Somehow, she knows exactly how displaced that young girl feels.

But soon it is her turn at the counter. She chats to the Man-with-the-Stamp and says she's on holiday and that she hopes the weather improves. He doesn't smile. He doesn't blink. Perhaps he's a lizard? He simply stamps her passport as he licks his fly-smeared reptilian lips.

Meg doesn't care.

Im'here!

Now, where's Catherine and the England of Big Ben, scones, strawberry jam and lashings of cream?

Chapter 3

The Pub and the Posh People

'ARE YOU SURE no one can see?' Meg anxiously looks over the long grass to the lights of oncoming traffic storming down the lane. The chilly wind slaps her red, cheeky backside.

'Course not. It's what you do when you've been to the pub. You stop on the way home for a *whiz*. It's tradition. It would be rude not to.' Cath chuckles with ale addled mirth and then hoists up her jeans and starts to march off in the direction of Mummy and Daddy's Manor house.

'Hang on, hang on.' Meg grabs at her jeans and half-tucked in shirt and stumbles over the field after her friend.

'Cath, wait up I don't know where I'm going.'

'Well rattle your dags. That's what they say in New Zealand isn't it?' She laughs again. 'You don't want to be caught out here with your pants down.'

Hearing 'rattle your dags' in Catherine's plummy accent makes Meg chuckle. Her friend was the best kind of nuts.

The village pub had been everything Meg had imagined it would be. The publican was jolly and red-cheeked, an old chap was seated at the corner table by the fire (a fire in Summer?) and there was even a gun dog snoring at his feet. Everyone had been full of chatter about Catherine's parents' wedding anniversary party. They were big news in this little village. In fact, for all Meg knew they were still big news throughout England, as they once had been in their day when women stayed at home preparing martinis for cocktail hour whilst their husbands graced The Club.

Meg had been delighted to be a no-one for a while. No-one's mother, no-one's daughter, no-one's wife. A traveller, itinerant and free. Now, marching over the fields towards the light of the estate's cottage, she realised she hadn't felt this free in a very long time.

It had been a busy couple of days in West Sussex with Catherine's family. She hadn't paused to gather her strength after jetlag. She wanted to see everything - in typical Meg fashion - right now! Arundel castle, the cobbled streets of Chichester, and the sands of The Witterings... Pubs and pints and Agas and bridleways. All of it, every last bit, all at once.

Secretly, she'd been impatient to get to London – the unrequited love of her teens – but first on the agenda was some time with Cath's wealthy family in their West Sussex home.

'So what do you think of England so far?' Cath asked as Meg fell into pace with her.

'It's amazing but different I guess from what I expected.'

'Really?'

'Well yeah. I've had this weird kind of childhood filled with Beatrix Potter, and Enid Blyton and you kind of expect to know England. And though it does feel familiar, it also kind of doesn't. I mean... it's like I expected to belong here... but I don't really.'

'Why would you expect that? You've never been out of the Southern Hemisphere before.'

'I have! I've been to America. I guess many New Zealanders feel like that. I don't have it as bad as some who still call England home despite living in Te Kuiti or deepest darkest Waikouiti. Murray's Mum still called England home even though she was born and bred in Northland.'

'Odd.' Catherine shook her head.

'Yeah I guess. It's like a cultural echo.' Meg was relishing her role as Social Anthropologist, albeit an inebriated one. 'As if we've been living a parallel life just off Wimbledon Common.'

Catherine was doubtful. Sensing dispute, Meg changes the subject.

'Can't wait to go to Paris on Wednesday.'

Meg wanted to admit she was busting to see London too, but it felt ungrateful somehow. She'd been enjoying her time with Cath and Dave and having a great time at Catherine's parents' place.

'But your Mum and Dad have been brilliant having me. I really am incredibly grateful.'

They wandered up the white shelled path and crossed the circular driveway in front of the old half-timbered country house. Catherine's parents had placed their daughter, grandchildren and their hanger-on, in the cottage, a separate two-bedroom house that had once served as the servants' quarters. Meg hugged her friend goodnight and headed into the small downstairs' room. Settling into the little bed she all of a sudden felt cold and alone. She grabbed her mobile and called a familiar number in New Zealand.

Jayne answered and Meg immediately started silently crying at the sound of her littlest daughter's voice. She forced a smile into her voice.

'Hello, how you are you hun? Are you having fun with Dad?'

'Oh hello Mummy. We went to Burger King and I got a Whopper but I took the gherkin out. Yuk. Don't like gherkin and Dad had a Double Whooper and so did Alex.'

'But what else have you done?'

'We went to the holiday programme at the Church and they had lollipops. Oh, you know what Mummy? Here's Sarah.'

Meg's oldest daughter was chatty and bright. It didn't seem as if they were missing her. In fact, they seemed ecstatic with their Burger King and lollipop fuelled holiday programme. Even when Meg had whispered into the phone 'I miss you' her daughter hadn't volunteered that she was pining.

She probably wasn't, but as Meg rang off and settled to sleep strangled sobs escaped and wet her dreams.

There is only one problem with being no-one... it is incredibly lonely.

The following day Meg wakes with the sun and pads across the shelled driveway to the kitchen in the main house. Andrea, the housekeeper, is preparing Mummy and Daddy's breakfast, standing, stirring porridge on the Aga cooktop.

'Good morning. How did you sleep?' she asks Meg.

'Not too bad. Still suffering a bit of jet lag, but I'll get there.' It was jet-lag, not too many pints at the pub; she was almost sure. The housekeeper continued her cheerful chatter.

'Are you heading over to Arundel today with Catherine Dave and the kids?'

'I think that's the plan. How far is it?' Meg asked.

'Only about twenty minutes or so, but it is worth it.'

'You've been?'

'Oh yes, many times. The castle is the high point, obviously, but aside from that it's a really quaint town. When I'm finished here and they are tucked up in bed and the other girl comes in to clean I'm free to pop off and go exploring. I've seen quite a bit of the local countryside and even popped over to France and Germany since I've been on this placement.'

'Have you been looking after Catherine's parents for long?'

Andrea paused. 'About three years now. It's not too bad. They sleep in till 9 or so and then read quietly in the conservatory most of the day.'

'Where are you from originally?' Meg asks noting an Antipodean accent.

'Timaru. So living here is much the same...'

Meg raises an eyebrow.

'Except, you know, considerably posher!'

They laugh and Meg dives into the cutlery drawer to prepare the breakfast table. Before long Catherine's father had been, breakfasted and gone off to read his paper in the study. An hour or two later, Catherine, Dave and the kids arrive, and the kitchen is full of loud chatter and laughter.

'We're going to head off to Arundel at about 11:30 Meg. You're still coming aren't you? There's this incredible cheese shop there I want to show you, and we'll grab some lunch at *Olivada*.'

'Ooooh yum Mummy!' Jamie piped up, his eyes gleaming at the thought of bowls of chips followed, inevitably, by bowls of icecream.

Catherine laughs and scoots him out the door. 'Come on silly we need to get you ready. Teeth, t-shirt, shoes...'

Her voice trails out the door after him.

'So Meg, how were they really on the way out here? I know you said they were fine when we picked you up at Heathrow but were they? Really?' Catherine is good-naturedly asking her friend whilst trying to coax some bread into her daughter.

'Really. They were great. We had fun didn't we guys?'

Sophie grimaced at her bread and Jamie wriggled.

'Have some chips then, honey,' Cath urges her daughter.

'There were a few hiccoughs,' Meg continues 'but it's a bloody long way and we all got a bit tired. And Singapore was a bit hairy.'

'Why what happened at Changi?'

'The kids were pretty tired and they wanted to run around a bit. I suppose I was tired too and didn't really want to run after airport trolleys. In the end I just let them go for it.'

Fly little birdies, race those trolleys as far away from me as possible.

'But we always do that don't we Soph? What are trollies for, if not to race?' Catherine puts an arm around her daughter and Meg catches a glimpse of a new colourful tattoo on her forearm, another example of her friend's exquisite eccentricity.

'And then there was toothpaste-gate,' Meg threw out into the conversation.

'What was wrong with the toothpaste?' Dave asked.

'Sophie didn't understand about putting it in the clear plastic bag. I was trying to progress in the queue towards the security officer at the gate, mobile phone and laptop battery in one hand, camera in the other, and my own clear plastic bag with all my toiletries hanging off my pinky finger. My jeans were missing my belt and with the weight I've lost over the past few months I could feel my jeans sliding down and I started to panic that I would be passing through Changi security in my knickers. I was grabbing at my jeans and trying to get Sophie to put her toothpaste in the bag... and she was fussing... I tried to explain to Sophie that it was a security precaution...And she argued that it was 'only toothpaste...So I tried to discreetly explain that, you know, terrorists can turn it into something...' Meg takes a sip from her glass, for effect.

'She wanted to know *how*. Being as it was only toothpaste and not a BOMB or something.'

'Sophie called out B-O-M-B in the security queue?' Catherine asked incredulously.

'Yeah everything stopped, people turned to look. I think the man behind me gasped. Someone in dark sunglasses talked urgently into his sleeve and I was expecting to be hauled off, any second now, to a life behind bars planning cockroach races.'

Dave starts to laugh loudly.

'And then you told the officers that you weren't travelling with us Meg,' Sophie pipes up.

'Really?' Catherine pursued her lips.

'No, *not really*. The Asian officer asked if they were travelling with me.... I said 'never seen them before in my life...' It was a joke! She didn't really hear.'

'She did,' said Jamie. 'She started to get really angry.'

'Nah, she didn't really. Not really. It was all good.'

Catherine wasn't entirely convinced but Dave continued to chuckle. 'But the flight was OK? he asked Meg.

'They did really well. I don't know how people do that trip regularly; it's a really long way. We had a few scraps over seats but it was OK, mainly.'

'See Meg, I told you to seat the kids behind you. Down the plane a bit. You know within view, just out of earshot...'

Sophie seethed. Nothing was worse than her Mum taking Megan's side.

'And how have things been at home Meg?' Dave asked kindly.

'Ok.'

'Have you managed to get a settlement out of Murray?'

Meg looked down. 'Not yet.'

Dave wasn't to be deterred. He dug deeper.

'What's wrong with him? You can't go on like this waiting for everything to be settled. He should just sign the house over to you and be done with it. That's the least he could do, after...' His voice trailed off and Meg shifted in her seat. She had made a custom of not talking ill of her ex-husband around the children, and even though they were 18,000 miles away in New Zealand, old habits died hard.

'Does anyone know what happened to it all?' Dave persisted.

'Nope. Two legal teams and still we don't know. I had a psychic tell me he gambled it.' But, who knows?' Meg's tone was bright; her face was not. Why hadn't she seen it sooner? Why did it take 16 years to realise the marriage was over? Why did she stay?

Seeing her discomfort, Dave changed the subject. 'Ah well, that's in the past now. History. Time to move on. Catherine says you've been having some fun with online dating?'

'Oh yeah, lots of fun dating Sun Worshipper and Secret Agent and LOL. There was this one guy, he seemed quite nice at first. Though, his handle was Creepy.'

'Creepy? You didn't go out with him, did you?'

'I thought he was being ironic. He wrote really well and how creepy can an articulate, well-read, well-travelled man be? So I decided to meet him in Mission Bay. That was my first and second mistake. I don't usually go to dinner on the first meeting nor do I arrange meetings so close to home. But

I suppose I wasn't really thinking. I went to all this trouble to get it all organised, too. I flossied myself up, bought new clothes, did my hair and makeup carefully...I even bought new earrings. I organised a sitter for the kids and rushed there ahead of our meeting time so I wasn't late. He'd suggested we meet by the toilets by the fountain so...'

'By the toilets?' Cath asked.

'It's not as bad as it sounds. It's central. It was just a good place to meet. Though I did get a few sideways looks. It's not as if it was summer. I suppose it looked odd, this dressed -up woman sitting outside the public loos. I waited feeling increasingly nervy and kept looking suspiciously at everyone who walked by. Was this him? Nope. This guy? No. This one? Oh hell, please, no...And then there was this guy hulking towards the toilets. He seemed a bit, ... um, rough-hewn...'

'Rough-hewn?' Cath was enthralled.

'Yeah. Like Stig of the Dump or .... Um... I don't know... Just really big, and thick set. A man-mountain, and not in a good way...'

'And that was him?' Cath quizzed.

'Yeah.'

Meg glanced down.

'I really did think he was being ironic with the name, you know. But yeah. It turns out he wasn't.' She shuddered.

'What did you do? Did you run?'

'Well no, I'd already promised I'd meet him and I shouldn't be so superficial, dismissing men at face-value. After all I'm not an oil painting. He could have been a brilliant guy with a sparkling personality...I hate it when men do that to me so I decided to stay and have dinner with him.'

'Men stand you up?'

'Not all of them. But this one guy. He said I was too short to go out with him. Prat.'

'So you did have dinner with Creepy?'

'I did. Me, Creepy and his halitosis had an OK time. Though the waitress, who knew me, did shoot me an 'are you kidding me?' look.'

'But did he sparkle Meg?' Dave asked.

Meg's face cracked into a broad smile as she shook her head vehemently.

'Er, no.'

They all laughed.

'But I'm tired of all that. New leaf, new phase, new start. No more dating. In fact, I'm not sure I even want to get married again. I think it'll be just me and the kids until they leave home. Then I'll be too old and wrinkly.'

'You will not! Don't be silly Meg.' Catherine rushed to her defence.

'You might meet someone in Paris!' she said.

'When do we fly out to Paris Dave?' Meg changed the subject. 'Monday afternoon,' he replied with a smile. Meg could see he was really looking forward to their trip. Dave was a good looking Englishman who had more than a little bit of Stephen Fry about him – the same quick, dry wit, and abundant intelligence.

'I'm so looking forward to it,' Meg said trying to swiftly move the conversation on, but Catherine wasn't to be deterred. She leant over to Meg and said softly. 'It will all happen at the right time.'

Meg tried to not wince.

*****

After the trip to Arundel, Meg caught the train from Chichester to London and on to Catherine's friend's home in Hounslow, one of the suburbs out near Heathrow airport. Catherine and Dave were hosting a family party at Catherine's parent's house and Meg had taken the opportunity to travel on to London on her own.

It had been good staying with Catherine's family. a salubrious introduction to English life, complete with a dinner party for twelve hosted by the aging couple in the formal dining room. She'd eaten quails' eggs for starters and tried to not let on that was for her, a gastronomic first. She'd even put the kettle on the Aga made a brew and served it to Mummy in the conservatory – just like a pro!

She would catch up with the family in a few days on their way to Paris, but first she would lap up London. Westminster Abbey, Big Ben, Baker Street – all of it! She would lap it up until she was quite drunk with it all and fell down silly and giggling in Briar's spare bedroom. As the green fields sped past the train window she smiled with delicious anticipation, at the thought. She reached down, grabbed her phone and texted her friend Ally, back in New Zealand.

Off to London for a few days now, then Paris. Excited, much? Woohoo. xx

When the train eased into the cavernous, domed Waterloo Station Meg was awed by the sheer scale of it all, by the huge glass arched roof, the ornate iron clock and the wall of electronic sign boards detailing the comings and goings, etched into the black background in neon orange. The concourse was massive and there it seemed to be heaving with bustle.

More than anything, Meg was caught off guard by the glamour of the assembled masses. Not the great unwashed at all, strangely, every second person seemed to be dressed in their Sunday best. She applied all her poise to not stop still and stare at the women in their heels and pearls and veiled hats, the immaculately groomed blokes in three piece suits and over there standing nonchalantly by the newspaper kiosk, a tall dark bloke wearing a top hat. *A top hat!*

Did everyone dress like this in London?

The excess of it all was overwhelming. The juxtaposition between the well-heeled and the down and outs was glaringly obvious. For just as she noticed the well-dressed, she also saw the have-nots dressed in track pants and soiled t-shirts dragging all their earthly possessions around with them in dirty sports bags. The crowds rushed on; talking, laughing, running for trains, yelling for friends to catch them up, and yabbering urgently on phones as they ran for the train. No one else saw. Only the invisible ones could see the invisible.

Meg stops to buy some lunch at Marks & Spencer's and asks the operator about the top hats, cravats and heels and the well groomed crowds. He replies that the Ascot races are on, and relieved that this isn't the typical dress standard for London town Meg cheerfully edges through the crowds to the overland train heading for Hounslow.

Briar's house stands out in the row because it is purple. Meg smiles broadly when she sees it, relieved to see such personality in the otherwise carbon-copy line of brick houses. She lugs her case through the first 'outside' door, and extra-carefully through the second 'inside' door, carefully guarding the exit so that not one of Briar's six cats can race outside.

Briar had warned her that they were inside cats only, and pausing to pet them Meg could see why. They were all Orientals and absolutely gorgeous. They reminded her of her own beautiful Tonkinese at home. Angels in fur. She lugged the suitcase upstairs and allows herself to sink into a deep sleep before Briar comes back home from work.

Later in the evening they are talking companionably by the fire, drinking wine and chuckling over their mutual friend's exploits. Briar and Catherine have been friends since they were teens and Meg can't help but warm to Briar's quick wit and quirky conversation. Briar was obviously very fond of their mutual friend.

'How did you get on staying at Cath's parent's place? It's quite posh...' Briar asks tentatively.

'It was interesting. Yeah, a little posh. But I'm not really worried by that. I've always had wealthy friends, back in school, you know. I take it in my stride. But what was kind of weird was *class*... '

'How so?'

'I've always thought of myself as upper middle class, if there has to be a definition, but it doesn't really matter in New Zealand. In Auckland, it's more about the old school tie, the suburb you live in, the holidays you take.' Meg explains.

Briar nods. 'It's still a thing here. Class, I mean.'

'And you can see that. Though after Cath's warnings I might have been pretuned to it.' Briar raised an eyebrow.

'Cath warned me not to wear bare feet and told me to say loo rather than toilet or bathroom. It's funny, I always thought it was polite to ask to go to the bathroom but she told me that was terribly middle class. Which is apparently, not such a good thing. She was quick to set me straight too. In fact, I think it was one of the first conversations we had on the drive down from Heathrow to West Sussex.'

Briar chortled. 'She was probably trying to be helpful and maybe even a little protective of her Kiwi friend.'

'I guess so. It was a bit different. It was interesting to see that the staff were all colonials. The housekeeper woman was from New Zealand too, and one of the cleaners was from Queensland, I think. And the bare feet thing was just odd. In the end, I did wear bare feet around her parents' house. At one point I even had to rush to help her with her Mum after she fell and I didn't have time to find shoes.'

Briar nodded.

'But probably more so for them than me! Don't get me wrong, it was wonderfully generous of them to have me, and you too of course. I'm really grateful. It was just *so different*. I guess things are a lot more laid back at home.'

They talked late into the night, Briar suggesting places that Meg should see and how to nab good cheap tickets for a show at *The Globe*, one item on Meg's must-do list. It was past one am when Meg snuck off to bed and settled down into the duvet with one of God's furry angels purring on her bum.

In the morning she roused about 10am and sleepily checked her email messages before lazily swiping to the news on her mobile phone.

She sat bolt upright as she read.

Police foil London Car Bomb Plot

> *A controlled explosion was carried out on the car, which was packed with 60 litres of petrol, gas cylinders and nails, in Haymarket, near Piccadilly Circus. It would have caused carnage if it had exploded, police say.*

Safe, little ole New Zealand felt a very long way away.

When she finally arrived back in London Central after a slow sombre trip through the suburbs, for her carefully planned day of sight-seeing, she could feel a palpable tension. There had been an eerie silence on the train and a no-nonsense expression on the faces of the London Transport staff. But most of all she noticed the Metropolitan police and their tightly gripped guns.

She tried to not stare and instead started her tour of London with an open roofed double decker Bus tour ride. It didn't take long to forget the threat of terrorism and get into the swing of it. She revelled in the tour and smiled as the guide pointed out the city's highlights. It was as if her entire English Literature reading list had come to life.

She pushed her fears over terrorists to the back of her conscious mind and lapped up the sights and sounds and when the day was over and her feet were bruised and blistered with walking across ancient cobbles, and she was sitting on the train heading back out to Briar's cosy spare room, she couldn't help thinking: It would be very cool to live here.

****

Meg's first view of Paris is of a grungy Montmartre. There is a buzz of accents, smatterings of French and German and then Swedish with its ooordles and boordles. Layered on top of the linguistic mash was a heavy slice of American and a garnish of British.

Meg's group strode across the cobbled terrace with purpose – misplaced purpose. Out in front, enthusiastically embracing the role of expedition leader, Dave is striding purposefully. He can't find the written directions for the hotel.

'It must be down this way' he says heading confidently down the cobbled passageway. Meg stifles her irritation.

We could just ask. Then we'll know!

I'm just not as used to having a man take charge. I've been on my own for 18 months now, and I lead my family. I find the hotel and destinations and I manage my passports and money.

Dave had taken Meg's passport and ticket at the airport placing it carefully with his own and his wife and children's passports. Meg knew he was only trying to be protective and organised, but it was driving her nuts.

Not that Dave, the intrepid good-looking British geologist used to leading teams of explorative scientists through the Papua New Guinean bush, could intuit. Meg was too busy trying to recall the French for 'where is the Croix?'

'Pardon! Ou est La Croix,' she practised under her breath.

Undeterred by their lack of a compass, map, or natural sense of direction, Dave led the party through the wild streets of Paris, past the tourist trap artistes with their berets and pencil drawings. Past the little supermarché on the corner and the wooden café tables en terrasse and their signboards advertising cheveux and beaujolais.

The Parisian streets narrowed and Meg's short legs ache as she struggles to keep pace with the long-legged family. And then, mon dieu, the hotel comes into view.

La Croix is a staid building not dissimilar to the apartment buildings on either side of it, bar for the sign in the front advertising cheap accommodation and WIFI. A tall dark skinned Algerian man showed Meg to her room on the fourth floor using the ancient grilled lift that wheezed past the floors.

Meg's room is as immaculately clean as a broom cupboard, and almost as big. Just outside the shuttered windows, there is a narrow balcony bordered by a decorative wrought iron balustrade. Beyond the view of the neighbours' apartments, way up past the balconies and rooves, high up on the hill was the Sacré-Coeur Its lit dome shining as brightly as an American show biz smile. Meg was mesmerised by it.

'Hiya God' she chuckles to herself as she throws her backpack into the space under the little china basin. She had only brought her day pack with her so that she could travel light on the Easyjet flight over to Paris. She had few possessions, the room was a cell - perfect for a chaste sleep, and she was conspicuously on her own. *Perhaps I am becoming a nun?*

On the Sunday before leaving, her Catholic friend Mike had taken her out for brunch at *Mecca* at *Mission Bay*. They'd sat in the cool winter sunshine and attempted to not acknowledge Meg's jangling nerves. Mike had nonchalantly placed an envelope in front of her onto the table.

'You'll be alright Meg, you will,' he'd said kindly, tapping the envelope forward to her.

'Yeah I'm tough'.

He guffawed and in his broad Kiwi accent explained the mysterious envelope. 'It's just some foreign currency I've picked up on my travels. I've no use of it. Thought you might though.'

'I can't accept it Mike.'

'Nah don't be stupid. It's not much, just a bit that was lying around. Let people help you!' He growled.

'I can't. I'm not programmed that way.'

'Well someone has to! I talked about you to The Big Guy at Mass the other day.'

'That's good. I guess. What did He say?' Meg was almost too scared to ask.

'When I mentioned your name, he just laughed.'

'He did not. We're on great terms. God and me, we're close, like this.'

Meg crossed her fingers. Then corrected herself.

'We just don't talk much. Typical bloke, God. Not a natural communicator!'

'Ah Meg, what are we going to do with you eh?'

'Er, send me back and get a new one?'

'He wouldn't have ya mate.' Mike laughed loudly at his own joke as Meg jigged her legs under the coffee table.

Standing at her hotel window in Paris now, she stares over the tops of the apartments across to the shining dome of theSacré-Coeur.

Look Mike! God's there on the hill, watching out for me.

She laughed quietly to herself. It felt right. And then, not directed to anyone in particular asked out loud; 'Now where's the bloody toilet, before Dave turns up to escort us to dinner?'

*****

The waitress appeared at the table and Dave started rattling off his order in impressive French.

'What about you Soph?'

'I can't see it. I don't want any of this, I want french fries!'
She was tired and grizzly.

'Sophie, there's more to French food than French fries!'

Meg shouldn't have said it, but tired and exasperated and
fearful that they would soon vacate the cute little café for
the nearest Maccas, she lost her temper. Dave turned to his
fuming daughter and tried to sell her on the benefits of the
incredible food which was every bit as good as french fries, if
she'd only try it, she'd see.

The waitress cocked her head, a little confused.

'So the French fries I am sure the cook can make these.'

Defeated, he sighed. 'Merci beaucoup.'

He ordered some wine with the fries and their entree
courses and launched into a story about his travels through
France as a student, that involved escargot and copious
quantities of cheap bordeux.

'What's the matter Jamie? Do you need the loo?' Catherine
asked the scowling eight-year-old. He nodded. Inwardly Meg
groaned. *This is why you don't bring kids to Paris!*

As Catherine took Jamie by the hand and led him down
the stairs to the subterranean toilet, Dave continued his story.
Meg smiled a tired smile. It was very gracious of David and
Catherine to take her out to dinner, but still tired from the
flight over from Australia, she had been counting on heading
down to that little supermarché around the corner and

getting some bread and cheese and maybe some beaujolais, and settling in with a glass of wine pouring over guide books and plotting her assault on Paris. She wanted to be polite and convivial but was failing miserably.

Catherine was positively glowing and Dave seemed jolly. The reunion had gone well then, Meg thought uncharitably.

Well why shouldn't they be happy? They were still in love after umpteen years of marriage, they were newly reunited after being apart for months with Dave working in PNG and Catherine living with the kids in Brisbane, and they were even having a wedding vow renewal ceremony next week! What's more, they were in Paris the city of a thousand lights.

And under every light were a couple of sodding lovers.

Dinner came to the table and the family chatted and joked around her. Normal, family in-jokes and squabbles and soon she felt the shroud of melancholy bind her shoulders. She tugged at it and pulled it close, losing herself within it. Dinner conversation continued around her like raucous birdsong in a frigid forest. It jarred.

The wine is delicious, the cheese superb, the company convivial. So why in God's name am I so miserable?

On the way back to the hotel they parted company and Meg walked alone across the cobblestones to the local shop. She found some brie, bread and a bottle of wine and made her way to the counter.

'Bon soir monsieur.'

He didn't laugh at me! Perhaps he didn't hear me.

'Bon soir!'

He replied in rapid fire French, leaving her smarting with confusion.

'Er pardon?'

'Je m'excuse. Je ne comprehend pas.'

'Parlez-vous le francais ?'

'Oui, un petit, petit, peu!'

And she laughed self-deprecatingly.

'Je voudrais, ...um.... Un botteile de vin rouge, une brie, un pain si'l vous plait.'

The shopkeeper studied her face. Her eyes were tired and her smile was stretched thin. Her curly dark hair hung in a frizzy mat across her shoulders and over the bridge of her nose there was a smattering of pale beige freckles.

'L'Australien ?'

'Mais non. Novelle Zéalande !'

She didn't mean to say that she was New Zealand - ALL of it - but she had no idea how to say she came from the other Land Downunder. Then it all fell apart into a rapid fire discussion about the All Blacks, and how they were giants...

'Les noirs, les noirs....' The short, balding grocer kept repeating.

Meg wasn't much of a rugby fan, but given the choice between mentioning the All Blacks or the Rainbow Warrior incident – the only two NZ/French connections she knew of – she felt the All Blacks was the safest bet. She nodded and smiled as the shop owner continued his ballad of praise for the All Blacks until she was mercifully saved by a little man wanting a pack of smokes. Paris hadn't received the WHO memo that promised smokers and those downwind of smokers, a phlegmatic death.

She paid her money, cheerily assailed all within earshot with an au revoir squeezed out with flattened Kiwi dipthongs and trotted down the street back to the hotel and up the lift to her room. Placing the cheese and bread on the small table, she opened the bottle of beaujolais and poured the wine into the little glass on the side of the basin - the one for rinsing her mouth out after brushing her teeth, not guzzling grog. Walking over to the window she opened it and carefully perched on its lip she sat, looking out into the Parisian night sky.

Over the road through the open window a woman was moving about her flat drenched in the blue glow of a TV set. Down on the street below there was a rhythmic drumming. When she looked down she could see a group of African immigrants dressed in tribal gear passing below, chanting to the beat of long missile shaped drums. Eerie sounds of a distant, mystical land French Africa. Beyond the tiled roofs of the apartments, and the wrought iron fretwork of the apartment buildings' narrow balconies, the white sandstone curves of the Sacré-Coeur Basilica was shining brighter than any other light in the City of Lights.

A thousand lovers are probably right now, sighing over glasses of wine or walking arm in arm alongside the Seine. She sat in the window and drank the beaujolais – close to tears - remembering her mother's words.

Is it true God? Is that it? That's me, done and dusted?

She slapped the rest of the wine down her soured throat.

'I am not looking God. You hear me. I'm sick of it. I'm sick of the compromise and the selling of your soul for what... what exactly? Selling who you are and what you are for a nice house in the suburbs with a pool and two trips overseas each year.'

Suddenly, the lights turned out over the Sacré-Coeur. Midnight obviously. Either that or she was about to be hit by a lightning bolt.

She poured some more wine into the glass and sipped it thoughtfully. Tomorrow, she would really see Paris. She'd see the Louvre and the Eiffel Tower and all those other things she had learnt about in fourth form French. She was alone, not lonely. There is a difference, she told herself. Not lonely. Just alone. Self-reliant and independent. Yeah, she could do that.

She undressed and climbed into the narrow single bed in the nun's cell. And just to reassure herself that there were people out there who gave a shit about her, she picked up her

mobile and texted a Happy Birthday to Ally and a Hi to Mike
back in NZ

Chapter 4

Dumped by an Eight-Year-Old

HER SLEEP WAS not restful and at 4am as the sun was stretching and downing the first cappuccino of the day in summertime Paris, she woke to a call from New Zealand. It rang off before she could take it and no message was left.

Are the kids ok?

Her heart raced in panic. Her mother was right. Once you became a mother, no matter how old they are, or where they are, whether they're at home with you or with their father, you will always be a mother. A mother, who worried, it seemed.

Lying in the narrow bed she wondered how different her life could have been. The 'If's' were capitalised and punctuated. IF she'd stayed on at that job, or not married, or stayed at Microsoft, or not had the kids when she did. It had started off so well. She'd gotten the degree early, she'd backpacked and seen the world, she'd had big jobs, she'd married an investment banker...

And then it all turned to shit.

She threw on a pair of jeans and a clean t-shirt and went in search of the communal toilets and shower. It was a nice enough little hotel. A French Fawlty Towers. The lift was old fashioned grille and the shower a humongous colander shower head over an austere wooden soaking mat. She probably should have kept her jandals on in the shower, she rebuked herself. Oh well. She darted back to her room and prepared for the day.

She reached for the lipstick.

'Bugger that.' She shook her head.

Why bother when there's no one to see you?

Instead she scrunched her passport and money into a travellers' belt and grabbed her camera, throwing it with professional nonchalance over her head. She was a travel writer! Single woman, out to see the world. PJ O'Rourke cataloguing witticisms in a Moleskine notebook or Kate Adie on holiday from Iraq.

They congregated in the reception. Dave and Catherine looking puffy eyed. Jamie hadn't slept well, and the presence of both of their children in their family room had defeated any marital consolation. Meg let slip a wry smile.

Welcome to my world!

'Ok everyone sorted? First up, the Louvre.' Dave had them organised.

'Dave, minor problem, it says here that the Louvre isn't open on Mondays.'

'Where?'

'Here in my guide book.' Meg passed it over to him.

'Ah. Ok.'

'What about that other museum you wanted to see...the Rodin or something?' Catherine suggested.

'We could walk to the Notre Dame and the Île de la Cité and then on to the Rodin place.'

'Ah yes, the Museé Rodin.' Dave stroked his chin. Sensing another recount of jolly old adventures, Meg resolved to assist the group's organisation.

'Ok, so what train do we need to get?'

She didn't want to let on that she'd actually never heard of the Museé Rodin. Whilst Dave checked the Metro timetables, she covertly scanned her guide book. Apparently it was a museum of French sculpture.

'Is there a McDonalds down there, Daddy?' asked Sophie.

Meg could see the allure of eating le Big Mac, - who couldn't - but it took every ounce of self-control to not roll her eyes. Dave appeared to not hear and instead opened the heavy glass door and led the group out onto the street.

It was already warm and a little humid and Meg had dressed in serious traveller gear with a heavy jacket, t-shirt and jeans and the money belt stuffed around her waist making her short-wasted figure, no-waisted. Her long hair was curly in the humidity, and for the first time in days, perhaps months, even years, she had not one scrap of makeup on.

The streets were busy but not yet bustling. Small groups of tourists were wandering aimlessly along the cobblestones stopping to admire the pencil sketches the artistes of the Marais had displayed on easels. In the cafés waiters presided over steaming cappuccino machines. The accordion man was unpacking his instrument and placing his cap on the ground as the group passed through the entrance to the Metro at Solferino, under the covered glass roof and down the stairs – sticky with dropped icecreams, split drinks and grime - into the Metro tunnels. The long white tiled walls of the tunnels were tagged with sooty graffiti and redolent of stale pee and rotting food.

The inner city commuter crowds were multicultural and urbane. Tall dark Algerians, chic Parisians, Romanians and Russians all hanging onto the straps in the train with the same uniform expression - sophisticated disinterest.

An older woman breathing heavily climbed aboard and scouted the carriage for an empty seat. Seeing none available she started to reach for the leather strap when Meg interrupted her with earnest French.

'Assez-y-vous, s'il vous plait.'

She hadn't meant it to be an order, but the startled woman obediently sat down. For years that had been the first thing she'd heard in her French classes. 'Sit down please'. But perhaps she shouldn't scare the locals with her attempts at speaking the lingo?

Emerging from the underworld they blinked hard at the sunlight and made their way through the city crowds. Outside the Notre Dame they came across an old man pigeon-whispering. He was surrounded by the birds. They perched on his outstretched arms and on his head and as they approached they could see he was encouraging the birds to settle on tourists' heads and shoulders.

Jamie ran towards them impulsively.

'Can I do it?' he asked the old man who smelt vaguely of sardines.

'Yuk, Jamie! You'll get bird poo in your hair.'

He ignored Meg and with his parents' blessing stood still whilst the birds with a million germs per clawed foot crawled over his head, arms and shoulders. They took photos, but Meg stood well back, not keen to encourage the old man who simply wanted his palms pressed with Euros.

Naturellement.

The Notre Dame was ominously dark inside, and somewhere in the hidden vestibule a low chanted Mass was keeping a melancholy refrain. Death sat in front of the main alter. His shadow a reminder of life's end. Hanging from the tall vaulted ceiling were the lights their incandescence subdued by the tears of the saints and of sinners. To the side, candles lit up the pained faces of the female supplicants. All light was throttled by the heavy lead light windows and when it was finally released into the church it fell like shards of glass – beautiful but deadly. A breeze from somewhere unseen, was teasing the candles. At the front of the cathedral the altar towered above them all. Meg found it decidedly unsettling.

How big was this God, if that was his altar, and by the same reasoning, how small and insignificant to Him must she be? She moved purposefully through the the cathedral searching for the famous Rose Window. It was stunning, but still not enough to settle her rising panic.

Meg hastily took a couple of photos and then scarpered out into the light. She was running from the sadness, the devastation of a thousands of years of heart rent, unheard prayers.

She waited patiently outside for her friends who had obviously not found the Cathedral as unnerving as she had.

Almost half an hour later they emerged from the cathedral and joined her standing outside on the forecourt.

'Where next? Where's the Rodin place?' Meg asked.

'It's not far maybe a mile or so.' Dave answered.

'Nooooooo. I don't want to walk anymore,' Sophie started to whine. 'I don't want to. Can we just find a McDonald's?'

Ignoring her dissent, they started down the road. It was quite possibly the longest mile in history. Sophie dawdled behind, whimpering and clutching her side.

'What's wrong with Sophie?' Meg asked Catherine.

'She's not feeling very well' Catherine replied. Why don't you go on ahead with Jamie and I'll walk with Sophie.'

Catherine was such a good mum.

Unlike me.

They trotted on past the shops and cafes, until finally they arrived at the Museé Rodin and joined the queue outside the entrance. Not long after Catherine and a pouting Sophie arrived.

'Helloo' Catherine said perkily. 'Sophie's not feeling very well. I think she's even got a bit of a temperature, Dave.'

'Oh that's not too good.'

He looked at his wife pleadingly. With the wisdom of a long-married spouse she caught his unspoken request.

'Tell you what. Meg can you go in with Jamie and we'll wander around with Sophie. I'll get her a drink and see if she feels a little better.'

'Ok. Come on Jamie.' Meg grabbed the eight-year old's hand and they wandered into the garden.

The garden of the Musée Rodin is not only the lasting tribute to the genius of sculptor Rodin, but is also one of the most tranquil spots in Paris. It features a large mansion house and manicured lawns peppered with sculpture that is so visually descriptive that when Rodin released his image of Anthony, Parisian society of the day suspected he had entombed a body in the bronze.

Meg was impressed. She mentally traced the line of the sinews underpinning Anthony's muscles. As she walked through the gardens she was awed by the incredibly realistic sculpture, again and again - the Burghars of Calais, the Gates of Hell, and then exposed to the elements, surrounded by hedges snipped into topiary cones, The Thinker.

What on earth could he be thinking? Does it change so much over the years? Don't we all have the same human need for companionship and love and life?

Ensconced in her own heavy thoughts, she let Jamie run along ahead. Like a spaniel let off the leash he enthusiastically skipped along and was now humming happily to himself tripping along the raised border of the pond.

'Jamie, get down. Come on, it's a quiet place.'

He pulled a face and started to jump on and off, the pond's siding.

'Jamie! Stop it!' Exasperated, she ran to catch up to him, and then grabbed his sleeve.

'Come on Jamie, you don't run around like this in public. It's not a playground.'

'But it's boring.'

That'll be the typical response to the incredible talent and skill of Auguste Rodin!

'No it's not.'

'Yes it is. It's BOR –ING.'

'Jamie!'

She couldn't think of anything further to say.

He did have a point - it wasn't terribly exciting for an eight-year-old. Sensing victory, he broke free and raced off down the path cutting in front of a guy trying to frame a photo shot. Meg jogged, red-faced after him.

'Come on Jamie, get out of it!'

'Oh no, sorry. He got right in the way of your shot didn't he? Sorry!'

The guy moved the camera from his face and turned to talk to her. It was a professional looking camera with a long lens. She noticed the tripod and camera bag slung over his shoulder, his face a study in concentration.

Maybe he's a photo journalist? He's definitely serious about it, whoever he is. She could feel the intensity emanating from him.

'Yes, oh, it's ok. Don't worry about it. I can get another shot.'

He was probably swearing under his breath!

Meg had stopped right in front of him now and could see his mouth was smiling. His eyes however, were not. She sized him up. His hair was cropped very short and sandy brown. Military short? He was dressed in jeans, a lightly tanned, fit torso visible through the crisp white cotton shirt. He'd barely spoken a sentence but there was something about him. Some mysterious something. A thinly veiled sadness? A secret? She couldn't put her finger on it. Jamie started kicking a stone along the path, and racing after it.

'They don't stand still for long do they?' He proffered the consolation. She rolled her eyes.

'Oh, he's not mine. I'm just looking after him for his parents.'

Is he relieved?

How old was he? Late twenties maybe? Definitely too young for her. But there was that accent - English, soft, educated. She was a sucker for an accent. A Brit. A good-looking Brit. His girlfriend was probably just behind the hedge.

'Are you enjoying it...the sculpture?' she asked.

'I am.'

She smiled. 'I'm amazed at how amazingly true to life they are. It's incredible too how they're staged out here in all weather. I guess it even snows out here in the winter.'

Of course it snows in the winter you stupid woman! It's Paris!

But she could not stop.

'It's so life-like. They said that the Parisian society thought he'd buried a real person in the bronze.'

'Really?'

She searched his face for a hint of mockery, but there wasn't any, only warmth. And he was still smiling, but this time his eyes crinkled too.

'Um, he's doing it again...' he smiled.

'What?'

'Your little boy, he's on the side of the pond. There.'

He pointed to a small figure just up ahead.

'Oh crap. I'd better go. Nice to meet you. Enjoy your morning.'

Enjoy your morning? What the hell am I? A tour guide?

She raced off to catch up with Jamie. 'You have got to stop being such a pain.'

'Do you know what?' He turned to her scowling.

'What?' Meg replied.

'Sophie told me she doesn't want you with us anymore.'

He studied her face. 'She just wants you to go away and leave us alone. I do too. I don't like you very much.'

Smacked in the head. Ouch. That hurt.

'Oh. Ok.'

She turned away for a moment.

Obviously I've been too strict. Well done Meg. Your success with the opposite sex extends to small boys. Dumped by an eight-year-old, now.

She turned back to the small boy, unsmiling and controlled.

'Tell you what, let's go back to the café and see your Mum and Dad.'

They walked smartly to the café where Catherine and Dave were sitting enjoying a coffee with their daughter.

'Everything ok?' Dave asked.

'Fine. Fine.'

'Do you want a coffee?'

'No thanks, that's ok. I'm just going to head off to the loo for a bit.' She walked off into the toilets sniffing.

Am I really that horrible? So witchy, that even eight-year-old boys dump me in public? But what about the cartoon, on the plane?

When she came out of the cubicle, Catherine met her at the hand basin.

'Jamie told me what Sophie said.'

'Oh, look that's ok.' She brushed it off with the water from the tap.

'It's only natural that they would want it to be just your family! They were really looking forward to seeing you and Dave! I'll just give you and your family some space to be on your own a bit and after I've seen the rest of the Rodin I'll head off and do some sight-seeing on my own.'

'But where will you go? On your own?' She winced.

'I'll be fine! You forget, I travelled all the way around Asia on my own, I'll be fine! I'll catch up with you tonight back at the hotel. And don't worry about Jamie, they just want some time with you, it's only natural.'

'Meg! Are you sure?'

'Absolutely! I'll just have a look inside the Mansion House and then I'll head off to the Museé D'Orsay I think.' She reassured her friend and headed off in the direction of the L'hôtel Biron.

The Kiss caged her breath.

There was something about the purity of the white stone matched with the purity of the emotion. The adoration on his face, the woman's submission to love. Pure love - complete submission one to another. His hand on her knee, consoling, adoring, claiming. 'This woman is mine', that hand says, and her hand around his neck, her face dipped slightly in acquiescence to his lips, responds with passionate acceptance.

Meg took the requisite photo with the camera she'd bought especially for her trip. It wasn't as long and cool as the smiley Brit's but it had been all she could afford. After looking over some of the other works she made her way through the busy Parisian street to le metro, placed her ticket through the automatic reader and trailed along the white tunnels.

The world walked past her and she revelled in her invisibility. The old man with his cane, the woman jabbering in French on her mobile - far too quick to catch a word - the young German students with their harassed teacher, the elegant Parisian woman effortlessly casting a shadow of dignified glamour. French, English, German, babble of all shape and colour, tone and intonation. Meg smiled at the dark brown eyes of the little girl whose hair had been braided in rows, and she smiled back generously. Her teeth stark white posts in the gate-way of her mouth.

The train was efficient and Meg took careful note of the line and the stations they passed. She suspected she was having a little tiki tour of Paris, and that she could have simply walked between the two museums but she enjoyed the challenge of deciphering the French instructions and finding her way.

At least there was only herself to worry about. And in that case, getting lost was a matter of perspective. If she eventually found her way to the house in the woods had she been lost at all, or was she merely taking the long way? If she had taken the wrong turn all she had to do was turnaround and take the other option.

Perhaps I should have left a trail of bread crumbs so I can find my way home again.

Chapter 5

The Tourist Trail

SHE GOT OFF the train at Solferino and walked up the stairs into the light, emerging blinking and gritty and headed in the general direction of the Musee D'Orsay. The sky clouded over and started to drool large drops of rain. Meg pulled on her rain coat. It was as efficient and stylish as a light blue, supermarket bag.

Her hair started to curl into coils and stick out of the fetching hood in all directions. Her camera strap hanging heavily around her neck left a large red smear and the money pouch around her waist created a special, unusual roll that was as obvious as a hi-vest emblazoned with the words 'Get all my money here!'

To cap off the charming picture of sophistication, the blue raincoat spilled over her body and camera like an emergency tarpaulin shrouding the disaster that lay beneath.

At least my mascara's not running.

She hadn't put any on! Hah!

As she turned the last corner en route to the D'Orsay she came across a long straggling queue of tourists, all clutching their Lonely Planets. Queuing seemed par for the course in the UK and Europe, and she had queued at the gates of castles and at the Tower and at trains since arriving in the Northern Hemisphere a week ago. It was the most obvious difference to everyday life in New Zealand, where a queue was not usually an everyday event. The British in particular had some strange conventions when it came to acceptable queuing etiquette and Meg – always a quick learner – had quickly realised that jumping the queue was a disgrace second only to public nudity.

'Pardonez moi,' she said quietly to the guy she bumped with her backpack.

'That's ok,' the man replied in a broad Texan accent.

It started to rain properly now as she stood pensive in the queue, listening to the conversations around her, happy in her invisibility cloak. Looking up briefly, she scanned the queue. Nope, Catherine and Dave weren't there, she was truly on her own. No need to urgently abandon her place to take a small child to the loo, no need to provide a constant stream of educational and upbeat chatter, no need to plan what next after this visit – where to go to eat, what to eat, how far was it, how late they'd be back to base....

No need to think about anyone else's needs. No snotty noses, or weak bladders, or rumbling tummies, except perhaps her own.

And it was bloody fantastic! For ten whole minutes she was alone with her thoughts. And then she saw him.

In later recollections she'll say she doesn't remember what made her look up, let alone call out. She was content, on her own, she will say.

'Oi, Englishman,' she waved. 'Over here.'

He was surprised to see Meg in the queue. Perhaps it was embarrassment, maybe he wouldn't even want to acknowledge her.

After all we've shared one short conversation about children, and no doubt the girlfriend was probably bringing up the rear somewhere.

She almost didn't want him to come over, and wished she'd not said anything at all.

But he did. Waking over to join her in the queue, guided in by her flaming cheeks - as clear a guide light as those little emergency LEDs on the cabin floor of the plane. She hoped he wouldn't notice that she was a human glow-stick as she subdued a recalcitrant curl and planted it behind her strawberry ear.

'Hi. Imagine seeing you here.'

'In all the gin joints...' she laughed.

'I wanted to see the Louvre but it was shut,' he offered almost in apology.

'I realised that this morning. It's a shame isn't it? Though the D'Orsay is meant to be wonderful. I vaguely remember from fifth form French.'

He nodded and pulled out his guide book and read out the description –

'The Gare d'Orsay was built at the turn of the 20th century and served as the Paris station for trains coming from southern France until 1939. After that, it continued to be used for smaller and more local trains until the station was closed in 1973. In 1977, the French government had the brilliant idea to convert the historic and beautiful building into a museum, and the Musee d'Orsay opened in 1986.'

OK, so he's a by-the-guidebook kind of guy.

He had a slight accent, a lilt in his soft speaking voice. She liked it, though she had no idea where in England it was from. At least it was a nice accent, not an obviously gobshite kind of 'where the fook do y' get off' accent.

'Well then. Sounds like we shouldn't miss it.'

Whilst waiting in the queue she had morphed into a fifth form History teacher, complete with chastity belt and fetching, red ears.

'I know it's a bit cheeky, but if you were to pretend you were travelling with me then you could join me here in the queue and then you wouldn't have to wait as long. I've already been here for an hour or so.'

He cast a glance over the queue trailing off around the corner and then mentally counted how many people were in front of them.

'Ok. Sounds good,'

'I'm Megan, by the way.' *Should I offer my hand or la cheek a la Francaise?*

'I'm John.'

'Hi. Nice to meet you John. Not Dave? I thought every male in England was a Dave.'

It was as comfortable as dragging fingernails down a blackboard. Or realising you've walked down the high street with your skirt in your knickers.

'How long have you been in Paris?'

'Where are you staying?'

'Sorry, you first.'

Be cool, stupid woman.

'How long have you been in Paris?'

'I arrived here yesterday afternoon, and leave tomorrow. Just a quick trip.'

'Are you from Australia.'

She grimaced.'New Zealand!'

'It's like asking a Canadian if they're an American. But don't worry, all my family live in Australia, my mum's Australian and I've lived there on and off too.'

'Sorry about that. I've always wanted to go to New Zealand. My parents are planning a trip there so I think they'll beat me there. I hear it's beautiful.'

'It is. And the people are lovely too. Polite and quiet. Like me!'

She smiled a smile that jumped from her face and hijacked his. 'It's got everything – New Zealand I mean. You can go skiing and surfing in the same day if you want to. Of course the South Island is the most famous for its tourist spots – with its mountains and snow and lakes – but the North Island has a lot to offer too... I live in Auckland, which is in the North Island.'

She did this. She talked too much, said too much, revealed too much, too quickly. It was fast too, almost breathless. She prided herself on being an open book, and was often hurt by how many people she met on the street, in the supermarket, on airplanes and other public transport, were simply not readers.

She wondered now if it was too much for this quintessentially polite, softly-spoken Englishman.

'How long have you been in Paris, John?'

'I came across for the Bourget airshow.'

'On your own? Are you in the Air Force?'

She had to keep reminding myself that this was not an interview, or an inquisition. Spanish or otherwise.

He paused for a moment.

'Well no, actually. I came across with a friend, but she and I had a bit of a falling out.'

Bingo. Girlfriend! See. The nice ones are always attached or gay. Sometimes both.

'Where are your friends you were with this morning?'

'I decided to give them some space as a family, you know. Just so they could be by themselves.'

And besides the eight-year-old dumped me.

'Did you come out from New Zealand with them?'

'Kind of yes and no. It's a long story. They live in Australia and I came out with the kids and then delivered them to their parents who had travelled to England to visit her parents about a week before. It's all very confusing. We've all had a few days in England together and now here of course.'

The queue had moved forward at a fair pace and as they reached the gates, John and Meg prepared to purchase their tickets. But just as they crossed into the foyer they were directed to the side and sidled in without paying.

'Great trick!' John laughed as they walked into the main room and were overwhelmed with the soaring roof and the huge old clock set against the ceiling to floor windows.

'Wow!'

'That's amazing!'

They spent the rest of the day wandering through the Manets and the Monets stopping to reflect on artworks that caught their attention.

The Degas L'Absinthe.

'Absinthe makes the heart grow fonder.'

'Oh hahaha. You're quite a funny guy.'

'Quite?'

'Well, yes.' She blushed.

They found the perfect vantage point and the best camera positions and slipped from masterpiece to masterpiece.

'We used to have a print of this picture in my room when I was a little girl,' she said pointing to The Ballet Class.

He looked at her carefully, and turned his head to one side.

'You're quite arty really aren't you?'

'Well, not really. I'm a writer. I mean, I run a PR/ Marketing business and I write freelance. What do you do at home?'

'I'm a Senior Electronics Engineer.'

'And that would mean you do.... what...?'

'Design stuff. Consulting. You know.'

'Wow an engineer interested in art. That's very impressive. The engineers at Varsity that I knew were known for their uncouth behaviour – peeing in gumboots, sleeping with sheep you know!'

'I love how you say that. Know – in.'

'Hey. No accent jokes. Why how do you say it?'

'No, it's nice. I think you have a lovely accent.'

She turned to look at him, but he had already moved along and was standing staring at a picture of a woman reclining on her bed, her hand placed suspiciously between her legs.

'Alone – Henri Toulouse Lautrec,' she read.

'She seems to be having quite a good time on her own.'

Meg nodded. 'Yes, well one has to keep one's hand in.'

Overwhelmed with silliness, she started to giggle. The feeling started in her feet and moved like warm water up to her head. Heady, round, joyous giggles. Before long her cheeks were sore from smiling. John playfully pushed her shoulder.

'I was thinking, Megan.'

He said Megan as if it was two distinct words – Meg – in.

'Uh huh.'

'It's almost closing time and we've pretty much seen everything, do you want to come out for a coffee with me?'

She stopped and thought quietly.

'Yeah, ok,' she said slowly. Then gaining courage she added...

'That would be good. Yeah. That'll be fun.'

After all, it was only coffee. Not coffee and dessert. Just a coffee. No harm in that. And besides it was too early to be launching into 'that kind of coffee' - the one that men often ask for after a night sharing cocktails and dancing. What's more, he was still too young for her which was a very good thing, given that she was *off men* and definitely hadn't come to Europe to 'find a man'.

He looked pleased and together they walked out into the late afternoon and around the cobbled corner until they spied a racing-green awning and the traditional terrace seating of a Parisian café. Above the awning flowerpots full of flowers and shrubs spilled out scratching at the café's sign 'La Flore'.

The waiter came to seat them and as they approached the table, John reached forward and pulled out her chair.

This is different!

This was a very different breed of man than the Antipodean version. Urbane, yet not effete. Strong but not overwhelming. An engineer who likes art!

Une tasse de café noir' s'il vous plait,' Meg smiled to the waiter.

'A deux,' John added.

'What a great afternoon! That was brilliant,' he said.

She smiled.

The day wasn't yet done yet, was it?

Chapter 6

A work in progress

DUSK FELL SOMEWHERE between the second coffee and the opening of the beaujolais. Then it's fair to say they were in engaged in a different type of outing - one that verged on being seen as a date.

The rules of dating are very clear. Thou shalt not discuss exes, nor children, nor baggage – emotional or otherwise. Thou shalt not discuss difficulties or reveal details. The rules are very clear. Thou. Shalt. Not.

Dating again in your late thirties is fraught with difficulties and the detritus of past relationships. The path to true love is strewn with the ruin of loves past. Meg had learnt all about the vulnerabilities of men who seemed articulate and erudite on the surface but were just as insecure and shaken by the destruction of their marriage or personal lives, as the suddenly single women she knew. All in the same boat – a leaky one at that – they clung on to the hope that past lives at least indicated that lessons had been learnt and that as recycled people they were therefore more cynically prepared for the future.

Not that they were on a date or anything! They were simply enjoying a glass of Beaujolais on a summer evening in Paris. Just the two of them.

'So what do you do in New Zealand?'

'I've worked through my own marketing communications consultancy for over thirteen years now. After leaving my husband in October 2005, I worked for a small telecoms company on contract that provided me with the financial means for my escape really. That first pay packet I received into my own personal bank account was so brilliant. I was like a knackered Roman slave or something. I could buy my freedom from the marriage. It was pretty much dead by then. I didn't immediately leave. I could buy stuff for me. So, I paid some bills first and bought myself some new shoes.'

'Shoes? Didn't you have any shoes?' he asked.

Good God what am I on, talking about buying shoes?

'Well yes, I had shoes, but my feet are really small and it's hard to find my size in New Zealand.'

'You're really petite, like my Mum. I can see why it would be difficult to buy shoes in the land of the hobbits.'

'Did you see The Lord of the Rings?'

'Loved it! I really want to go to New Zealand, but I've been saving pretty hard to buy a house, so apart from the odd trip up to London to see the shows, I haven't been going very far.'

'What sort of shows? Airshows?'

'No the West End. It's great fun. It's been brilliant being able to get out and do stuff, my ex-wife wasn't very well and we didn't go out much. Since we divorced, I feel as if I've got my life back. I feel a bit guilty about that. Do you feel guilty about leaving your husband?'

'I do.' She shrugged. 'But you know what? I did try. I tried really hard to make it work, but in the end I realised that he has to try too. You know? He has to take some of the responsibility...He could do a hell of a lot more you know, to help himself, but he just didn't seem able to do it... not even for me... or the kids.'

'I know what you mean about feeling guilty,' He leaned in.

'I felt so guilty about divorcing my wife.'

She nodded in sympathy.

They fell silent for a moment.

'Locks? You said earlier that you were writing about locks at the moment.'

'Er, yes, just call me Madame Lash!' She made the corresponding thrashing sound of a whip to illustrate.

'Well that's certainly interesting.'

'Not really. It's not like I grew up desperate to write training manuals about hinges and locks, but it was a contract

I could do from home and I needed to be around the house for the kids. It's not terribly salubrious, but it brings in a good income and between that work and the ex's child support and the rental income from the lodger I've installed in the downstairs' room, financially the kids and I are ok. I even managed to buy myself a new Landrover last year to replace the Ford Exploder.'

'Ford Exploder?'

'Yeah it finally died last year. It was ancient.'

'So you've got your decree nisi?'

'My *whatsy*?'

'Divorce papers.'

'Oh, the divorce hasn't settled yet, the ex has decided to leave it for a year until we sell up and split the money we've made on the house St Heliers. I'm really grateful he's given me and the kids some time, but can't help feeling that somehow I'm going to pay for the kindness. You know I thought before I started all this that we could even have 'happy divorce'.'

'Is there such a thing?'

'Well I thought so. Once upon a time I thought we could get together and have Sunday dinners as a family, from time to time. But that was before the nasty emails and text messages and all the crap. I always have this fear that eventually he'll stop paying support for the kids. Then I will be screwed!'

'How many kids do you have?'

'Three. A son and two daughters.'

'How old are they?'

'Alex 13, Sarah's 11 and Jayne is 7.'

'Where are they now?'

'They're staying with their Dad while I'm travelling. It's a good opportunity for them all really, he hasn't spent very much time with them since we separated in 2005. You said before you were here with a friend... won't she be wondering where you are?'

'Oh it's not like that. We're just friends. We just came over to see the air show. We had a bit of a falling out this morning really and I needed some space. We just don't have anything in common any more.'

'Oh.'

'It's true. We really are just friends.'

He trailed off. She couldn't read his face. Was this a no-go subject? Did he want to talk about it?

'I'm really enjoying the wine. This is lovely John.'

'It is lovely. You're great company!'

'I am not! So far I've told you all about my horrendous divorce and that I write about locks for a living.'

He laughed.

'Well I think you're amazing. Your own business and kids and everything.'

He smiled and all at once she felt hideously self-conscious about the tarpaulin she was wearing and the building renovations it covered, not to mention, the lack of makeup.

She longed to step back in time to the basin this morning and that opened lipstick. Just a smear. A touch of mask. A hint. If only...

The waiter buzzed them.

'I think they want us to order some more...it's getting late.'

'Megan would you like to join me for dinner?'

'Wow, that would be charming John!'

They both started to giggle.

'Oh and call me Meg.'

'Why don't we see if we can find somewhere nice around the corner. I'll just pop to the loo, back in a minute'.

She watched him wander through the café, full of the evening crowd, fresh from work. It was getting late and she was going to go off to dinner with this strange bloke she'd picked up in a queue in Paris? Unbelievable.

Incredible that they should both like the same things – art, musicals, music, travelling, photography – and that they had parallel problems with their respective exes. She picked over the memory of the conversation.

Had he seemed bitter and twisted about the failure of his marriage? Not really. Maybe Catholic guilt?

She'd clocked the cross on a chain around his neck.

In which case, my womanhood is safe. Isn't it?

She watched him pick his way through the tables back to the expensive camera gear he'd entrusted to her and paused at my elbow.

'Ready?'

'How much is it?'

'I've paid already!'

'You have not!'

'No, it's all sorted. Come on let's go and find a lovely French meal.'

Paying for the meal was often seen as a down-payment on after dinner entertainment, in Meg's recent experience. When she'd first been turfed out into the dating scene, she had learnt very quickly that going Dutch was the only way to avoid this embarrassing fait à compli. John didn't seem the type though. There was something endearingly old-fashioned and chivalrous about him. They walked down the street side by side, falling into easy stride with each other and then John swapped to the street-side.

'What are you doing?'

'Walking on the road side to protect you.' He blushed.

'From what? Marauding Frenchmen?'

'I was taught that it was good manners.'

'Wow, things are different over here. They sure as hell don't do that in New Zealand. You'd be lucky to get a guy to open a door for a woman at home. Hey, can you help me with something. I promised my kids that I'd see the Eiffel Tower and tonight is my last night here. Would you walk there with me after dinner?'

'I saw it yesterday, but I haven't seen it at night all lit up. Yeah. That would be great. What about this one?'

Meg looked over the deep windows and the wooden framed doors. It looked lovely, more a local café than a tourist trap. She nodded and he stepped forward to open the door as she passed through in all her anoraked gorgeousness.

Over dinner they talked about everything that is typically banned in a date time conversation - politics, religion, failed marriages, and hopes for the future. She spoke about the IT industry and being her own boss and asked him again what he did for a living and he changed the subject.

For a brief moment she wondered if that would be the sticking point. The place where their agreeableness and compatibility wavered. Was he in the army? Was he a spy? Why wouldn't he give details? Funnier things had happened in her life and ever the journo she tried rephrasing the question.

But still, he revealed nothing.

It wasn't worth ruining the evening over, so they talked some more about music, and films they both loved. They discussed God and religion, and he claimed he was a Christian guy, but not Catholic.

At one point during dinner whilst she was studiously cutting her chicken breast she caught him watching her. She thought she saw *that look*. And her stomach rolled over. He reached forward and touched her hand – lightly, a little hesitantly – and then curled his fingers around hers. A loud roar of laughter from the table of local men seated behind them, filled the cafe.

John's eyes moved past her to them. She turned to look and saw them all raising their glasses in bonhomie.

'To the happy couple.'

Or something similar in French.

So this is a date?

Chapter 7

The City of Lights

I T WAS CROWDED on the Parisian streets, and the air was buzzing. A light frivolous energy, a Tinkerbell magic that darted and kerned and every now and again illuminated with light. Uncertain of directions and the most efficient route to the Eiffel Tower they ambled along avenues and streets – John would likely call them lanes – until they found themselves walking alongside the Seine. There seemed to be no shadows in the city of light. It was as if everything was glowing with reflected light from the street lamps to the neon lights of shops and stores, and standing sentinel above it all the long necked Eiffel Tower, itself glowing like a lighthouse.

'I think we should be heading in that direction,' Meg pointed.

He didn't seem fazed.

'Let's just head up here onto the road and follow it round.'

He could have said let's just go and lick shop windows and she would have smiled her agreement. A large man with a smudge for a face walked past them, murmuring something. Meg bristled slightly, ever wary.

But there was something about John that reassured her that he would protect her from zombie attacks or slave traders or even dark suspicious men loitering through the streets of Paris. She sized John up as a potential protector.

He wasn't tall or large framed, he was lithe and taut. He'd spoken about his martial arts training and she suspected that behind that benign smile there was a steel resolve. He was completely opposite to her ex-husband's large bulk - there wasn't a scrap of fat on John.

They were walking along the Champs Elysee now dodging couples arm-in-arm walking past, and cyclists pulling up onto the footpath. The traffic was manic, a melting pot of taxis and vans and cars of all descriptions.

'You're quiet.'

'I'm ok. Just thinking.'

'I think we should head across that way,' and he reached out to take her hand to cross the road.

Imagining that death at the hand of speeding taxi was imminent Meg took a leap of faith, grabbed his hand and ran with him to the traffic island in the centre of the famous avenue. Laughing, scrambling and trying to calm their racing breath they paused at the traffic refuge. Meg reached inside her top to yank up a travelling bra and as she did, John grabbed his moment. With one strong move he pulled her in close to him and then he kissed her.

Meg hadn't been expecting that.

Nor had she been expecting the volt of electricity that swept through and subdued the sensible brain that noted that she hadn't known him all that long, that she was in the middle of Paris and that she would surely wake sometime soon; probably just as a taxi collected them. She fought hard against logic and simply acquiesced to the magic. Somehow it was just right. Not logical, not sensible not entirely comfortable and yet, it was right.

Recovering from the kiss she cocked her head slightly to one side and paused to drink in the unusual feeling of having absolutely no words. And then, as if it had never happened John calmly took her hand and lead her, running, giggling like a fourteen-year-old, through the traffic to the other side of the street.

They walked a while in companionable silence. They weren't far from the Eiffel Tower and Meg reckoned they had been pretty much walking in circles. She didn't really care.

'Hey, what time is it?'

John looked at his watch. 'It's 11.45. Oh no.'

'What?'

'It closes at midnight. I don't think we'll get there in time.'

Meg fought her disappointment.

Is the night over already?

She didn't want it to be done.

'Do you need to get to your train?' she asked.

'Actually, I think I've missed the last one.'

'Mmm. Can you catch a taxi?'

'Not really, it's way out of town. It was cheaper.'

She thought for a moment.

'You could come back to my hotel if you like. It's pretty basic but it's better than being on the streets all night or sitting in the Metro.'

She'd seen Betty Blue she knew what the Metro was like, at night. In her backpacking days she'd slept behind the toilets on trains, in bus stations bolt upright and laid flat across a row of seats in airport terminals, a floor guarded by a locked door would be preferable.

'That would be great. If that was alright. I'll sleep on the floor...'

Of course. He's a good Christian guy and I've just met him.

'Why don't we grab a taxi and head back to my place. We seem to be wandering in circles anyway...'

'I hadn't noticed.'

And with that John confidently stepped forward and hailed a taxi. It wasn't long before they were sitting in the back of the cab snuggled in together cheerfully tossing directions to the driver, quietly serenaded by cool jazz.

The streets flew past in a kaleidoscope of colours and a cacophony of sounds – horns, drums, music, laughter and before long they pulled up alongside La Croix. John paid the cab driver and grabbed his day pack before taking her hand and leading her through the door into the hotel.

The night receptionist smiled a cheeky smile and she blushed.

He's sleeping on the floor!

He just smiled more in response to her panicked look and John and Meg climbed into the ancient grilled lift and rode up to the third floor.

'Here we are, then.'

She breezily opened the door to the little single room – her nun's cell – and nonchalantly put her bag down on the little table. As she turned back to chat he pulled her close. His mouth finding hers after several wayward assaults on her nose and chin.

As he pulled her down onto the bed, one hand on her shoulder and the other sweeping her face with tender fingers, she noticed that the view out through her window was dark.

God had pulled the plug on the Sacré-Coeur.

Chapter 8

See you later

'You are coming back...aren't you?'

Meg looked at him anxiously as he rushed to get out the door of the little hotel room.

'Of course I am,' he said with reassuring gusto.

And then he disappeared for an agonising forty minutes whilst she lay on the little single bed and waited. She hadn't told him that a guy had once left her before in similar circumstances and was simply never heard from again. She didn't tell him that because, well, ... he might think she was that kind of girl. The sort that men have dark second thoughts about, turn around and flee away from as fast as they can!

Waiting for your lover to return is not something you do terribly patiently.

But ever the Girl Guide she had wanted to 'be prepared', and on discovering he did not carry any supplies she had insisted he head off into the dark rim-around-the-bath-dirty Montmartre to get some. She'd already broken the rules. She'd brought home a stranger for the night, and allowed him to take refuge in her room, and her heart.

But he'd told her solemnly that he was a Christian kind of guy, and didn't really do the one-night stand, to which she'd nodded. She wasn't a one-night-stand kind of girl either so they were in agreement that he might kip on the floor. But when they reached her room, a funny thing happened – all her clothes fell off. His hand – so sleight – had something to do with it. Then there was the kissing... that was a dead give-away! You don't tend to kiss your mates, well not like that!

Waiting, waiting, waiting....

Should I position my pose on the bed? Nah, too film star sex kitten. Should I nonchalantly look out my window, over the wrought iron balcony to the Sacré-Coeur on the hill so that as he walked in I could casually throw him an 'oh hi' as if, you know, we were meeting for sandwiches.

At two in the morning. In my bra.

Could I get away with appearing to be reading? You know as if we were an old married couple sitting up in bed?

Be cool Megan!

Men just don't realise the agonies we go through trying to be attractive for them.

She jumped off the bed and sprayed on a little more Versace and put on some lipstick. Then rubbed it off. So it looked like it had worn with the day. Casual like. Now she had lipstick on and no mascara. That's uneven. You either do a full face with the full works or a little mascara, eyeliner, and lipstick. He wouldn't notice mascara would he?

She didn't want him to think she'd made an effort. She wanted the overall impression to be casual elegance. (To make up for the previous slovenliness.)

Why don't I just find a ribbon for around my neck, tidy up my trotters, stick an apple in my mouth and lay down on a serving platter for his delectation!

As she primped and preened he raced through the dishevelled streets of Montmartre desperately looking for a chemist. He'd forgotten the French word (le preservatif, just so you know) and had to demonstrate by gesticulating to the pharmacist what he required, in the crazy hours of the morning, and then he had to find his way back to the hotel where Megan was waiting.

Back in the hotel room, nervous and exasperated with herself for being so, Meg jumped under the covers and pulled up the mustard blanket to her chin. She didn't get the chance to feign sleep or boredom. She didn't get the time to feign anything. Unrehearsed, unprepared, the door opened and flushed with early morning cold, he peeled back the covers, took her in his arms and unbelievably, quite unexpectedly, they fell into love.

*****

When she woke her eyelids heavy, she felt panic at not being able to lift her arms. Struggling to get free, she lifted up the strong muscular arm that had curled around her pinning her in place. He didn't stir. Breathing softly and rhythmically she quietly rolled back to survey the scene in her little single bed.

He'd slept curled around her as if they'd been together for years, and she'd snuggled in close, revelling in the warmth. She'd not been chaste since her marriage split but there was something completely different about this morning. No regret, no bitter taste of wine and second hand smoke on her breath. No anxiety about what to say and no race to the bathroom to scrub clean her conscience.

He was quite literally sleeping like a baby!

All that energy quietened, those sparkling eyes shut now, long lashes pinned to his cheeks like butterflies in a display case. Intricate fragility against his smooth, lineless skin.

No laughter lines? OMG how old is he?

As if hearing the voice screaming in her head, he started to rouse.

'Good morning gorgeous.'

He rolled over back towards her as his smile-rise gently dawned across his face. His grey-green eyes opened and found hers.

'How are you?'

'I'm good. You?'

'I'm good.'

Well then, let's all go and have a cup of tea!

The problem with romantic movies is that they never cover off what new lovers actually say in the morning. They never explain that the breath that was only last night so sweet with desire is often a little, shall we say, tired. That the body is ravenous and in Meg's case, desperately aching for coffee.

She leaned forward and kissed him gently on the cheek.

'Shall we go and find some coffee?'

'Mmm. But where's the loo?'

'Oh it's out the door down the corridor and to the left.'

He grabbed his jeans and bare chested headed off in the general direction, leaving Meg to lay back down on the pillow put her hands over her eyes and burst out laughing.

It occurred to her that she could just quickly nip over to his wallet on the side table and look for some ID; an age, an occupation. Yet as she was about to do he was already through the door and pulling her out of bed.

'Come on. Up you get. There's all of Paris to explore.'

'And coffee to find.'

'Well tea, anyway.'

'Hey, weird question but um, how old are you?'

'32. Why?'

Oh thank God it's in the thirties.

'Really?'

'Yeah. Why? How old are you?'

'38.'

'You don't look it.'

'No? Well neither do you.'

'Come on let's find breakfast, I'm starving.'

It didn't take long for them to gather their things and head downstairs in the ancient lift. He stole a kiss in the lift and Meg's heart fluttered. She felt as light as Pavlova.

Which deflated swiftly when she heard the familiar voice before the lift doors opened. Catherine was loudly telling the kids to stop yelling. The doors opened and Meg slapped the UP button before sliding through the closing doors.

Catherine didn't see the flummoxed Englishman heading back upstairs in the lift, she turned only as the lift doors closed.

'Oh there you are! We've been so worried. Where did you go? What happened Meg? Are you OK?' Catherine asked

'I'm fine. I went to the D'Orsay and had dinner out and came home about midnight.'

'On your own?'

'Mmm. I wanted to see the Eiffel Tower but kind of missed it.'

'We were so worried. We looked everywhere at dinner time. David was really anxious. You just disappeared. We thought something had happened to you.'

It kind of did.

'We're going to head down to breakfast, coming?'

'Oh I met someone yesterday and I'm meeting them for breakfast.'

Catherine's eyes widened and then narrowed. 'You're meeting someone you don't know for breakfast, in Paris?'

'Well I kind of *do* know him. We looked around Paris last night.'

'Meg!'

Meg knew what she was thinking, but she didn't have time to stop and explain. Instead she became acutely aware of the lift doors opening behind her and knew that within seconds John's smile would escape and introduce itself to Catherine's alarmed face. Meg impulsively reached forward and pushed the UP button once more shooting John back up to the third floor.

Catherine, distracted by the kids, didn't see and assumed Meg's flush was due to their conversation. She started to muster the fidgeting kids.

'Well we're going to set off now. We'll catch up here at 3.00. Don't forget the flight is at 4.30,' she called out to Meg. And then they bustled through the door and out of sight, just as the lift doors opened behind her.

'What was that all about?' John looked a little put-out.

'Oh just my friend, she's a bit protective. She's gone now to find some brekkie.'

'Clever woman. I think we should do the same. After you.'

She checked Catherine was well gone and then stepped out with John into the Parisian sunlight.

They spent the day wandering from one café to the next, with side jaunts to the Louvre where they laughed about the Da Vinci Code and John jostled the crowds to ensure that she, being only five foot one inches tall, got a decent view of the Mona Lisa.

It was as if they held their breath the entire time. They walked arm in arm, joked and smiled until they realised that they could not beat the clock.

By 2:30 Meg felt the sadness of a closing chapter.

'I need to head back to grab my pack and go to the airport.'

He didn't speak.

'My flight's at 4.30. Back to London.'

'Are you heading back to NZ then?'

'I have a couple of days with a friend in London and head back home next Friday.'

She could see him thinking.

'I'm here until tomorrow.'

They walked in silence to the Metro and waited in the fluorescent light for the train back to Montmartre. He reached into his pocket and started writing on a used billet.

'Here's my email address. Do you want to give me yours?'

She looked at the ticket, taking a moment to decipher the tiny scrawled writing.

'What's thermite?'

He looked away. 'I shouldn't really use that anymore. It's an explosive reaction...'

'Mine's a bit easier. Just my initials - mjsinclair@xtra. co.nz.'

The train pulled up alongside them as he pulled her into an embrace.

'I don't want to say goodbye.'

She noticed the high emotion on his face and briskly refused to acknowledge or return it.

'Well how about, 'see you later'? You could come visit me, in New Zealand.'

His face said 'not likely' but his eyes argued with his face.

With a final kiss and a garbled 'see you later,' she climbed aboard the train and collapsed heavily into an empty seat. When she looked back over to the platform he was still there standing still. Forlorn. As if the train might somehow change direction and return to him. But the train did not. It headed into the dark of a tunnel and there, unseen and unashamed, she let go her tears.

Chapter 9

Don't Dream It's Over

'Alex get off the loo and go to the bus, PLEASE!!'

Meg swished through the kitchen collecting plates half full of cereal and milk and dumping them into the sink. She shouldn't yell but, oh God, they've got three minutes to get to the bus stop or miss the bus.

'Alex! Hurry up!'

'I can't find my shoes.'

Sarah barged past, pushing her mother into the side of the bench.

'Ow. Stop it.'

'Well, you said hurry.'

'I know. But... Alex where the hell are you?'

All the time Jayne sat nonplussed at the counter watching the pre-school rush. Sarah ran to the other side of the room and started pulling on her school shoes.

'Have you seen Alex's?'

'Nope.' She made her way to the counter.

'Mum, we need money for our trip tomorrow and my bus ticket's out of clicks.'

Meg's eyes whitened. '*Now,* you tell me?'

And then she yelled down the passage so loudly that the inhabitants of Nauru wondered what the commotion was. As did Alex, who appeared, eyes blinking lazily against sleep, shoe laces untied. Again. She was about to let rip at Alex when over the fence came a loud call from the Czech neighbours.

'Why you always yelling? Why you always yell at the children.'

Crap. I'm in deep.

She was trying so hard to get them off to school and get them organised, but nothing worked, nothing that is, except yelling. Yelling seemed to lend urgency to her instructions, whilst also helpfully releasing some of the pressure. If she were a kettle she'd be whistling by now. Instead, she started to crumble.

'Come on guys. This isn't fair. It's just not fair. No matter what time you go to bed you're never ready. Why didn't you check your bus tickets last night? Why didn't you get your shoes on while I was in the shower, Alex? Why?'

She started to wail. 'I'm going to have to take you into school now.'

And dodge Social Welfare who are coming to get me after this morning's performance.

'Do you want to be taken away? Do you? Do you want to be farmed out to some other sensible capable mother?'

Little Jayne's eyes widened and her lip started to tremble.'No Mum we love you.'

Alex and Sarah, cautiously grabbed their lunchboxes, ejecting the rotten apple core or mouldy orange peels down the waste master.

'Mum, there's no bread,' Alex said.

Shit.

'Ok, everyone in the car."

There was no choice, she would have to drive them through rush hour traffic to their Parnell based school. On the way she would gather up sandwiches from the little bakery and try and regain her sanity.

To think, two months ago, I was in Paris.

As commutes go, it wasn't bad. She chose to drive down to the waterfront at St Heliers and weave along the bays – Kohimarama, Mission Bay, Okahu – so although the traffic was bumper to bumper it was moving and the view was stirring. The 8km stretch from the CBD to St Heliers Bay is a jewel in Auckland's crown, a waterfront esplanade that provides a pretty slice of golden sandy beaches and the blue waters of Auckland's magnificent harbour. All the while the islands stood sentinel. Brown's Island (which was winter-green now but turned hay-brown in Summer) Waiheke – long-time retreat of the creative and alternative, Motatapu with its treasured farm, and attached to it, its bush clad foil, Rangitoto.

As the Landrover stuttered in the traffic, past the joggers and the dog-walkers, the latte drinkers and the spirulina ingesters, Meg's dark mood started to dissipate.

'What was it like on the Eiffel Tower Mum?' Sarah asked.

'Gosh what made you think of that?'

Stall for time.

'We were talking in class about how it was built to commemorate the French Revolution. I told everyone you'd been there.'

Bugger.

'Uh huh.'

'So, what was it like?'

What had they said in Fifth form French? Views for miles, City of Lights...

Of course, Meg hadn't made it to the Eiffel Tower at all, by the time she and John reached it after their romantic interlude along the Seine waterfront, it had closed for the night. That had been her last night in Paris.

'It was really beautiful. You could see for miles. They don't call it the City of Lights for nothing.'

Memories of the warm white glow of the Sacre Coer, the jazz in the taxi and the smell of his aftershave, flooded in.

'Mum! It's red!' Sarah screamed.

The traffic light was indeed red. She slammed on the brakes and sat wistfully remembering her time with John in Paris. She'd spoken with him almost every day via Skype, since she'd returned to New Zealand, though that had been a surprise. She had wondered if maybe it had been a one- time 'thing.

When she returned to the UK from Paris there were no passionate messages from him on email, and she started to fret that maybe he had been a break from her day-to-day. Simply a glimpse of what her life could look like once she'd finalised the divorce from Murray and gotten herself and the kids settled.

He was too young for her.

He was too handsome for her. Too slim. Too fit.

Too far away.

Of course he was! When she'd applied for online dating she'd had a few restrictions on age and social status, but not many. The one thing she had been clear on was that she didn't want to date anyone who lived out of Auckland. It was too hard, she reasoned. After compromising to what Murray wanted for fifteen years, she wanted to be sure that any new relationship would be grounded on what she wanted. And the kids, of course.

She didn't want to move them from their home, or their school. In time she may have to sell the house but even then she didn't want to move them from the Eastern Bays and the same mates, doctors, soccer club and netball teams. She especially didn't want to move Alex and Sarah from their brilliant school, and little Jayne from her football club and swimming lessons.

Murray had been applying pressure about the school fees. It didn't escape her notice that as the kids no longer lived with him, the salubrious environs of their private school would no longer afford Murray with networking connections.

She hated that. She hated the way that despite all her best efforts she hadn't managed to keep her kids' lives untouched and unblemished by her marital problems.

'You're divorcing me not the kids Murray,' she wanted to scream at him, but she never did. Instead, she forwarded all his emails to a 'Shitty Murray' folder and read them when she was feeling relatively zen. From time to time she would fire off an email salvo but it was usually forced by some pathetic excuse of parenting – almost drowning their seven-year-old through not watching at the water park, forgetting birthdays or not calling, or returning them early from their weekends together – like sandwiches that had gone stale and were no longer appetising.

Strictly speaking, she was divorcing him, and in that disloyal act she had single-handedly ruined the kids' lives.

Hey There Delilah came onto the radio. She turned it up and started singing along. It had been on the last night in London as she checked her messages and she saw one from Thermite. She smiled when she read the name. It read.

Hi Meg, I've just got in from work and realised that you didn't receive my first message. It bounced. I have been having a few problems with email. Anyway, I just wanted to say how much I enjoyed meeting you. I smile whenever I think about the time we shared in Paris. You brought out the best in me, I think. I'd love to share some photos with you and if you did have that one of The Kiss I'd love to see it. You made Paris for me. Anyway I better sign off its late and I need to get my beauty sleep.
Talk soon. John xx

The traffic crawled past the Parnell baths and alongside the train tracks. Meg flicked her indicator and turned up towards Parnell Rise.

'Dad said he couldn't see us this weekend.'

Meg silently pulled a face and forced a calm voice. 'Why's that Sarah?'

'He's going to Germany again. He's really, really busy.'

'Really busy' murmured Jayne from her seat in the back.

His lawyer had asked that she be reasonable. He was, after all, a very busy man. Too busy to see his kids once a fortnight.

And she wasn't? Meg scowled. She slid the car into an empty space alongside the brick school building. The older two tumbled out and without so much as a wave or a kiss they raced off to be with their friends.

'Bye, love you!' Meg laughingly yelled after them.

They knew. Didn't they?

It took another half an hour to weave back around the Bays to Kohimarama where Jayne went to primary school. Meg stopped to walk her to her classroom and then continued on through the back suburban streets to home.

Walking into the kitchen and open plan lounge she grabbed her coffee pot and started making a coffee. Above the sink she'd hung a canvas that made her smile:

IN MY VERSION OF HELL, THERE'S ONLY DECAF.

She had just finished pouring the water onto the grind when the familiar tones of Skype started. She hastily grabbed the plunger, spilling a little coffee on the floor as she did, and slid into prime viewing position behind her laptop, at the dining room table.

There was a fuzzy picture at first and an English 'Hang on a min..' and then big black boots came into view. He was pulling them on. They matched the black trousers, black socks, and black long-sleeved polo shirt.

'Oh hi, how are you?' She called to the screen.

'Good, keeping on the straight and narrow. Just getting ready to go on exercise.'

'At night time?'

'Yeah. We do sometimes.'

Weird.

'Do you always wear big heavy boots when exercising...'

'Not always, but sometimes.'

His picture came into view. He was red-faced and seemed distracted.

'I just wanted to see your lovely face before I went.'

'Oh, OK.'

Now she was blushing.

'How are you?'he asked.

'Good. I've just got in from dropping the kids at school. It's a beautiful day here in Auckland. See, it's lovely and sunshiney. Bit cold though.'

She lifted the webcam so he could see the sunshine pouring in through the living room windows. She didn't know why she always felt obliged to give a weather report when they talked on Skype. What was he supposed to say in response? 'It's dark, wet and cold'?

She started to gabble.

'I had to drive them in to school along the waterfront today because Alex was late and Sarah couldn't pay for her bus and they didn't have bread. And the neighbour almost reported me to the police.'

He looked back to the webcam and peered down it.

'The police? What for?'

'Oh nothing really, I was yelling and it was a bit chaotic. Not too bad. She was over-reacting. All good now though.'

She lifted her coffee mug up to show him.

'You got a nice warm one?'

He grinned.

'Coffee. Yes. But only coffee.' She sighed dramatically.

'I could do with you warming my toes.'

'Thought you said it was sunny,' he countered.

'It is. But. Y'know.'

She took a sip. This conversation wasn't really going where she wanted it to go.

'So where are you going to exercise?'

'Wales. I'll be gone for a few days. "

'Oh.'

He quickly changed the subject. She didn't press him. Who exercised in Wales in the middle of the night?

'So, Meg,'

'Yes, John,' she laughed, lightly.

'Well I've been looking and I have two week's annual leave in September. I've been looking at flights.'

'Really? That would be amazing!'

'I was thinking I'd book it for middle September.'

Meg's mind was racing. When were the school holidays? Was he serious?

'I'd love to see you again.'

'I'd love to see you too. I think about Paris all the time. Arrrrgh!'

The webcam frame slid out of Meg's view and she caught a delightful eye-full of John's jacket. It was black – of course.

'Arrgh?'

'I'm running late... I'm going to have to go love.'

'Oh, ok.'

'See you later! We'll talk about my trip to see you when I get back.'

Her quiet 'bye' was lost in the sound of the muffled bumping and thumping and then black screen. He was gone. To exercise. In black. In Wales.

Meg wasn't having it. She knew that he wanted to steer her away from the subject but she wouldn't be deterred. Like hell he was exercising! So why was he going to Wales, in the middle of the night?

She had long suspected that he was military. It filled her with simultaneous dread and excitement. There was something WWII RAF cool about it.

How awfully dashing!

She didn't know much about the military, in fact she wasn't even sure that New Zealand still had an air force, or whether they'd flogged all their planes in the 1990's asset sales. The air force was as far from her everyday life as coal mining or nuclear physics. She didn't even know anyone in the forces, save for a couple of guys who'd joined the RNZAF when she was in her early twenties.

But there was something about John. The haircut. The love of planes. The fit physique. And of course the fact that he wouldn't directly answer her questions – that was a dead giveaway.

He wasn't going to like what she was going to do. She pulled up another Google search screen and typed in the search phrase

What is thermite?

Thermite noun; a mixture of finely powdered aluminium and iron oxide that produces a very high temperature on combustion, used in welding and for incendiary bombs.'a thermite grenade'

She couldn't see him welding.

For bombs?

She couldn't stop now. No, now she was really curious, and irrespective of how many lives this cat had or whether she was in fact a cat, Shroedinger's or otherwise - she just had to keep digging.

She typed into Google.

RAF bases in Wales.

Google was particularly helpful, and the screen flooded with listings. She dismissed the listings that featured mechanical bases but honed in on the one major base that seemed to concentrate on fast jets – RAF Valley.

She'd once seen a documentary on TV about these Harrier jets. The guys had seemed smart and cool despite being hurtled through the sky at frightening speeds. She clicked on the photos but couldn't see any recriminating photos, but then would there be?

Instead there was the cheerful mug of the Station Head Honcho, she wasn't sure of the military term (was it Commander or Commandant like Hogan's Heroes?) and there in black text on the menu bar was a word that she'd heard a great deal about this morning.

Exercises

They weren't talking aerobics.

So that was it. He was an air force guy, and at this very moment he was out there in the night doing some sort of dangerous exercise in deepest, darkest Wales. With thermite.

Bloody hell!

She should probably be worried, but instead she just grinned like The Joker.

Chapter 10

Pokarekare Ana

ŌKAREKARE ANA, NGĀ wai o Waiapu
Whiti atu koe hine, marino ana e

It's not every day that you're treated to a Maori Cultural Group performing *Pokarekare Ana* at Auckland International Airport, whilst waiting in arrivals. Some big wig was obviously arriving, but Meg found herself humming along with a particular Maori-Rhubarb version. She'd once learnt the words to sing in front of a group of WordPerfect executives on the snowy slopes of Sundance, in Utah. She'd forgotten most of the words now, but it still seemed poignant.

The love song was about Hinemoana swimming across the lake to her forbidden lover, and here she was waiting for the arrival of her lover arriving from England. She hadn't seen him in the flesh for two and a half months.

Does he still want to see me?

It had taken ages to get ready this morning. She'd been running an extra couple of km's each morning to try and keep herself in shape and then treated herself to a slim fitting red blouse. She argued with the mirror in her bedroom; she thought she looked pretty good.

She just wasn't sure he would think so too.

But she'd carefully worked it out that if he wasn't 'into her' any more then that needn't spoil his first visit to New Zealand. She would still show him around and he could stay up the road at her friend Tom's house.

Tom had once been a bit more than a friend but she hadn't – yet – told John about that. He would look after him and show New Zealand off to him.

Standing in the waiting crowd she almost convinced herself that she should immediately, with haste whisk John off to Tom's house, so that he could have a great time in New Zealand. She shifted her weight onto her other foot and gave her face a quick respite from smiling. She'd reapplied that lipstick four times already.

Her lips would be permanently dyed red.

He would take one look at her – in the flesh – and turn on his heels and run back to the plane. Or to Tom's. She would drive home alone, with matching lips and burning cheeks.

That was how it was likely to go. She'd had other love adventures that had turned out as similarly unusual. There'd been the guy who had been keen as mustard, until he met her.

Then he'd decided she was too short. She hadn't heard from him since he left to go down the road to get some cigarettes.

Probably a good thing.

Then there'd been the guy who had freaked that she had womb-fruit. He'd glared at the kids' portraits as they sipped wine in her living room. How dare she have kids. How old was she, again? He'd disappeared too, after the wine, to watch the game at home. Must have been a long game – that was twelve months' ago.

Meg's inner critic was in her bitchy prime. It took all her strength to reason with the cow.

But he's met me. He knows what I'm like. In. the. flesh.

And just as she was about to turn and run, there he was. Dressed in a crisp white t-shirt and clean jeans.

Who travels across the world for 30+ hours without a wrinkle or a sweat stain in their t-shirt? Who?

This man had secrets.

He broke from the corralled masses and ran over to her, throwing his arms around her – almost knocking her off her feet – and then (in front of everyone) planted a big kiss on her red, red mouth.

****

A week later

The drive north from Auckland to the Bay of Islands had been leisurely and easy-going. They grabbed a coffee in Whangarei, and then stopped again at Kawakawa and gave the Hunderwasser toilets a quick once over. Meg drove, giving John a chance to catch the view as they headed to the north of New Zealand. John was quiet as she drove, quietly clocking the lush dense bush and the aquamarine bays. Every now and again he placed his hand on top of her hand, which was resting on the gear stick. She didn't feel the need to fill the silence with chatter. Instead they pressed on further and further away from the city, and into the countryside. By the time they drove into Paihia they were feeling weary of the road and ready to turn in for an early night.

The motel Meg had chosen wasn't flash. A double storied long concrete block painted in a cheerful white. It was just a short walk from the Paihia waterfront and Meg had specifically chosen it for its location. She'd wanted to walk everywhere, to the Waitangi marae, along the foreshore and past the touristy shops.

'I was thinking we should swim with the dolphins' she informed John as they unpacked in their room.

'Are you sure? I thought that the dolphins got all stressed from the boat'

'No it's not like that. Actually they are really sensitive about it. You go out on a boat which is run by the local tangata whenua, and actually get into the ocean with them. They're free to swim away and they have really strict regulations about swimming when there's babies or if there's pregnant mums. They've won all sorts of awards for it. People say it's amazing.'

John looked impressed. Meg could tell that this was something a bit different than what he could experience in London, or Wales for that matter.

'You can swim?'

'Yes. Of course I can swim.'

'Well I just thought maybe you know.... It's cold over there... you might not swim so much.'

'We just turf the ice off the top of the pool and then it's good to go.'

A deadpan face for two seconds longer would have sealed the story. Meg playfully shoved him.

'Awwww. You had me there.'

He intercepted her arm and in a fluid movement pulled her close to him and collapsed with her in his arms onto the bed.

'That was very sneaky.'

'I thought it was the epitome of smooth.'

'Yeah, I guess.'

He lightly kissed her face and then leaning in – his breath warm on her cheeks – he started to kiss with passion.

'But what about the dolphins?' she murmured softly.

*****

The assembled dolphin fanciers were a veritable United Nations. A Japanese couple on their honeymoon, a family from one of the Scandinavian countries – all with impossibly white hair and teeth and eyes marine-blue, like the ocean itself - a couple of guys from Aussie, tanned and tattooed, sporting backpacker threaded bracelets and wielding iphones, and the over-tanned Brit gapsters.

And then there was Meg – a short dark curly haired Kiwi – and her sandy haired Brit. He had brought the Canon along and was trying to frame shots of the bush and hills and the rocks and sea. It was overcast and slightly damp and Meg wished that it had been a stunning spring day.

She knew how pretty the Bay of Islands could look when everything was shining in sunlight, but John didn't seem to know any difference.

'We could live there,' he pointed out the large wood and glass home tucked into the bush covered bluff overlooking the ocean.

'That's amazing' Meg agreed.

'But what would you do all day? You could photograph the local wild life and maybe send it off to the *National Geographic,* or something'

'And you could bring me cups of tea and write the accompanying text.'

She laughed.

'I'm not so sure about the tea. Coffee, surely.'

'Eeew coffee mouth.'

'Didn't seem to worry you this morning, 'she teased.

She was quietly thrilled; he was talking as if they would one day live together. But where? Here, amongst the bush and by the coast, or there – amongst the clipped hedges and stifled emotions? Or would his career take them somewhere else?

The boat started to slow and then burping in the water the engines stopped.

She knew she was being silly. They'd known each other for precisely two and a half months. How could they know enough about each other to want to make it permanent? Hell, she wasn't even free of the last husband yet.

The boat pulled into a small bay and the captain, a Maori guy dressed in a t-shirt and shorts, grabbed the microphone.

'Yeah, Kia ora koutou everyone. I think this is a pretty good place to stop. Our spotters saw a pod of dolphins here yesterday and they were quite happy to have a play with us. So while the crew get the wetsuits ready I want to let you in on a few house rules. We take the conservation of our local dolphins really seriously. Some of our crew members have been visiting the dolphins for over twenty years and pretty much know their personalities. Giz a wave Floppy! There she is over there by the stern. Chances are we will see the most common species of dolphin in our waters, the Bottlenose dolphin. They're really friendly and playful and tend to want to hang out with us. If for any reason they signal that they're at all unhappy, then we'll need to get outta here. If we don't see any dolphins, we'll give you a return voucher so you can come back again. But yeah, I don't think that's going to happen today.'

There was a squeal and a kerfuffle from the other side of the boat. Meg and John raced over to see, John with camera in hand.

'Oh folks it sounds like we have some visitors. Can I just remind you of a few more things before we suit up and get into the water? So, if they're distressed or if there are calves in the pod I'm sorry folks but we won't be getting in. We want to protect these guys, and respect them. After all, it's their ocean. If you want to get in go and see George, yup, see him just over there on the starboard side of the boat. He's got wetsuits and snorkels and goggles. If you're not a very good swimmer we also have life jackets. No shame in wearing one folks, these guys can swim better than Ian Thorpe. So go grab your gear and get into the water with them. Let them come to you and have a play.'

Meg and John didn't need to be prompted further. John placed his camera down safely inside his day pack and joined Meg in the queue for a wetsuit.

Meg was quietly praying they had her size. And that she could get into the suit without forging a hernia. Thankfully there was and she eagerly zipped up the front, washed her mask in the sea water and then quietly slipped over the lip and into the water.

Meg could feel the water's cool temperature even through the wetsuit. She gasped a little and started a gentle breast stroke over to where the dolphins were playing. She wasn't a stylish swimmer, but a strong one. It wasn't very choppy but occasionally the waves splashed over her and cooled her cheeks. She turned and looked for John.

She watched him slide into the water and swim carefully over towards her. As she watched Meg felt something swim between her legs. She squealed and then quickly stifled it. The dolphin was surprisingly fast and once it had swum through her legs it swam quickly away. It was fleeting but surreal. Exactly as special as she thought it would be.

She tried to keep up with the pod, but they were swimming faster than she could. The cold water licked across her face. It was exhilarating! She lifted her head to see if John was enjoying himself. About 10 metres from where she was, he was swimming madly, and then beneath him and then alongside him in the water, she could see a flash of grey.

She couldn't see his face but she could see that he was fully in the moment. It filled her with pride. Her beautiful country hosting this incredible experience. The dolphins played with the swimmers for about ten minutes but then they were off and the skipper called the swimmers back to the boat.

Meg was cold and weary as she climbed aboard. She tugged at her wetsuit and then quickly wrapped a towel around herself. The deck hands started preparing the boat and the skipper started the engines. The other passengers were excitedly swapping stories and cradling hot mugs of coffee. The backpackers ticked off swimming with dolphins from their travel bucket list and started researching the 'Cream Run'.

Meg looked for John, but couldn't see him amongst the drenched passengers.

Concerned, she walked first to the loo – but it was empty – and then back to the side of the boat and looked out to where they had been swimming in the water.

Amongst the green waves, a lone figure was swimming hard for the boat.

'Tell the skipper to hang on a minute!' she hollered.

A moment later, John wearily climbed on board and the moment he did so, a crew member closed the side gantry. Meg gasped when she saw him; he was translucent. His skin was yellow and his lips were shivering purple. He looked completely spent. She raced over to help him ease out of the wetsuit.

'That was amazing,' he said between gasps.

'One of them swam between my legs and nudged my knee. They really wanted to play.'

'You look horrendous. I thought you were from England, where it snows.'

He brushed the comments aside with a grin, and as he vigorously rubbed the towel over his body the colour started to return to his blanched skin.

They cuddled together on the hard seats at the back of the boat – body warmth being the first rule of survival in the wild – all the way back to the Paihia wharf. There was no need to talk. The colour had returned to John's face too and his lips had stopped shivering. Meg had towel dried her hair and woven herself into his arms.

It was a short trip back to the wharf, the skipper all too aware at how tired and cold his passengers were. But he reckoned they were happy. Cold but happy. 'That's close enough', he reckoned.

After swimming with the dolphins they warmed up in a shower back in the motel unit and headed out to dinner. He chose a fish restaurant down by the Pahia waterfront, and ordered oysters for her. He'd even been game enough to try one, licking the white iodined slipper tentatively off the spoon and then pulling a huge face at the after taste. Loosened by wine and the romance of the dark cloth skies and the lights from Russell twinkling on the harbour waves the conversation was easy and free, just as it had been on that first dinner date in Paris.

They talked a bit more about *real life* – the life that was other from the *now life*. Emboldened by the wine and the intimacy she asked him outright what he did for a living, and for a moment he unpeeled the covers.

'I work for the MOD,' he confided.

'What's the mod?'

'Ministry of Defense.'

She cocked her head to one side and squinted slightly. 'But you said you were an engineer.'

'I am, I'm an Electronics' Engineer.'

She was confused. 'But you said at first in Paris that you were a consultant?'

'I am. Something like that.'

And then it slipped away, again, and she was none the wiser.

Just as he'd done that first night in Paris, he paid for dinner and started to walk back with her to the unit. Arm around her shoulders, his step in stride with hers, he smiled at how petite she was.

'You fit just under my arm,' he smiled.

She smiled back but was deep in thought.

First he said he was an Engineer. Then he said he was a Consultant. Now he says he works for the MOD.

They walked a few hundred metres when suddenly he stopped, as if there was a stone chip in his shoe. She waited patiently as he thought hard and then said in mouse-tones something she couldn't hear. He turned towards her and stopped to find the words.

The night, the stars, the sea – everything was electrified. Time was shocked into pause. She waited for the storm of revelation.

'Meg, I think I'm falling in love with you.'

She knew.

Chapter 11

Where there's smoke there's fire

Jumper in 5 – 4 -3 – 2- 1 minutes

Jumper ready!

Meg swallowed hard. Was it possible to sweat from the soles of your feet? This morning, the idea of a Sky Tower Bungee Jump seemed like a good idea.

'Bungy was created in NZ' she'd told him. 'It's part of the Adventure country thing. You should do it' she'd said.

That was when they were lying in arms under the warm down duvet with the dog at their feet.

Now it seemed like a perfect way to kill your lover. She glanced up at the electronic sign.

Jumper ready

But was she?

No one else in the observation deck was watching as intensely. What if he didn't go through with it? What if he was a wuss?

What if he did?

But then, there he was, dressed in a yellow and blue jumpsuit (aptly named she thought) wearing a slightly concerned face - as concerned as the stiff upper lip action man guise would allow. He cracked a nervous smile and then – face first – he dived off the Sky Tower.

Meg lost all feeling in her lower limbs and abruptly sat down. John was on his way down also, speeding through 192 metres of space at 85kms per hour. Meg couldn't look, yet was transfixed.

And then it was done. He was on terra firma, or at least on the squishy landing pad outside the Sky Tower building and before long he appeared on the observation deck, still kitted out in his jumpsuit.

'OhMaGawd, OhMaGawd, OhMaGawd' She was having problems with words.

'That was incredible.' He threw the words out there at a 100 kms an hour.

'Such a rush! I'm going to do it again.'

'You what?'

'The guy asked if I wanted to have another go so I'm going to.'

Meg knew it now. 'You're nuts!'

'Yeah but it was incredible. You should do it with me.'

'Nah, nah, nah, nah. I'm terrified of heights.'

'So am I.'

'But you just jumped off the Sky Tower, one of Australasia's tallest buildings...'

'Yeah. But...'

She shook her head. 'Nuts.'

'Yeah, I have some!' he grinned.

'No you are NUTS.'

'Look I better get back up there before he changes his mind. See you in a bit.' He pecked her quickly and then Action Man was gone.

Meg wandered through the crowd of tourists to the nic-nac bar and bought a bottle of water. Somehow her mouth was very dry. Then she moved back into position in front of the electronic sign.

Through the tall glass she could see the city stretch out towards the watery horizon of the harbour. The plumped up cushions of Waiheke and Ponui Island smudging green into the background blue-grey of the distant Coromandel ranges. Ferries worked the sea-stretches of the inner harbour and out to the East she let her eye graze through the white squares of homes and shops.

She lived out there. She was born way out there in Howick, 23 kms from the CBD, had schooled in the posh precinct of Epsom, had babies in Remuera, was married in Mt Albert, divorced in St Heliers. Had loved and loathed and felt and numbed, all that minutiae of everyday life, out there amongst the blue-grey of the waters, the green of the parks and the tidy boxes of homes and shops. She'd grown up here, and until now she'd not ever seen a reason to live elsewhere.

Her eyes flicked up to the electronic board; the countdown was back on.

As she waited for him to jump she thought about the past week. It had been amazing. Everything was light and sparkling, everything was magical. She'd loved it all – the trip out to Waiheke Island, sitting amongst the vines toasting their adventures together; the walk along Muriwai's black sands at sunset, arm in arm, smiling in unison at the shadows and the last golden sunbursts as they rained down on the sands. He'd loved her cooking, and her driving – well if not loved, he hadn't criticised her mercilessly as Murray had once done. In fact, he hadn't criticised her at all. Not even once. Not even on the way to the Bay of Islands. Her heart jumped a little. Where he'd told her he loved her.

Stirred from her reverie by an excited gasp from the German couple standing next to her, Meg checked the electronic sign.

JUMPER IS READY

'That's my boyfriend!' she said to no one in particular.

The Germans nodded, smiling, confused.

'He's already done it once,' she gabbled 'but he's doing it again. He's a bit of an action man.'

More smiles.

Then the sign turned.

Jumped!

*****

'See that over there?' John lifted his hand from the steering wheel of the Landrover and pointed to the mountain in the near distance. 'What's that?'

Meg looked up from her book. 'That? Probably low cloud or something.'

'Looks more like smoke to me. See it's moving.'

'Just 'cos it's a volcano doesn't mean anything. It's just cloud. Hear hooves think horses.'

He was doubtful but continued to drive through the mustard desert towards the snow-capped mountains. She was irritable. They'd spent most of the day lazing around in bed and now there was only an hour or so left to ski before the mountain closed for the day. His jet lag seemed to last forever. And now he was seeing smoke when it was only cloud? She hated being late.

But then, everything had been a whirlwind. As it had turned out there hadn't been a need to ring Tom and emergency eject John out to a boys' own adventure trip of NZ. They'd enjoyed each other's company, and yes, she wondered if perhaps she was falling in love with him too.

Hell, she knew she was, but she couldn't just let it happen. There was too much she didn't know. How much of the smiling kind-hearted John, was Holiday-John? How much was real? How would he cope when he met the kids, or when she was struggling to get Murray to pay his child support? When things were mucky not magical, how would things be then? And where, would they live?

A wave of anxiety smashed over her head. She was enjoying the fall, but worried about the hard landing.

'You're Hurricane Meg,' Mike had once told her. Tom had said that too, as had the boyfriends of years ago. They'd all said that. Mostly meaning that she was fiery and passionate and created an impact. But Murray hadn't subscribed to the PR version - he called her that too, but he had simply meant that she was the singular most destructive force of nature he had ever met.

The car sped through the brown tussock sliding along the black snake tarseal and then slithered up Mt Ruapehu itself. In the car park she slipped out of her jeans and sweatshirt into a woollen sweater and leggings. John was bemused.

'Good trick.'

'Yeah, I once worked as a nurse aid after school and had to get into my nurse's uniform on the school bus. I managed it without anyone seeing anything.'

He laughed. It was soft, bubbled and bursting with mirth.

The harassed twenty-something at the Ski Hire was confused. Why did they want to hire gear for the last hour or so of the day? She didn't understand, but grabbed the skis and poles and boots and within ten minutes they were walking like penguins across the snow to the lift.

The spring snow was patchy at the Bruce and even beginners needed to jump on the chairlift to get up to a decent run of snow. Meg quietly wondered how John would cope with the chairlift. She'd been skiing a number of times – here on Ruapehu, in the South Island on the Remarkables, and even on the ski fields of Sundance in Utah. She wasn't an expert skier but she knew she could stay upright and manage a snow plough and a few turns. Most of all she'd wanted him to enjoy the mountain – the crisp air, the crystalline snow and the peace that came with the muffled sounds of the other skiers.

John hadn't ever been skiing. She knew that and wondered if this might be the one thing she could do, that he couldn't. After all, until now the man had seemed invincible. He jumped off buildings in a single bound, he mountain-biked (for fun!) and knew the dark arts of several martial disciplines and then there was the whole... exercising in Wales thing.

Maybe, just maybe this would be her thing. Not that she was competitive or anything. They joined the short queue for the lift.

'So how do I do this?' he asked her.

Pleased, she showed him how to get onto the lift and eased the tension by retelling the old story about how she'd been too scared to get off the chairlift and had gone around for a second time.

She climbed onto the chair lift first and confidently moved over to allow him space to sit down, but John paused for a moment, missed his turn, and ended up seated in the next chair that swung around. The lift sashayed them both up the mountain, threading them up the hill, over the rock heads peeking out of the icy snow and stumbling over the pillar connections.

She sat back in the chair taking a moment to suck in the mountain air and feel the last of the day's rays on the back of her neck. She was supposed to be scared of heights, but chair lifts didn't count. One day she'd tell him that she'd conquered that fear – on chair lifts only – during her teen years in youth group. In those days she'd been a Youth Group Leader, a veritable Happy Clappy. He didn't need to know that, yet. He wasn't the only one with secrets.

Way off to the western edges of the ski-field a man was creating yellow snow. She giggled to herself and sucked in the cold mountain air. The top of the chair was fast approaching.

She rearranged her legs so that they were braced for the landing and in parallel and then with an astonishing amount of grace she skied off and waited patiently at the side of the lift, for John to alight. He did, though not gracefully, instead falling head over ski into the snow. She laughed loudly.

This is fun.

The rest of the afternoon they took to the spring snow with enthusiasm though John bemoaned his skiing inadequacy.

'I don't get it; I can ice skate really well.'

Meg continued to smile. 'I can't believe you've never been skiing before. Don't you have snow all the time at home?'

'We do, but it's not like here,' was all he managed.

The drive back to Auckland was long and winding. Meg started the long drive home but soon aftwe the long day of exercise caught up with her and she passed the driving baton over to John and dozed quietly in the passenger seat whilst John sang along to the music from the stereo.

Past the country towns he drove, until finally stopping at Huntly to grab a greasy burger from a roadside café. They switched driving duties once again after the coffee and burger and Meg capably drove over the Bombay Hills until they reached the light ribbons of the southern motorway and Auckland city stretching out in front of them as far as they could see. On the far horizon, the needle of the Sky Tower was glowing red.

Meg drove through the southern suburbs and then down the familiar stretch into St Heliers Bay, and finally up the driveway and into the garage. In silence they parked the car and then wearily thumped up the stairs to bed.

***

Meg's muscles pulled in complaint as the next morning she gingerly walked down the steep driveway to the letterbox to collect the NZ Herald. John was still fast asleep, gently snoring, but she had woken with the sun and was keen to find her first coffee of the day.

Stifling a yawn, she grabbed the paper from the box, spread it out between her hands to read the front page headlines as she staggered back into the house.

'Bloody hell! He was right!'

RUAPEHU ERUPTS, INJURIES REPORTED

Mt Ruapehu began erupting tonight spilling lahars down two sides of the mountain. One lahar ran down through the western boundary of the Whakapapa skifield on the mountain.

Chapter 12

Incommunicado

'Nothing?'

'Nothing at all, not even a quick text.'

Ally's brow furrowed and her coiffured dark hair bobbed as she spoke. 'He's probably just tired. It's a long flight back to England.'

Meg nodded. 'I know.'

'You haven't texted him have you?'

She knew her friend. When Meg was in she was all-in.

'You don't want to scare him off. Let him come to you.'

Ally walked back from the large kitchen and placed a glass of Pinot Gris in Meg's hand, and then taking a thoughtful sip from her own glass she settled into the plush cushions on the opposite leather couch.

Ally's home was spectacular. Sitting high on the cliff overlooking the bay it was a large brick home with dedicated media room, gym area and several living spaces. Carefully decorated with modern art and elegant sculptural pieces the living area spilled out onto a topiary fringed patio and large swimming pool. In the distance, across the waters of the Auckland harbour Rangitoto kept watch, shrouded in verdant bush.

Meg was struggling to speak. Finally, she found some words. 'I sent him a message on Skype telling him how much fun I'd had when he was out here. That was four days ago. He's read it, but...'

'He's probably just tired.' Ally insisted. 'Remember how exhausted you were when you came home from London?'

'Yeah but I didn't go to ground for four days.'

'You probably wore him out after keeping him up all night every night for ten days' Ally giggled.

Meg pulled a face. 'I just thought he would call. We had such a brilliant time together...' She sipped her wine.

'He will. But don't chase him. Men hate that. Meg, are you listening?'

She was. But she wasn't. She was reading a text on her mobile phone.

Mum, we're back home now. Where are you?

'I've got to go home Ally, its Sarah they're back from their weekend.'

'Already? But it's only 4 o'clock.'

Meg stood up and resignedly picked up her bag. 'Yeah.' She shrugged and started walking to the big wooden door, Ally walking behind her sensing Meg's mood, struggling to keep her dark thoughts to herself.

'But what about your weekend? This is your time. He can't just drop them off because he's sick of them. What about you?'

'But he does. And I can't leave them at home on their own, so I'd better go...Thanks hun.'

She drove home absent-mindedly, slipping across the suburban streets until she reached her steep driveway. Sitting on top of the stairs outside the front door was a huddle of her womb fruit.

'I wasn't expecting you guys back till 5 at least.'

'Dad had work.' Sarah said.

'He really is very, very busy.' Jayne repeated throwing herself tearfully into her mother's arms.

Meg opened the front door and waved them in. Alex looked tired and was sporting big dark circles under his eyes. The girls were chatting excitedly, telling her all about their weekend adventures. As they did, Meg switched back into Mum-mode; made dinner and ran showers and stacked the dishwasher. It wasn't until 9:30pm that all three of them were curled up in bed. She'd been into Sarah's room three times after bedtime to take various books off her and had growled at Alex for sneaking back into the kitchen for a glass of water at 9:00pm but by 9:30pm they were all finally settled in for the night and Meg gingerly poured another glass of wine and opened her laptop lid.

She clicked through to Skype and scanned the chat column to see if he was online. He wasn't. There were no messages left for her either. Dejected, she opened her Gmail inbox. There were several emails from friends and clients, and one unread message in the *Shitty Murray* folder, but nothing from *thermite*.

Maybe he'd texted whilst she was doing dinner and bed?She rifled through her handbag and pulled out her mobile phone. Nothing.

Maybe that is really it. They'd had some fun and now it was over.

Back to reality. She picked up the TV remote and turned up the volume on McDreamy. But she wasn't really watching. She was thinking about Paris and the Bay of Islands, and Ruapehu. And then, his broad smile, his strong arms framing her shoulders, his body close to hers under the duvet when she had finally breathed out and was no longer Mum, businesswoman, pseudo-Dad cook, driver, accountant and lawyer. When she let go all the weight of responsibility; the weight of the struggle with Murray, the fear that she was ruining her kids' lives, the dad-shaped-hole in Jayne's life that saw the little girl throw herself into Meg's male friends' arms...

This couldn't be happening, to her, again.

Why was she 'Hurricane Meg?' What was wrong with her?

She was drinking too much, she knew it. She smiled wryly as she poured the last dregs of the bottle into her glass. It was liquid calm. In between the yellow bubbles and the tang on her tongue lay quiet unburdened peace. She knew there weren't answers there but she also knew there were no questions. She closed her eyes and sitting in front of the TV, glass still in her hand, she dozed.

The dog's bark startled her awake. Drowsy, Meg followed the noise to where the Labrador was standing at the lounge window barking loudly at something on the driveway. 'Shh Bailey. Shh.'

She walked over and opened the curtains a crack and looked out. She couldn't see what Bailey was barking at. In her imagination the driveway was full of danger, P-addicts were just waiting behind the stairs, and gang members were crouching behind the garage... She stroked the dog's long silken ears and scratched her muzzle. 'Nothing there Bailey.'

Nothing she could see. When she had first separated from Murray she had been on high alert and panicked every time the dog had barked or fussed. Some nights she had lain awake all night fearing that unseen danger, but now she was only occasionally worried; she'd grown used to being alone and in charge. She was the head of the household. Warrior woman, a vixen who would protect her kits at any cost. Besides, it wasn't late. She looked at her watch. 11:00pm

It was 11:00pm which meant it was 10:00am in London.

Dammit, she was going to ring him.

He had somewhat begrudgingly given his landline to her before he flew home. It had annoyed her at the time ('why all the secrecy?') but she had carefully saved it in her contact list. She found it now and before she lost her nerve she dialled the number.

'Hello?' the woman's voice was brisk as if she was running. Meg was taken aback. Who was this?

'Hi is John there please?'

'Sorry, what?'

'Could I speak to John please.'

'OK.'

She could hear the woman calling out for him in the background. Her voice was laced with irritation.

Who is this chick?

'Hello?' He sounded tired and very distant.

'Hi, John, it's me.'

'Sorry, who is it?'

Surprised, and a little defensive, she replied. 'John, its Meg. From New Zealand.'

'Oh hi'.

A pause.

'I haven't heard from you since the airport and I wondered if you were OK,' she said.

'Sorry, what was that?'

'I wondered how you were. I haven't heard anything from you, at all.'

'I can't really understand you. Sorry.'

'It doesn't matter. Sorry to bother you. I'll send you a message on Skype.'

'OK'.

And the phone rang off.

Sorry to bother you?

Who was this polite woman? Seething Meg opened the Skype window and typed.

Hi John, sorry for interrupting you. I just hadn't heard from you since Auckland airport and wondered if you were OK. Send me a message when you have a minute. Meg

She didn't sign off with her customary 'love Meg xx'.

Petty. She knew.

At midnight she gave up waiting for a reply and trudged off to bed and a fitful sleep. Obviously that was it. Chapter end. If not, *story* finished.

When dawn broke and her alarm roused her from her fitful sleep she was relieved that she could finally get out of bed and get away from her troubled dreams.

The lounge was shrouded in grey light and she held off from flinging open the curtains and letting the world inside. Her laptop was silent and still, displaying the screensaver of 'The Kiss'. She winced a little as she saw it and then taking a deep breath she opened her Skype window.

Hi Meg, sorry I couldn't talk on the phone earlier, I was rushing out the door to work. I haven't been up to much since I got back, just sleeping mainly. My brother is staying with us before he's deployed to Iraq. Hope everything is ok with you. Love John x

Who's us?

Does he have a girlfriend?

Feeling queasy Meg typed in her response.

Hi John, sorry for the telephone call I didn't mean to interrupt you. And sorry to hear your brother is going to Iraq, that must be very worrying for you. I was really surprised that I hadn't heard from you after our close time in New Zealand. It made me wonder if perhaps I had misinterpreted your feelings. I'm not going to call you again, don't worry. Meg

And who is that chick?

As she sat staring at the screen, willing it to change and magically return everything back to being wonderful, Alex wandered into the room behind her. She wiped her eyes and flicked away tear-buds, replacing them with a careful smile.

'Hello hun, how'd you sleep?'

Alex looked up sharply. 'Are you OK Mum?'

'Yes, I'm fine. All fine. All good.' She stood up briskly and started the breakfast routine, pretending for hours that felt like decades that all was fine, all was good.

It wasn't until after the school drop-off and Meg had quietly written in her journal and said a prayer or two that she allowed herself to check the Skype messages. There was one from John, and as she read it she sucked back the bile rising in her throat.

Hi Meg,

I've just been sleeping! I haven't been doing anything else – just work and sleeping. When Tina, my landlady called me to the phone I was running late for work and then I couldn't hear you properly on the phone. I'm sorry if that caused you any offense. I have been thinking a lot since our time together in New Zealand and think that I would like to tone things down a bit. When I divorced my wife I didn't want to jump into another relationship. I need to take some time to sort myself out. Love

John xx

Right.

What happened to 'I think I'm falling in love with you'?

Chapter 13

Flying away

'HE'S IN JAMAICA?' Ally was incredulous. 'What about the school fees?'

Meg looked surprisingly smiley for a woman whose ex-husband hadn't paid child support for two months and had jetted off to Jamaica.

'Paid 'em.' Meg grinned. 'Actually, that's not quite the full story. I helped him pay them. As he should. Bloody Murray!'

Ally leaned in closer to her friend. Meg always had a story, and they were often good. 'What did you do?'

Meg's face lightened as she warmed to her story. 'We still have a joint account for the mortgage and he forgot that years ago he made me a shareholder of his company. Not a director – so I can't be held responsible for anything he does ...' she shuddered.

'...but a shareholder with access to his business account. I've been watching his income for the past twelve months.

Every time he's whined about having no money to pay his share for the kids I've watched money come in and out of his account. Sometimes, quite a lot of money. I haven't told anyone, except my lawyer. I just watched.'

Oh this was good. Ally cocked her head, listening intently.

'So when he said he had no money to pay for Sarah's school fees and no money to pay child support I was surprised to see a rather large amount of money disappear from his account, earmarked for House of Travel, tagged 'Jamaica trip'.'

'What a bastard!' Ally said.

'Yup. But I didn't say. I just watched and waited. I knew he was getting some money in from a contract on Wednesday, so that night as soon as it struck midnight and the money fell into his account... like a ninja of the night, I slipped in under the cover of darkness and removed the money we need for his share of child support the mortgage and the school fees.'

Ally's mouth fell open. 'You took it?'

'Yup.'

'All of it?'

'Nah, I left about $3000 for him to live off. I'm not a total bitch.'

'Wow.' She was dumbfounded. Her friend never failed to surprise her.

'Does he know?'

'Oh yes he knows. First thing the next morning I get an email from him written in capital letters: 'YOU BITCH'.

Which, is probably fair. But, I didn't have a lot of choice. We don't have anything in the cupboards to eat and I got an email from school on Thursday saying they were kicking her out. And anyway, the accountants and the lawyers haven't come up with anything... I'm never going to know where it all went. So I figured, I may as well show my hand.'

'He probably showed you the finger.'

'I reckon.'

They both laughed and Meg reached forward for another brie cracker.

'And what happened to your boyfriend?' Ally asked.

'Ah well, that's another story! He's coming over on Boxing Day.'

'Here? The last I heard you weren't talking to him and he wanted a break.'

'That was ages ago. He did have a break, it lasted about a day. You were overseas in the Bahamas, and then Australia, I've barely seen you since October.'

'I'm barely at home! Elliot wants me to fly here and fly there. I'm never here... So that's exciting. Is he going to meet the kids this time?'

Meg shyly smiled. 'Yes, I think it's time. We've been on Skype every day since that last time. Sometimes, twice a day. We're really close.'

'On Skype?' Ally asked doubtfully.

'Yeah. Weird eh? But when you talk on Skype you focus completely on the other person… I reckon we're closer than if we were living together and there were all the distractions of the TV and kids and stuff.'

'So what was all that needing a break business about?' Jane asked.

'His brother was just about to go out to Iraq – he's in the army, his brother I mean - and he was really worried about that, and he seemed really tired and moody. Maybe a bit of jet lag too. It was all a bit intense, I think.'

Ally understood. Meg could also be intense.

'But you made up, and now he's coming out. Ooooh, that is exciting.'

'I'm going to take him down to Whangapoua with the kids.'

'We'll be in Matarangi then so you'll have to introduce us.'

Meg agreed. It was about time she got some input from her friends; was he right for her?

And if so, what then? Where would they live?

****

Christmas in New Zealand is frenetic in the heat. Meg spent most of it driving her Mum-taxi through the haze, avoiding tropical down-pours and sun-drunk Aucklanders ready to finish work for the year and head to the beach, bach, or boat. From ballet recitals to school prize-givings, and then when school finished for the year, to the shops on endless trips for Christmas food and presents, she drove, trying to focus completely on steering her little family through the busiest time of the year.

Christmas Day went off beautifully. She played a perfect Santa, an excellent home cook, and had managed to find just-right presents for the kids. She'd phoned her family in Australia and texted her friends – Tom, Mike and Ally – and now she was sitting quietly watching the Christmas tree lights flash on and off in the dark.

The peppermint tea was working – calming the butterflies as she thought about John's flight on its way out to New Zealand. Where was he now? Probably somewhere high above the Asian sub-continent.

Murray was picking the kids up in the morning to whisk them off on his version of a family Christmas and then in the afternoon John would arrive.

She gulped the tea. In two weeks she would surely know whether John was the one. Or rather, he would know if it was real or some elaborate fantasy. She was pretty sure. It felt right. She had faith it was right, and after all she had been through surely that in itself meant something.

The crowds poured out through the Arrivals doors, but not one of them was John. Meg paced. Then stood and watched. Not seeing him, she paced some more. *I'll text him.*

No answer. Maybe he hadn't turned his phone on yet?

She glanced at the Arrivals' board. The letters and numbers tick-tacked over and Emirates 502 from Brisbane was no longer processing. In fact, it was no longer there on the board. Everyone had been processed and had swept through the doors to the waiting arms of relatives, friends, lovers...

Everyone, but her Englishman.

Where is he?

Did he get the flight wrong?

He'd texted her during the night saying he was just about to board the plane to Melbourne. Which was very strange as she had checked his flights – all six of them from Newcastle – and the last flight was from Brisbane to Auckland.

He is coming. He just missed the flight. When's the next one from Brisbane?

She grabbed her mobile phone from her handbag, logged on to the Auckland Airport website and checked the time of the next flight. As she was flicking through Arrivals, she felt a tap on her shoulder. She turned around, and there he was.

'What happened? I thought you'd missed the flight!'

'We landed on time but they wanted to talk to me for a bit.'

'You didn't have an apple in your bag did you? They're really strict about food into NZ now.'

'No apple, no, it wasn't that. Anyway, hello.'

Weird.

After the hello kisses and hugs they drove out through the bright Auckland sunshine to the brick house in St Heliers. Then, after ruffling the Labrador's ears and flinging his bags into the corner of the bedroom, John took Meg's hand and sank back into the feather-down peace.

'Welcome home darling.' Meg managed to squeak. If this visit went well, maybe he would move here and truly make Auckland his home.

John didn't say anything in reply. 38 hours ago he'd left the snow and ice, Yorkshire stone churches, and country lanes, driven to Newcastle where it was bitingly cold and now here he was in sunshine so hot it seared straight through him. Where was home? The last time he'd asked himself that question, home hadn't been so hot.

The Immigration Officer at the airport had wanted to know that too, along with answers to other tricky questions. John had been warned years ago this type of investigation could happen when he travelled. He'd kept his cool, answered the questions quietly, shown the officer *the letter* and after a slight nod he'd been stamped through.

Two weeks later

New Chum's sand squeaked softly as the small group walked along its curvy stretch to the shade created by a massive Pohutakawa tree. All along the bush-clad headland the birdsong rang out amongst the tree ferns, the Toitoi and Flax. The beach was quiet – only a few determined souls had walked down the Whangapoua beach, crossed the little sea-fed stream, pinched their way across the boulders and then climbed the narrow dirt path over the headland, to swim in the New Chum surf and sunbathe on the white sands.

It was a stunning day. The surf was curling in long rolls of white-flecked turquoise and then ravenously biting through the sand at water's edge. A little girl was playing chase with the waves and her shrieks were carried by the afternoon on-shore breeze. Down towards the other end of the beach Meg could see a young couple walking hand-in-hand along the beach.

'Oh, it's busy!' Meg wrinkled her nose.

John could count only four other groups on the beach. 'Busy?'

'Yeah. It's a Kiwi thing. If there's another group on the beach it's too much for us. We get used to having beaches pretty much to ourselves.'

'But they're miles away!'

What's more there were no Winkle sellers, no amusements, no lifesavers, no donkey rides for little kids and no crowds of white flesh. John noted that no one had laid a towel out on a striped deckchair, there were no sandcastle competitions and there were no rows of umbrellas.

On this pristine Kiwi beach there was only sand, sea, sky and the bush. And a couple of brown faces.

'Yeah. But...'

Over the past week there had been a few moments when she had felt the distance between them. First at the airport when he hadn't told her why he'd been detained, then later at the shops when he'd been scornful that there were only two or three different Pizza brands to choose from, and even this morning when Jayne had barged in on them. John had blushed beetroot and seemed rattled by her intrusion, whereas she'd laughed it off. It wasn't as if Jayne had seen anything. After she'd shooed the little girl out, he'd leapt out of bed to the shower, as if his bum was on fire.

Meg placed her towel on the sand and announced that she was ready for a swim. She scanned the sea through her sunglasses and puzzled, she turned to quiz John.

'Hey, what's that?' She pointed out to the dark shadow just beyond the breakers. She couldn't see whether it was black or forest green.

John was framing a photo.

'Pass it here' Meg said. Meg raised the camera to her eye and pointed the long lens out to the sea.

'Nah, it's OK. It's just seaweed. We're all good. Come on. Race ya.'

And with that, she raced down to the sea and without stopping, hurtled into the breaking wave. The current was strong, it tugged at her legs, grabbed her soles and twisted her body under the crest of the wave, finally flipping her head over heels until she was prone on the sand and spluttering salt water.

'It's really dumping,' she yelled out to John. He couldn't hear. No matter, he'd learn soon enough.

She picked herself up, spat out the sand and waded through the swirling water to the breakers. It felt good to be back here. Whangapoua and New Chum beach was her favourite place in the whole world. She loved it here so much that she never wanted to leave. Though it seemed she might have to, soon.

Sarah had waded in also and was flapping about in the shallows with her little sister. Sarah had demanded that she lug her boogie board over the track, and as Meg had predicted, she had passed it to her mother half way along the beach. Meg had ended up carrying Sarah's board, the picnic backpack, as well as her togs and towel. John had his hands full with his camera and towel. Oh well, she reasoned. They were her kids after all.

He probably hadn't even thought that they would want help carrying their gear. Just as he probably hadn't realised that the bach she'd hired had cost well over $1000 to hire for the week. And that Murray had given her an earful about taking the kids to the beach with him.

From Pavlova to Pork Pies

She had been forced to place the house on the market just before Christmas and had already had a few potential buyers through the property. She had not been able to find the money to buy Murray out and when she obliquely mentioned it to John, he'd startled.

It was too early to start thinking about shacking up together. Too early to borrow two hundred thousand dollars from John. Too early to know – for certain – if they would choose Auckland as their new family home.

Meg rode the wave, pushing out the water in front of her as she body surfed towards the shore. John was coming in.

Finally!

He'd stopped every three minutes on the track over to take photos. Yes, it was beautiful. But every three minutes to take a photo?

She waded back out to catch the next wave, mis-timed the break and held her breath as the white water smashed over her head. John waded through the water to her side.

'You ok?' he asked.

'Yeah. Just miss-timed it.'

'But you're ok? Other than water up your nose?' He wasn't just talking about the surf. He scanned her face. She was scowling slightly.

'I'm OK.'

'I was thinking about our discussion this morning...' he started but she didn't have a reply.

Sensing she didn't want to talk, he moved closer to her and took her hand and together they leapt up high, facing into the breaking wave. The wave broke over their heads and forced them backwards into the cool clear water. Meg saw a shadow slide past under the wave. More seaweed.

John shot her a look. Her face was gleaming with sunscreen and under the sheen her cheeks were freckled brown. Her curly hair was trailing in long sodden ropes down her brown back.

'You're beautiful,' he told her. She brushed it off and nodded doubtfully as another wave broke over their heads. His hand found hers in the swirling water and he pulled her to her feet. 'I've got you,' he said.

She let him pull her close. She closed her eyes and just breathed in and out as she jumped.

In.

And out.

She banished thoughts about house auctions, and divorce settlements and panic about where they would live and what she would do. She lay there in his arms, the blue-brined water holding them up. For a moment or two her salty peace was broken only by the seagulls' caw and the occasional kiss from her amorous Englishman; but then, somewhat inevitably, it was broken by the insistent calls of her thirteen-year-old son across the waves.

'Mum, what's there to eat for lunch?'

The picnic was a feast of ham sandwiches, bottled water and sand. The kids had eaten hungrily, and now sated were milling around waiting for the requisite half an hour after eating before heading back into the water.

Meg was lying in her tankini with her head in John's lap. He had pulled the cap down over his face was lying on his beach towel, and browning his chest in the strong sun. Meg was keeping quiet, listening to the intense discussion her two eldest children were having with her boyfriend. She was staying out of it; but she was listening to every single word.

He was trying to explain to them what he did, without actually saying very much at all. So far, they had got the name of the company he worked for...but that was all.

'But we don't want nuclear weapons,' Sarah insisted.

'Which is why we do what we do,' John countered.

'But how can you say you don't agree with nuclear weapons if England makes them?' Alex asked.

Meg looked over at her clever son. He was squinting in the sun, and his freckles and dark curly hair matched her own. He was tall for his age and so skinny she could count each rib in his white chest. He seemed to be standing up straighter since Murray had left the home.

John was obviously used to this argument. After all, he'd heard it pretty much every single work day from the protestors lining the barbed wire fences at work. They had been regularly told not to reveal where they worked for fear of exactly this kind of reaction.

'We don't make them Alex. We belong to the Nuclear Non-Proliferation Treaty. We just maintain them. The UK's existing arsenal in case we need them. They're a deterrent. If we didn't have them there would be nothing to stop them. Anyway, I don't work on that side of the business. I make sure people are kept safe.'

'But doesn't that make the UK just as bad as them?'

'No, we're the good guys. We keep the peace. If we didn't have nuclear weapons well...'

'If we didn't have nuclear weapons no one would be killed by them. We read Sadako and the *Thousand Paper Cranes* at school. I think there shouldn't be any nuclear weapons anywhere,' Sarah said emphatically.

'But then who would stop the wars in Iraq?' John asked.

'We don't have any here,' Sarah retorted.

'Yes, well New Zealand is one hundred percent for the taking! Like that vid on YouTube'

Sarah pouted her displeasure but Alex laughed.

Meg listened to the argument and didn't say anything. *John and the kids need to find their own way together. I can't sort it out for them. Please God, let them like each other.*

The next day

From Pavlova to Pork Pies

Meg was sitting on the deck at Ally's beach house looking out to the surf-lined Matarangi beach. Elliot was lazing on his sun-lounger in the sun – book open on his brown round belly, his eyes closed under a broad rimmed hat - and John had borrowed a long-board and headed down the beach to try his luck at surfing. The kids were out roaming the beach and Ally and Meg were enjoying a cold bottle of Pinot Gris – or two – on the deck.

It was a heavenly spot. Elliot and Ally's beach house was in a perfect position right on the beach front of the long sweep of golden sand. At night you could hear the surf crash on the shore and the Morepork owls calling in the bush, high up on the hill behind the beach. Meg had often enjoyed the generous hospitality of her friends, and could count off numerous occasions involving good champagne and late night runs to the surf.

Turning to check that Elliot was out of ear-shot Ally started caught Meg's eye and spke conspiratorially. 'So Meg, how old is he? Really? I thought he was one of Alex's friends when you came in.'

Meg swallowed and was about to answer when Elliot called out from the lounger...'Is he your toy boy Meg?

'No...not really...I mean...he is younger.... but...'

'Get in there Meg' Elliot laughed.

Blushing Meg continued...'Not that much younger only six years.'

'He looks fifteen,' Ally giggled.

'Wahey....go Meg...' Elliot said.

'Oh shut up Elliot!' Ally laughed as Meg blushed red and hid her face in her wine glass.

'Do you think he's OK?' Ally asked. 'It's been a while since he left. He can swim can't he?'

'I did ask him. He should be OK. As long as the sharks don't get him.'

'Sharks? Are you trying to leave your lover again Meg?'

'Noooo....But last night we were going through the photos from New Chum and I'm sure I saw sharks in the water with us. I'd checked the water before we jumped in and thought it was weed and everything. Then this morning there was that story in the Herald about the 'Shark Traffic Jam', and Whangapoua is just around the corner from Matarangi.'

Ally was laughing hard now. 'So the first time he came out here, you almost deserted him to the ocean to drown after swimming with dolphins, threw him off the Sky Tower not once but twice, then you almost fried him in a volcanic eruption and this time you turn him into shark bait? And yet he still keeps coming over. He must love you!'

'I guess he does.' Meg pursed her lips.

'You don't seem sure Meg,'

'No. It's OK. I mean he says he does but...he can be a bit moody that's all, and then yesterday we had a fight about where we're going to live. I want him to come over here. He doesn't want to leave his job. I've got three kids to think about Ally! I can't just up and leave.'

Ally nodded slowly. 'But if you look at it from his point of view, taking on a whole grown up family is a lot for one guy. And he loves his job. It really is him. All that jumping out of helicopters and playing goodies and baddies. Has he told you yet what he actually does?' Ally asked.

'It's not as if he has to do anything for them anyway. I do it all. I do everything. I always have done.'

She didn't need rescuing from knights or Englishmen for that matter. It was true, but Ally knew that sympathising with her friend wouldn't help.

'He doesn't really jump out of helicopters anyway. He works in an office, mainly. I think,' Meg said airily.

'But he does work with the army right? And dress in black. And do dangerous stuff?'

'Yeah,' Meg nodded, 'but he could do that here.'

'Do you think so?'

Meg was irritated that Ally wasn't listening.

'You'd love England, Meg. Elliot reckons New Zealand is too small for you. You should go over there, and take the kids. It would be a great experience for them. Alex might even get into Cambridge or something. Would Murray let you?'

'Probably. He's over there half the time anyway, working in Germany. He'd probably see them more than he does now,' Meg said.

'Does he not see them very often?'

'He's seen them for 10 days out of the six week Christmas holidays.'

Meg pulled a face. 'I know I'd love England; I've always wanted to live there for a while. Back when I was backpacking, when I was young I had this huge map of the world on my hostel room wall and I'd plot how far I'd got towards the goal of living in London... but I was on my own then. It's different with the kids...' Her face darkened as she considered finding new schools and new friends and ripping them away from their Auckland home.

As she looked out to the beach she could make out a figure coming towards them carrying a long board. He was bare chested and his shoulders were brown from the sun.

'I know I'd love England but I love it here too. Once the house was sold I was just going to rent for a while until I've got enough money to buy something. I don't really want to leave this,' Meg gestured to the sea and the sand.

'You could leave the kids with Murray, it's about time he took some responsibility!'

Meg's face registered shock. 'I'd never leave them Ally. Never. And I think honestly that they would all want to come with me if I left. Even Sarah.'

'Or you could always travel back here every year, it wouldn't be any different from putting them in boarding school...' Ally started to say and then trailed off as John climbed the stairs up onto the deck and gingerly pulled out a chair. He looked exhausted.

'Where have you been? You were ages!' Meg asked.

'I couldn't remember where the house was and the rip took me all the way down the beach. I've been walking for about half an hour trying to find the right place.'

Meg was incredulous. 'Carrying the board? Right along the beach?'

On a roll, John talked over them. 'That's not all. I'm sure there were sharks in the water, something kept on slipping under my surfboard. Oh and I did this.' He removed his hand from his stomach to reveal a gaping sore just above his belly button. It was pink and angry and looked exceedingly painful.

'Didn't you wear a rash vest?'

'What's a rash vest?'

Ally rolled her eyes. 'Didn't Meg tell you? I know he's a bit of an action man Meg but the 'toughening him up in New Zealand thing' has to stop. You've got to look after him a bit better.'

John grinned broadly.

'It's good for him. Toughen up the old softie. Anyway there are sharks in the water all the time, you just don't see them,' Meg retorted.

John reached for a glass, cracked open a beer and started to gulp it down.

'Did you see the Herald?' Ally asked as she passed the paper over to him.

Shark Traffic Jam in Matarangi screamed the headline.

'After yesterday?' His mouth fell open. 'So we were swimming with sharks then at New Chum,' he said slowly.

'Good thing I'm heading home tomorrow, I reckon. You're a dangerous woman Meg Sinclair.'

'You're flying home tomorrow John? Ouch, that's going to sting.' Ally pointed at the oozing sore on his stomach.

'I'll go and get you a dressing.' She paused before leaving the table, leaned forward conspiratorially and whispered to John: 'I'd be careful John! I think Meg's trying to kill you. If she can't have you, no one else will.'

She caught Meg's eye and the two women burst out laughing.

Behind the sunglasses and the smile Meg's mind was working overtime. *How many jobs working with the defense force are there in New Zealand?*

Chapter 14

April is the Cruellest Month

April is the cruellest month, breeding

Lilacs out of the dead land, mixing

Memory and desire, stirring

Dull roots with spring rain.

Winter kept us warm, covering

Earth in forgetful snow, feeding

A little life with dried tubers.

The Wasteland - T.S Elliot*

2 AM IN THAT weird 24-hour clock that circumnavigates the globe like a bicycle inner tube with a slow leak. The only time, time itself is truly flexible, and undefined. Down below, Meg could see fires around Karkatov.

Where the hell is that?

Completely horrified at her lack of geographical knowledge she flips through to the flight map in the guide panel in front of her. There's an incessant buzzing in her ears.

The aircraft jerks suddenly, as if sliding on a slab of ice, and then it corrects but Meg isn't concerned; she's a good flier.

Her early years were spent flying from New Zealand to Australia to see the grandparents, and then later in the early 1970s commuting between her home in the Fijian goldfields and base in Auckland. As a student she had flown stand-by up and down the country, countless times, to and fro from university in Dunedin, to her parents' homes in Auckland. At 15 years old, her mother finally gave her luggage for a birthday present and two months after graduation, at the tender age of 20 years old she left NZ for adventure; first backpacking solo around Australia and then up into Asia. It was during those hard months on the road in Thailand that she had learnt the traveller's biggest lesson - the journey itself was way more important than the destination.

She had revelled in the domestic façade being lifted and life in all its glorious colour and raw reality revealed, with not a takeaway dinner or corner office in sight. She had wanted so desperately to make the classic OE pilgrimage to Earl's Court where she would live with a rowdy bunch of ten others, eat bread and cheese and pull pints in a low beamed English pub. Of course, it would all work out in the end and she'd end up with a plumb role in publishing or something and settle in London writing successful novels on the side.

It hadn't worked out like that then, would it now?

Meg wasn't sure, but she was flying over to see for herself. But she had no illusions of the OE dream life she'd wished for when she was younger.

For a start, John didn't live in London he lived in a small town 40 miles out in the country. His family were from Yorkshire but he had moved to the south of England for his work at Chairon Holding Ltd. - the company that serves as the guardian and maintainer of the UK's nuclear weapons. Meg had helped him negotiate the house's purchase during late night discussions over Skype. He had been adamant – he couldn't, wouldn't, leave his job and move to New Zealand – and she really would love living in England.

At first, Meg had panicked and wondered whether she should call it quits. Let him get on with his life, find a suitable young English woman and start a family. She would continue to rent in St Heliers, holiday at Whangapoua, pick up marketing contracts and make endless Vegemite sandwiches. The Sunrise-Sunset kind of romance didn't happen to real people, like her.

But he had been insistent.

He loved her, he said. He would buy a home for all of them and they would live happily ever after in the little country town in North Hampshire. She would find a job in the M3-M4 IT Corridor, he would spend his days saving the world (dressed appropriately in black) and Bambi would live in the nearest woods.

And so – with a little encouragement from her – he had bought the house, and moved in yesterday. She was on her way now to help set up home and to evaluate how an English life together could look. She wasn't sure how it would end, change was cruel and harder still when three kids were involved.

Restless, she eases past the empty seats next to her and walks to the tail of the aircraft. The plane is half empty; visiting England in early spring doesn't seem a popular thing to do. Out of the cabin door window she can see a halo of light far off on the horizon. That was where the plane was heading – towards the light. Six more hours and she would be in Heathrow, for the second time in a year.

The plane shudders once more and the overhead lockers rattle. Then suddenly it lurches downwards forcing Meg to reach over and grab the top of the last row of seats. The seat belt signs ping and light up and obediently she crab-walks back to her seat and buckles in.

Buckle up folks it's going to be a bumpy ride.

Years of flying experience had taught her that there was no point fussing over turbulence. Most fights hit a rough patch and when they did the best thing for her to do was shoot a prayer upwards and close her eyes to the jolting and jerking.

Her mouth is dry and she reaches forward to lift the plastic cup of water to her lips. In moments she is asleep, cup still in her hand, her eyelids jerking slightly as her busy brain ran the dream-reels inside her head.

She's picking the daffodils off the banks of the Dunedin Motorway overpass. Using a pincer action, she examines the bright yellow heads for signs of damage. Yes, Yes, No. She says out loud. All the while she's keeping one eye open for snakes in the grass. The kids are there – Sarah's trying to make a daisy-chain out of daffs, - it's gaudy and impractical but Sarah is forcing it to work. Alex is digging the bulbs out of the hard ground with a spade – making hard work out of it - and Jayne is tossing the rejects back to her mother.

'This one's OK Mum.'

'No, it's got a spider in it. There are better ones. Perfect ones. Like this one.'

Chastened, the little girl sniffs.

And then the clouds drew in and a wind starts to whip their jacket hoods. Meg draws the children close to her just as she did when they were babies and pulls her own jacket off to hold it above them as a makeshift umbrella. The wind is biting at their cheeks and lips and Meg realises in numb shock that she is almost naked in the cold. Jayne is really crying now whilst Sarah is absorbed in her gaudy necklace.

'We're going to freeze to death' Meg cries out and on cue, it starts to snow. White snowflakes tickle her chest with butterfly drops. The droplets turn into a trickle that forge a wet path down her naked breasts and onto her stretch-marked stomach. Meg tries in vain to close the jacket zip and as she fumbles she wakes suddenly.

The empty paper cup is upside down in her hand, its contents now pooling in her lap.

Snow has always been a positive motif in her dreams.

...and your sins will be washed white as snow.

It had always meant that something new was going to happen. It meant change. Big white change.

*Can I just start again God? Dare I disturb the Universe?**

The cabin lights have come on and the cabin is filled with chatter now, as the passengers rouse from sleep. She can smell the acidic smell of coffee and the cloying fat drenched stench of bacon wafting down the aisles. Her stomach turns - half at the smell of the breakfast and half at the sudden thought that if the cabin crew are serving breakfast they will be landing within a couple of hours, at Heathrow. The hardest thing about it being Spring is that it hurts when winter's cold thaws off you. She was feeling again and it was a kaleidoscope of pain.

The trolleys clink and rattle as the crew edge down the cabin. The Singapore Girls look fresh as daisies and Meg is envious.

She has breath that would frighten Satan. Her hair is lank with the cabin's lack of humidity and in defeat Meg has put it up into a pony tail. She's fished out her glasses too and cannot help but feel fraudulent. She is on her way to meet her boyfriend in London?

Yeah, right. She could see the Tui ad billboard now. The passengers finish their breakfasts and join the fast-growing queue for the toilets that conga-lines up the Economy class cabin. Meg watches as a young mum tries to coax her toddler into the queue whilst placating a screaming baby in her arms. She shoots her a sympathetic smile.

'Do you want me to hold her for a while so you can take your little one to the loo?'

'Oh would you? That would be amazing! Thank you so much!'

'No worries. I know how hard it is. I travelled quite a lot with my kids when they were younger.'

'Where are they now? Your kids...'

'They're back in Auckland with their father. Hopefully they're having a good time.'

Meg winced. *Hopefully!*

'We separated a few years ago and he doesn't see them a lot so it will be good for them to have some time together. I'm heading to London to spend some time with my boyfriend.'

The woman looked startled at the large download of information but Meg gabbled on.

'We're going to see if we can all make a life together in England.'

The toddler grizzled. Flustered, the woman handed the baby over to Meg.

'I'd better take him.' She grabs the red-faced little boy's hand and leaves Meg standing in the aisle holding the baby.

Meg studies the baby's face. Her little dark eyelashes are dotted with tears and her cherry nose and the skin under it is slimy with green snot. The child has a baby comb-over of straw and a large round head. Her mouth is framed by a meagre arch of pink lips and her cheeks are flaming scarlet.

Teething probably!

Meg gently peers inside the baby's mouth and just as she does so the baby pulls her head back, opens her mouth and releases a fountain of stale yellow milk, all over Meg's right sleeve.

Meg retches a little at the smell and is relieved to see the baby's mother walking towards her. She passes the child over – handling her as carefully as a primed device – and dashes to the toilets to remove the drenched long sleeved t-shirt from under her black tunic top. The remaining tunic is low cut, which was the very reason why she had worn the long-sleeved t-shirt in the first place. Without it the tunic's neckline falls just below the tops of her breasts.

Hi, my boobs and I are pleased to meet you.

She knows full well that she will spend the rest of the day trying to convince male eyes to raise their glance to her face, preferably her eyes.

A pastor had once told her that she was to blame for her boyfriend's sin. She and her wicked breasts. The pastor didn't know that shifting the blame to her sinfulness meant her boyfriend didn't have to stop curling his hands into fists. They broke up and she'd left that church – and any church at all - soon after.

Meg reapplies a little makeup, sprays on some perfume to counteract the stale smell of regurgitated baby formula and self-consciously pulls up the front of her top. Hopefully he will be so mesmerised by seeing her – in the flesh – he won't notice. It would appear she would be arriving in England half-naked.

Literally if not figuratively!

The plane was starting its descent as Meg returned to her seat, stomach full of anxious butterflies and head mulling over the ever-growing list of things she still didn't know about John.

What does he actually do? I know vaguely, but there has to be more to it...

Why is he so secretive?

Does he want kids? (*He's out of luck with that one I've jumped out of the gene pool!*)

Why is he so moody? (*Can I live with that?*)

They were things she probably should know by now.

And then there was that other list...

Would the kids want to come to England to live with her and John?

Would they get a visa?

Was it forcing their relationship to move in with John? Should she just live somewhere else and continue their relationship as boyfriend and girlfriend and not live together?

And most important of all. She looked down at the low cut tunic top where the sodden long sleeved t-shirt was supposed to be.

Will he notice that I'm half naked?

****

Later that night she's standing at the window sill in only a t-shirt (his) and her knickers in the dark quiet. John is curled up under the duvet snoring softly but she can't sleep. It's 3 o'clock in the afternoon on the day ahead, in her time clock.

She's not used to the quiet.

There's no sound. No traffic noise, no distant owl's calling, no foxes in the distance calling to their vixens. Even the neighbours can't be heard through the walls of the little brick terraced house. She opens the yellow curtains a little and peers out to the shadowed dark branches of the old oak tree in the neighbour's yard. The neighbours are so close! Even though it's the country.

He had been pleased to see her. Overwhelmed really. Teary-eyed. Their reunion in the half-empty house in Bottom Hedgeley had been passionate and Meg was feeling tired but wired now.

She was starting to feel again, and as the blood ran back to her head and her heart after being numb for so long, it started saturating her sad bloodless pores. The restoration of feeling, stung. She was in the country yet she couldn't see any pin pricks of stellar light through the dark curtain.

Where are the stars?

And as she watches the sky breaks into a million shards of white confetti.

'John!' she yells. 'Wake up! It's snowing!'

The good-natured Yorkshireman - who had seen snow pretty much every single year of his life - eased himself out of the warm bed to stand with his crazy Antipodean girlfriend, arm around her narrow shoulders, he quietly laughed at her big-eyed wonder.

He had pulled favours from heaven and earth to be able to bring her home and stand here with her. He had still been without abode only two days ago, when he had received a call from the conveyancing lawyer on his mobile phone, whilst on exercise in the English countryside.

He had to put one hand over his other ear to hear the woman's voice. 'How far away are we? I have my girlfriend coming all the way from New Zealand on Wednesday and I need to be in the house by then,' He shouted down the phone, his other hand covering his empty ear, eyes closed to the manoeuvres around him. He pulled into a quiet space behind the breeze block shelter.

'...we haven't heard back from the vendor...' the woman was stalling.

And then, suddenly, not far from where he was sheltering there was a gigantic explosion, the sound reverberating off the walls of the shelter, the shockwave shaking the ground around him.

At first there was stunned silence on the other end of the telephone. And then a small shaken voice...

'.... I'll get right onto it.'

He moved in the very next morning.

Chapter 15

Liar, Liar Pants on Fire

MEG LOOKED DOWN the stretch of Oxford Street, past the streams of people walking, talking, laughing, bustling forward, past the black taxis and the red double decker buses and the London Explorer bus with its open top and its collection of red-cheeked tourists.

'It's down here I think.'

John studied the Google Map on his mobile phone and absent-mindedly nodded.

As they walked hand in hand down the street Meg focused hard on the people blocking her path in front of her. She skipped and sidestepped to avoid bumping into people walking in the opposite direction all the while holding onto John's hand for dear life. He was walking purposefully with a surprisingly long stride given his short stature and her legs were struggling to keep in pace.

The cloud hung low in the skies above London, and despite the calendar heralding Spring the temperature was still a chilly 10 degrees celsius. Meg tied the scarf around her neck and pulled at the buttons to close her leather jacket. Her feet ached even though it was still only halfway through the day. Bloody cobblestones!

Following a dance of big steps and little steps and skipped steps and sudden stops they walked down through the crowds. Past the large wide shop windows of Top Shop with its models flaunting singlet tops and cropped shorts, a display of modernity incongruous to the ancient stone arch and black iron fretwork of its building. Past the red awnings of Hamleys' toy store and the bubble blowers standing at its doors beckoning customers to step inside, and down the street past the signs advertising Money Transfers and O2 mobile phones and the tacky tourist souvenirs – fridge magnets with double decker buses, bears wearing Union Jack sweaters and the mass produced prints of Big Ben – all undoubtedly made in China.

The offices of Sampson & Sera were hard to find. Meg double checked the address details on her phone and then looked for a sign on the building's entrance. It was as if the offices were hidden away on purpose. Perhaps this was the first hurdle in the immigration quest.

Finally, she spied a modest sign pointing down to the sub-floor below the street level. Curious, they climbed down the slippery stairs and into the dark little office. It wasn't at all what Meg had expected.

'Hi we're here to see Lyla,' she told the young bespectacled woman with the dark cropped hair.

'I'll just go and see if she's available.'

'We have an appointment at 1.00,' Meg called after her as the woman disappeared into the bowels of the building.

The makeshift reception area consisted of two school chairs and a brochure stand. Sampson & Sera were the Number One Immigration consultants in England, the brochure affirmed. And yet, the stuffy office and dowdy fraying green carpet suggested more a backstreet dentist's practice – one that had seen better days.

The receptionist appeared from nowhere and asked them to follow her into a small office crowded by a massive mahogany desk and piles of files.

Lyla Johnson was a short round woman with a penchant for Jaffa Cakes and a dislike of toothpaste. Meg noted that Lyla was quick to request her passport, birth certificate and other key documents, and when she did so she didn't smile, not once.

Meg handed over the documents and the carefully prepared application form, and Lyla nodded cursorily as she read through them.

'So your date of birth is 16th April 1968? Today?' she asked.

'Yes, it's my 40th today actually,' Meg replied with a short smile.

'Well, let's hope we can make your day by getting your visa application in order,' Lyla said. Though her words were reassuring her face told another story. 'Like hell' it said.

'Being older, you will need to apply for a work visa under the Highly Skilled Migrant category. I will need all your bank statements for the last twelve months before the date of your application. And, you will need to find a job here in England. But not just any job – it has to be advertised first to English nationals and the employer will have to stipulate that they cannot find someone of your ability and skillset in this country before offering you the job. The job will have to have remuneration of more than £45,000 per annum. Have you started looking for work?' Lyla asked.

Meg paused, feeling flustered. 'Not yet. I'm on holiday really.'

'Well I suggest that you get started as soon as you can. In the meantime, I will start preparing your application.'

'How long is it likely to take?' John asked.

'At least six months. The biggest thing is getting the job offer. The company will have to advertise it first for at least six months before offering it to you. What sort of work do you do in New Zealand?'

'I run my own Marketing business and do a lot of work in the IT and Finance areas.'

'It shouldn't be so difficult to find the right job here then,' Lyla nodded. She glanced over to the big white clock hanging on the opposite wall. 'I'll get Anna to photocopy your documents and we'll see you back here when you've found a job. Have you paid your deposit?' Meg could see a speech bubble above Lyla's head. It read: Next!

Later that afternoon Meg and John were lying side by side on the grass at Hyde Park. The skies had cleared and a pale yellow sun was shining over London. They had stopped at Marks and Spencer's on the way back from Lyla's office and were now chomping on a special late lunch of crab and watercress sandwiches. John took his camera off his neck and was pointing the lens at Meg's face as she not-so-delicately munched on salad.

'Do you think it will be hard to get a job?' Meg asked, waving the lens away. 'John, I'm serious. Don't.'

He ignored her and pressed the button clicking a series of photos capturing his girlfriend with little wisps of green hanging out of the corner of her mouth.

'Shouldn't be. You've worked with all those big names. For someone of your experience, it should be pretty easy.'

Meg flushed. She wasn't as accomplished as he thought. 'But nobody knows me here.'

'Microsoft is still Microsoft wherever you go in the world!'

'Hmm.'

'Anyway, let's not talk about serious stuff. Look at me...'

Click click click.

John studied the camera's viewfinder and smiled in admiration. 'Not bad for a 40-year-old!'

'Huh, you'll be 40 one day too!' she pouted.

'But not for *six* years!'

'I can't help it that you like older women who know what they're doing!'

'True,' he confirmed and leant over to kiss her.

She eased into his arms and together they lay back on the grass squinting at the sun above them. The lunchtime crowd at Hyde Park were starting to dust off the crumbs and head back to the office, while tourists pulled out day packs and recounted their morning adventures as they sipped on water bottles.

They lay there quietly and Meg's mind wandered over their morning. John had woken her with a champagne miniature and breakfast in bed. When she went downstairs to the kitchen she couldn't help noticing a huge sign in shaving foam on the kitchen window.

Happy 40th Birthday Meg

She smiled as she remembered. John disturbed her reverie.

'Have you heard from the kids?'

Meg immediately sobered. 'No, not yet.'

This was the first birthday since she became a mother that she'd had apart from her kids. Yes, it was wonderful being in London (LONDON!) with her man, but oh, her kids...

Everything felt bitter sweet, then. Clouds shaded the sun, the grass was a little less green and the sound of a siren could be heard over the top of chatter. Sensing her mood, he tightened his arm around her and squeezed comfortingly. 'Why don't we go and have a look around the National Gallery before *Phantom of the Opera* tonight.' Meg nodded in response.

The theatre audience is enthralled in the dark. Meg and John are sitting in the middle of the circle mesmerised by the spotlight and the performers in the middle of the shaft of light. Christine and Raoul are singing their celebrated duet. Christine's voice is sweet and pure and Raoul's is liquid amber. Not one member of the audience shuffles, or talks or rattles a bag lest they disturb the shared hypnosis. Romance has taken its place centre-stage.

Christine's treble sings out 'Say the word ... I will follow...'

Meg can feel the words form silently in her throat. She glances over at John who is watching the stage with absolute focus.

This man or that life.
Choose.

The music swells and the emotion in the theatre is high. Someone is sniffing in the seat behind them. Meg daren't look; the sentimentality could be catching.

The music is sweet and poignant.

As Raoul rushes to Christine to affirm his feelings, John reaches in the dark for Meg's hand and squeezes it. On stage Raoul confirms his love and in the circle John's lips move to the words.

'Love me, that's all I ask...' the soprano trills and together the actors duet...

But Meg barely notices. All she can feel are his hands cradling hers. She daren't look at his face for fear of dissolving on the spot but the music and lyrics play on above their heads all the way home – through the night streets of London, onto the Tube with the canned air and the blank faces of its passengers, and drowning out the music on the car stereo as John drives down the M4 takes the first Reading exit and then steers the little Astra up through the woods to the narrow streets of a sleeping Bottom Hedgeley.

She can hear the music in her head as she remembers playing it on the cassette player in her mother's car as they drove down the Gold Coast, decades ago, when the musical had first been performed. Back then she had sung along promising herself that one day she would go to London and see that musical for herself. And now she had.

The music leads the way from the estate's communal car park to the front door of the brick house and then up the stairs to the double bedroom with the bed that almost fills the space. It's there as they undress and tumble into bed and turn to each other, and it's there when they turn off the lights, and it answers – simply, sweetly, - when the questions begin to rise in Meg's tired mind. It simply answers –

'Love me...'

****

The Skype tones chimed just as John went out the door to work. Meg grabbed her coffee and raced to answer them, plucking the laptop screen open as she slid onto the leather couch. Sarah's face, framed by straight dark hair, came into view.

'Mum...'

'I'm here. Hang on. I'll just turn my camera on...'Meg flicked the camera button and positioned the laptop screen so she could be seen in the viewer window.

'How are you?' Meg asked somewhat anxiously.

'Good.'

'What have you been up to?'

'Not much. Dad's been busy working.'

It took all her willpower to not roll her eyes. Instead, Meg nodded, not daring to speak.

'But Mum...' Sarah looked hesitant. 'Mum...'

'Hey, yes. I'm here. What's wrong?'

'Dad wants to take us swimming today.'

Meg nodded cautiously, brow furrowed. 'Who's going?'

'Dad and us. But I've got my period.'

'Oh. I see the problem.'

Poor Sarah. All of a sudden Meg wasn't as worried about whether there would be adequate supervision of little Jayne in the pool – Murray was surprisingly slack around the water- but more concerned about poor teenage Sarah who really needed her Mum.

'Can't you get Sheila to help you?'

'No Mum. I don't want to!' Sarah was angry now.

'I wish you were here.'

Meg nodded. 'I wish I was there too darling. Only a few more weeks. Would you like me to tell you what to do?'

Sarah paused for a moment and then hissed in reply.

'I just wish you'd come home. Dad said you'd deserted us to be with your boyfriend in England. He said ...'

'I did not desert you. I'm coming back. In a few weeks. I didn't leave for good...'

But it was too late. Sarah was red-faced and crying now, and Meg watched helplessly from the other side of the world, trying desperately to placate her.

'Don't cry darling. I'll be back soon. Only two more weeks and I'll be back...'

But it was no good. Empty words. Not heard.

In defeat Meg signed off and sniffing back her own tears reapplied a little makeup, grabbed the jumper cables from the counter and headed out to the carpark. It took ten minutes of driving before Meg had calmed down. She turned up the radio and sang along to the music.

I will not let Murray get to me.

But she knew she would. He already had. He'd already blasted her when she'd informed him that she was going to stay two weeks longer in England than planned. She wanted to look for work and to register with the recruitment agencies before she headed home, but she didn't tell Murray that news. She didn't tell Murray that she had sized up the local school, considered beds for the children's rooms and even started stocking the cupboards with food for when she returned with the kids.

She wouldn't let Murray get to her, but it did appear as if he was getting to her budding teenager.

Meg turned the radio up as if the music would build a comforting distance.

She'll be OK.

I'll be back soon.

The car bounced along the tarseal bordered with daffodils and Erlicheer. In pockets of velvet dark under the canopy of trees and bushes, bluebells raised their indigo heads. The country roads were pretty in spring; the hedgerows now a stunning verdant green, the ancient trees now bedecked with leaves. Through the old Roman town of Silchester – which she'd studied in Latin in form five when she'd known it as Calleva – she drove, dodging farm traffic in the single laneways between tall hedgerows.

The sun was out and everything seemed to sparkle in its light. No-one had ever told her how beautiful England was in the spring. She drove past old thatched houses with their crooked beams and whitewashed walls; chocolate box houses that belonged to another time.

Everything is so old!

She drove past old brick farm houses and barns and laughed at the antics of the horses in the paddocks. Feeling lighter now she drove past a clutch of houses surrounding a local pub.

And as she did the little Astra lost power and rolled to a stop. John had warned her that the car was a little unreliable. He hadn't had time to get it serviced, 'take these', he said as he had placed the jumper cables on the counter. 'You probably won't need them. Do you know how to use them?'

'Oh yeah. No worries.' Famous last words.

Meg looked around for help. The traffic continued to drive past her as she sat in the car with the hazard lights flashing. Meg picks up her phone and tries to call John at work. The call goes through to the answering machine.

Bugger!

There's nothing else for it. She picks up the cables and pulling her skirt down over her thighs she carefully crosses the road to the pub.

The Red Cock is quiet for a lunchtime. Built in the 17th Century the pub has a thatched roof and beer garden where customers can exhale cigarette smoke amongst the roses and hollyhocks. Inside, the walls are wooden battens and turned wooden posts reach for the low ceiling which everyone – except Meg - has to slouch over to avoid grazing with their heads. The inside is decorated with curios from around the village – old rowing paddles, a straw broom, signs from the '30s for Pears Soap and day trips to Brighton by rail. Behind the dark wooden bar there's a selection of gold taps and levers marked helpfully with London Pride, Seafarers and even the Aussie pretender; Fosters. The pub smells of centuries of spilt beer left to soak into the carpet and of mud from the nearby fields. The old regulars are sitting up at the bar but apart from the three old boys the pub is virtually empty. They look up as Meg flounces into the pub.

One of the old boys clocks her pretty face and her skirt and heels. He smiles quietly, on the inside.

'Oh hi, I wonder if you could give me a hand,' Meg starts. She easily slips into a smile. All three boys are looking now. Unblinking. She has their attention. Their eyes widen as Meg strides confidently over toward them, cables by her side and breezily asks: 'Who wants to jump me?'

In reply there's a loud commotion at the bar. Someone spills something, one man's mouth falls open and one of the old boys half falls off his seat. The other two sit there smiling - cats with cream.

Now there's something you don't hear every day at The Red Cock.

Thankfully, a moment later the barman walks out and on hearing the damsel in distresses' problem walks to the car with her, pulls his own car alongside and does his thing with the jumper cables. He's a young guy, a uni student training to walk the Marathon des Sables.

'What's that? Meg says.

'It's famous. Called the Toughest Race on Earth. You walk through the Sahara desert for 156 miles carrying all your food and a ration of water. It's brutal.'

'And you do this for fun?' Meg asks.

The barman adjusts the cables under the hood. 'Mainly. I'm hoping to get into Sandhurst when I get back.'

'Sandhurst?'

'Officer training for the army,'

Meg nods. Of course. Wasn't everyone around here in the army/working with the army/been in the army/married to the army?

Peaceful, nuclear free New Zealand with its population of hippies and chartered accountants was a very long way away.

The Oracle shopping centre is busy. Everyone in Reading is taking time off to grab lunch or visit the Thorntons chocolate shop. Meg raced in to look around the shops and to grab a slab of chocolate as a surprise for John. He was heading away on exercise tomorrow and she thought it would be nice to surprise him with a note and some chocolate smuggled into his holdall.

She felt at home in the Oracle. It was familiar ground for her, with its shops of Esprit and Disney – it could be anywhere in the world. Any mall in Singapore, Australia or New Zealand. She knew this space well. There would be a clutch of Dead Sea people peddling soaps and moisturisers somewhere in the centre, the loos would be downstairs under the escalators and at each end of the mall there would be an anchor department store – a John Lewis or a Debenhams, David Jones or Farmers. She mooched around the stores, stopped for a coffee at a Starbucks and then people-watched to while away the afternoon.

It was late in the day when she finally headed back from Reading and stopped in to pick up John from work. The front gates were guarded by armed policemen dressed in black, the perimeter fence was topped with barbed wire and shadowed by another line of tall fencing about a metre away and patrolled by armed police with dogs.

'It's like a small town inside,' John had told her, 'it used to be an old air force base. There's an onsite police station and health centre and a main street where the runways used to be... There's everything you could ever need...'

'Except people from the outside...' Meg added.

Even staffers wearing their lanyards around their necks were searched before entry, and it seemed no one ever met their partner for lunch or popped in to say 'hi' to their partner's workmates.

Meg drove the car into a car parking space turned the radio up and watched as people came and go. As each car approached the gates it was stopped and papers checked. It felt like something out of the movies, or at a stretch The Simpsons. Meg half-expected Homer to appear clutching a bag full of donuts. Instead, a truck appeared and two policemen waved him over to a layby and started searching the vehicle. Meg was fascinated and yet somehow overwhelmed with guilt.

It was like walking through customs with an apple when entering New Zealand. Or driving with a traffic cop behind you. She glanced nervously over at the policeman with the long armed mirror device that looked like a massive version of a dentist's in-mouth mirror.

What do they call those?

As she pondered the correct name - Mouth viewer? Tonsil telescope? Mouth mirror? - the policeman carrying a large black semi-automatic rifle approached her car. She wound down the window.

'Hello. May I ask what you're doing here?' Unsmiling. All business. This wasn't an *Allo allo allo* what's 'appenin' 'ere bobby at all!

He peered into the vehicle, not looking at her face, his eyes methodically searching through the car. All of a sudden her seat felt slick with sweat.

'Hi. I'm waiting to pick up my partner from work,' Meg replied confidently. And then she smiled, though in her head she was singing 'I whistle a merry tune, so no one will suspect I'm afraid..."

'Could you step out of the vehicle please.'

'Um. OK.'

Bloody hell!

Meg stood by the vehicle as the officer carefully searched through the seats and behind the dashboard and inside the cubby hole under the gear box where parking tickets and shopping receipts met their mouldy demise.

'It's pretty messy in there' she warned as he went to open the glove box. He studiously ignored her and pulled out a used tissue and an empty Thornton's chocolate bar wrapper. Meg flinched and was sweating profusely now. Obviously she looked every bit the perfect terrorist because his partner soon joined him with the massive 'mouth mirror' and together they looked under the car, behind the wheel arches and then at their request, she opened the hood for them to search inside the engine.

Don't look guilty. Smile. Be cool. Not too much, just a little. NOT too much! Oh you idiot they'll think you have something to hide now. Exactly what kind of gun is that? Do they call it a gun? What else would they call it?

HOW THE HELL WOULD I KNOW?

She assumed it was loaded and ready to fire. Policeman number one with the troglodyte forehead was grimacing. He wiped his brown sticky fingers on the back of the crisp packet he'd also mined from the back of the glove-box. *Yup, that chocolate bar wrapper had been smeared with a slick of chocolate.*

If they had been Weight Watcher's police they would have been successful, and she would have been hauled off to diet detention but as they were not they didn't find anything of interest. No devices tidied away under the wheel arch or hidden inside the engine. No explosives in the glove box or tucked under the front seat. Meg who had only ever been confronted by armed police once previously in her life – on the tarmac in Denpasar - was struggling to keep her composure. That was whilst travelling through a troubled country, this was different. This was everyday life. You didn't confront this type of security when you clocked in to your office on Queen Street. In fact, she couldn't remember ever seeing armed police on the streets in Auckland.

After a solid investigation Meg was free to get back into the car and although she desperately wanted to drive off as fast as possible and never look back, she sat back in her seat and willed the time away.

And this – guns, bombs, threat of terror - is just up the street from home.

It felt like years passed whilst she was confined in the car, too scared to move or turn up the radio, before John appeared at the gate. After a cheery wave goodbye to the guard he came to her rescue in the carpark. How can he be so nonchalant? Their worlds were so different.

'Good day?' he asked her.

'Kind of.'

Really?

'Well not really. I felt a bit Kiwi today.'

'What does a Kiwi feel like?'

Meg thought about the laughs at the pub, the questions at the shopping centre (mainly about her accent) and even the suspicion of the armed guards a few minutes ago and then Sarah's tears on Skype. She felt very, very small.

'I spoke to Sarah on Skype. Murray told the kids I'd deserted them,' she blurted out.

John looked alarmed. 'What did you say?'

'I said I was coming back! I said ... I'm sorry I just can't talk about it right now.'

They drove silently back to the house and spent the night quietly as John prepared to head away on exercise. Meg watched from her spot on the couch.

'Where are you going?'

'I can't really say.'

'You can't expect me to not know. What if there's an emergency or something?'

'You could ring my mobile.'

'Yeah. But what if I need to come and get you?'

He couldn't see the need. 'I'm heading over to Wales.'

'Is that what I should say to people?'

'What people?'

'People, people. Friends, family – you know people!' She could feel anger rising.

'You shouldn't really say anything to anyone. Just say I'm away for work. Tell them if you told them you'd have to kill them.'

'Ha. Ha.' She wasn't laughing.

'Don't you think you should be a little more open with me? I don't know anyone in this whole country, or in this hemisphere really and you're heading off to God knows where...'

He silenced her with a kiss and playfully toyed with her pouting lips. She seethed.

'Don't be grumpy. I'll be back from Wales on Sunday. Have you seen my black boots?'

He was gone first thing in the morning and by the time she woke to the telephone ringing, the sun was pouring through the oak tree's branches into the little bedroom.

'Hello.'

'Oh Hi, Meg is it? We haven't met but I work with John. Can I have a quick word with him?'

'He's gone already.'

Her lips felt like sandpaper and someone had poured bleach down her throat during the night.

'Oh right. He's already on his way to Inyin then?'

'Um. I don't know. Wherever he was going, he's gone there already. Can I take a message?'

'No, it's ok, I'll call him on his mobile.'

With remarkable restraint she clicked off the phone and placed it down carefully on the bedside table.

Inyin? Liar, liar, pants on fire.

She had barely settled back under the duvet when the phone rang once again.

'Hello?'

A man's voice replied.

'Hello, may I speak with Megan Sinclair please.'

'Speaking.'

'Oh hello Megan, it's Luke Stone from Samson & Sera I've some unfortunate news about your application.'

She held her breath.

'I've been reviewing your case with my colleague Lyla Peters and we've discovered there's been a bit of a mistake. To cut a long story short you can't apply for the Highly Skilled

Migrant programme because your income in New Zealand hasn't been quite enough.'

'But I've been working part-time as I single parent my three kids and with child support I have enough income to meet their criteria.'

'That's not enough, I'm afraid to say. The UK Border Office don't accept child support payments as a legitimate income and they won't accept part-time work income either.'

'But Lyla said...'

He interrupted her. 'Yes, I understand you must be disappointed. But we have had a good look over the regulations and I'm afraid recent changes mean that they are really cracking down.'

'So, what can I do?' Meg asked between gritted teeth.

'My best advice is to find yourself a job offer here in the UK and apply under the Working Visa category and whilst you're doing that get your income up so that your income in the twelve months preceding entry meets the criteria. If you have any more questions, please don't hesitate to give me a call.'

He repeated his telephone number but Meg didn't hear it.

Fan-bloody-tastic. What do I do now?

She reached over to dial John's mobile but it went straight through to voicemail. She was disappointed but not surprised.

Chapter 16

Haere Ra

JOHN TRIUMPHANTLY BURST through the front door.

'Honey, I'm home.'

Meg found a smile to greet him at the door but moved her head slightly to present her cheek when he leant in for the kiss.

John didn't seem to notice.

He looks good, Meg admitted to herself. Wearing dark shades and a deep tan he swept past her and placed his black holdall in the centre of the lounge where everyone would fall over it during the evening and went into the kitchen to make a cup of tea. Meg looked at her watch.

Surely it is wine-o'clock.

'So, how was it in Wales?' She leant on the word *Wales*.

Oblivious, he poured the boiling water into his mug.

'Good, really good we got the job done...'

Glancing at Meg's thunderous face he stops.

'What?'

'You weren't in Wales were you?'

'Yes I was...'

'Except Andy called from work. Did he get hold of you in *Inyin*?' She spat the word out and walked slowly over to the kitchen sink. John moves over and places his hands on her shoulder.

'It's the same place! It's about ten miles from Wales.'

She rounds on him eyes dark with anger. 'You lied to me. I told you how important it was for me that you were truthful and honest and you lied.'

'I did not lie. We're not supposed to talk about where we are going and what we're doing.'

'Well you didn't. And I didn't ask what you were doing. All I want to know is the truth about where you are. I'm not just a passer-by, or someone down the pub, I'm your girlfriend. Is it that unreasonable that I know where you are? You said one thing and did another. How many times have you lied to me? Huh? Like the time you were here and I was in New Zealand you lied about your landlady. You were living with her weren't you?' she hissed.

'I was not. She was *just* my landlady.'

'But if you're not truthful all the time how do I know? How do I know you want me to stay here with you? How do I know you're not just stringing me along? It could all be bullshit.'

With that she marched out of the room and up the stairs to a safe huddle on the bed. John stayed downstairs for a time wondering what on earth had happened. He had never encountered anyone as fiery as Meg.

The day turned into night and Meg's anger dissipated with the light. It was replaced with a deep sorrow that ached like a stretched muscle. He wasn't the first man to say he loved her and then walk away.

It was 2am when she woke to the sound of the barn owl screeching in the oak tree. It sounded painful. She lifted her tired body out of the bed and walked over to the window, opening it slightly to see the owl high up in the tree, its white face haunting the branches.

She felt his arm curling around her waist. She could feel the warmth of his breath on the back of her neck.

'He's beautiful.' He said. She nodded. That was true.

'Please don't, Meg. I didn't lie. There's only you.'

She drew back slightly. 'You know how important it is that you're honest with me. You know *why*. I can't be completely in the dark. I don't even know what you do and you're expecting me to cross the world with my kids and live with you.'

He nodded sombrely. 'OK. I work up the road as an electronics engineer. Sometimes I work with the guys heading out to Afghanistan. I help teach them how to make devices safe.'

'Devices? Like bombs?'

'Yup.'

She sat down on the bed, her mind reeling. 'Oh wow.'

Outside the window the barnyard owl screeched as if someone was flaying it alive. The screams chased the panic down her throat as the window sucked in the cool night breeze. She wanted desperately to ask but couldn't find the words.

Is that dangerous?

Clearly it was. And clearly it was completely outside of her experience and comfort zone. They talked in low voices for an hour or two side-by-side on the bed. She asked if 'they ever go off' and he corrected her 'they don't go off; they detonate'. He told her that he couldn't ever tell her the full story, he was sworn to secrecy – quite literally it seemed – and that secrecy would protect him and her and their family.

Their family.

She silently repeated the words. At one point in the dark night she stopped and said it back to him. 'Let me get this straight. You work at an atomic bomb factory, you teach people how not to blow themselves up and half of your life you can never share with me. You're asking me to move across the world with my three kids and all my earthly possessions to share a life with you – a life that I don't really know anything about?'

He nodded.

She paused. *So different from anything I've ever come across. The most dangerous thing Murray ever did was piss off a fund manager.* Slowly she said 'I guess I better find you a cape.'

****

She felt different in the morning. As if everything had changed and she was no longer fighting something in the shadows. It's certainly different; she told herself as she made the coffee and prepared his cup of tea. She dangled the tea bag in the hot water and absent-mindedly stirred in the milk. John was heading off later this afternoon and then she would have a few days searching for jobs alone in the little house, before flying back to New Zealand Friday week. She grabbed the tea and slipped upstairs. He was still sleeping, his head under the pillow and his feet sticking out of the end of the duvet.

'Wake up Sleepyhead I've got you a cuppa.'

'Mmmmmm.'

'Come on! Wake up!' Meg laughed. 'How are you going to manage getting up at 6am to get the kids to school?'

'Worry bout that when I get to it.' He reluctantly tossed the pillow off and reached for his tea whilst sliding up to lean against the headboard.

'But really, 'Meg persisted. 'How are you going to manage? There'll be no sleeping in with early soccer mornings and school drop-offs...'

'We'll get there,' he said. 'We'll make it work.'

'But what if it doesn't. What if I can't get a job, or a visa? What if the kids don't want to come, what if...'?

'What if? We just don't know. Yes, there are lots of 'what ifs' but they're not all bad. What if you do get the perfect job? What if the Visa just happens? What if it all falls into place? It could. Don't give up. I'm not. I'm not giving up.'

Meg nodded half-heartedly.

'Come on. I'm not giving you up for anything!'

'Really?'

'Yup. Really. I love you. I think it will all work out. You'll see.'

Not wanting to argue Meg relented and fell into his good mood. What ifs could be good after all. She had a job interview just this afternoon with a recruitment agency in Reading, maybe that could be it. 'Ok. Ok. I'll trust you. You sure you don't want to come to live in New Zealand?'

'Nah,' he scoffed. 'You'll see; you'll be here living with me before you know it.'

John went off to his exercise that night and Meg pottered around the house popping off to visit recruitment agencies and in between times dreaming of what the future could look like. The days passed quietly and calmly and before long Meg was ready to return to her kids, pets and friends. It was John's turn to be emotional at the airport, but Meg was resolute. She kissed him goodbye, slung her handbag over her shoulder and cheerily smiled through tears.

'See you soon.'

With that she walked through to the departure lounge, not daring to look behind her.

Two weeks' later

There was a panicked message from John on Skype.

A recruitment company called for you today, he seemed quite urgent. You'd better get in touch with them.

He left the details and the telephone number, and once she had fed the kids and thrown the dishes at the dishwasher she pulled her laptop into her room, shut the door and dialled the number. They were keen to set up a call with the company, they said. 'They're desperate for someone with your experience' he said. She made the call at midnight and the woman running Faberge Marketing did indeed sound keen. So keen that after one phone call she requested Meg meet her for an interview, in person.

Which was problematic given she was in Auckland, about 12,000 miles away.

But they were keen and she was desperate to get on with their life with John – her crazy Englishman – so she got on a plane and travelled from New Zealand back to England for for the second time in three months.Thankfully she passed the interview and was offered the position – General Manager of Faberge Marketing.

Over the following three months she met with Murray and cleared the way for the kids to travel with her, sold up her fridge, bed, microwave and other possessions and prepared the furniture and pets for moving. She moved out of the little flat they were renting and waited out the visa application process in a motel room at Auckland Airport, for six weeks.

The holding pattern was exhausting yet somehow liberating. Released from school commitments and day-to-day domesticity they pretended they were explorers preparing for an expedition – which in effect they were doing.

After dozens of frustrated phone calls in the middle of the night to Lyla the liar and a panicky trip to the British High Commission in Wellington their visas were finally cleared and they were ready to travel.

'I wish I was as brave as you' Ally told her at their last farewell dinner.

Meg looked at her friend with sympathy. 'I don't know if I'm brave or stupid. I just know I have to do this. It's hard to explain,' she said lamely.

Ally's dark eyes smiled at her in piercing admiration. She passed over a little gift bag. 'It's only little. To keep you safe. You can always come back y'know. If it doesn't work out.'

Meg opened the bag and retrieved a silver Pandora bracelet and on it was a single suitcase charm.

'Thank you dear friend. I'm really going to miss you.'

She knew she could come home, but she wouldn't need an 'out'. There was only one way and that was forward.

Later that night at 11:55pm Meg, Alex, Sarah and Jayne were sitting expectantly in their Singapore Airline seats. The seatbelt signs were on. The engines were revving in that pregnant pause before take-off. Jayne was clutching Bearie and excitedly chattering away to her sister. Sarah was wired up to the entertainment system even though it hadn't yet started for their first 12-hour flight. Alex was particularly, pale faced quiet.

The engines roared, and the jet whipped down the runway, then with a thump the landing gear wheezed back into storage, and the flight truly began.

Meg is overwhelmed with emotion.

Brave or Stupid?

Quite possibly both.

Haere Ra New Zealand. God please let it all work out. We've been through so much to get here, please let it all work out. Please...

Chapter 17

Home is where your passport is

MEG COULD HEAR Sarah's voice before she rounded the corner on the path leading from the carpark. Sarah had never been a shy, retiring girl but her voice – so loud – hanging in the frosty night air at 7:30pm, seemed particularly shrill. Meg groaned and fought the urge to turn on her heels and sprint back to the car and head back down the M3 in rush hour traffic to work.

Twelve hours earlier she had dropped Jayne at the pre-school breakfast club and sleepily joined the throngs of commuters heading towards London. The morning commute was slow and stop-start all the way from Basingstoke to the Surrey hamlet just outside the London metropolitan border. It was not unusual for the trip to take an hour and a half, and occasionally, up to two hours if there was an accident on the motorway.

Morning carnage didn't even raise an eyebrow anymore. It was to be expected. As was the rain and sleet and the grey curtain of displeasure that hung over the country in November. She had been in England since mid-August and had enjoyed a summer honeymoon with John and the kids, a trip to Israel for work and a naughty weekend in Las Vegas. Everything then, was fresh and new and exciting. Even grocery shopping for the family could take two hours by the time she had carefully evaluated all the choices. The kids had been amazed at an entire aisle of Pizza and the food from all over the world and they had gleefully chowed down on the offerings of the mid-range 'family restaurants – Pizza Express, TGIF, and Zebra. They had started back at school and were settling in as they were settling with everything else – slowly.

On her first day at work Meg had been asked to deliver a pitch presentation on behalf of her new team, in London. By the second week she was working 12 hour days and talking to clients around the world then crawling home and repainting the lounge with John until the wee hours. In October she had travelled to Israel leaving John and the kids home alone to sort their relationships out.

It hadn't gone terribly well. She had returned from her trip to find John sitting rocking silently in the corner whilst all three children created merry havoc around him. If not literally, definitely figuratively.

Meg's not surprised to see the scene in front of her now. It's been coming for a while. John's face is thunderous as Sarah shrieks dramatically at him.

'I'm NOT making dinner. Just because I'm the girl. Why can't Alex do it?'

'Because I asked *you*, Sarah,' John is saying evenly.

'Because I'm a girl!'

'No, *because* you can cook. Look Mum's had a long hard day at work and she doesn't want to come home to this mess.'

'Well, why don't YOU cook?'

John throws his hands up, mumbles something and starts up the stairs to retreat, smiling perfunctorily at Meg standing in the doorway. He almost bumps into Alex who's hurtling down the stairs at an alarming pace.

'Alex, watch out!'

Alex pushes past and storms into the kitchen. 'What's all the yelling about? All I can hear is yelling...'

His 14-year-old body is all long limbs he doesn't know where to put them, his eyes are flashing with fury. He daren't acknowledge the shocked look on Meg's face. 'Sarah just make the bloody dinner!' he yells at his sister.

'NO. Why don't YOU!'

'Because I don't know where to start.'

John turns back to the kitchen.

'Alex, you could put the rubbish out, it's bin day tomorrow?'

Alex swears loudly and slams his foot into the side of the metal rubbish bin, which crumbles on impact, and then he turns and rushes past both Meg and John standing shock still in the hallway. Everyone turns to look. Mouths drop open in shock. Alex, always quiet Alex, no one has ever seen him like this. He storms up the stairs and Meg can hear his bedroom door slam at the top of the landing.

That went well.

John and Sarah are still at it, needling each other over dishes and dinner and whose turn it was and who was working and who's had a hard day at school and work. Meg wants to run. Mentally she has her trainers and sports bra on and she's gone. Instead, she places her laptop case down, hangs up her coat and scarf, retrieves a packet of chicken nibbles from the freezer and pops it into the microwave to defrost.

The argument rages for the next half an hour, whilst Meg pours a large glass of wine and on autopilot cooks up the family's Five Spice Chicken Nibbles. This is the third time they've had this meal this month.

Meg knows, she just doesn't care anymore.

As she cooks she remembers asking John about kids, way back in Auckland when they were getting to know each other.

She'd asked if he liked them. He said he did. She countered with the thought that raising kids was hard work.

He had considered that carefully and then with a straight face said calmly: 'I love kids. I do. I love having my nieces to stay.' Oh, how she'd laughed. It had seemed impossible back then to explain the difference between living with kids day-in day-out and being able to hand them back when they were difficult.

Dinner is consumed in front of the TV in sullen silence. The lounge come dining room is too small to accommodate all of the furniture that Meg had brought with her to England. They could set up a dining table, they just couldn't sit at it as a family, without rearranging the furniture. The house that had seemed like the perfect love-nest in April is now woefully crowded with five people living there, and no amount of redecorating would make it easier to manage. By the time the family have stopped eating, *Autumn Watch* is on the TV and the mood lifts.

'I saw a fox behind us on Church lane when I was out on my run, the other day,' Meg starts.

'Did it attack you Mum?' asks Jayne.

'No, but I did wonder if it would. I haven't come across a fox before.'

'They're usually quite shy,' John nods, 'they might attack a cat but not a dog or an adult.'

'Crap. So we should be careful about the cat going out at night?'

'Maybe.'

Meg files 'fox' alongside the other items in her mental 'present danger' folder. Alongside terrorists on the Tube in London, an Atomic Bomb Factory just up the road, the dire economic peril of the Global Financial Crisis, Avian flu and potential Snowmaggedon.

Sarah is still pouting, seated on the couch with the cat on her knee.

'How was school today, Sarah?' Meg asks.

'Ok.'

'Just OK?'

'Hmm.'

Sarah is distracted, typing furiously on her laptop that's perched on her knee.

'Who are you messaging?'

'Dad.'

'What are you saying?'

She rolls her eyes. 'I'm telling him about how the girls at school said I was poor and didn't want to hang out with me.'

Meg's shocked. 'Hang on. Poor? How do they know?'

'They said they knew where we live, so obviously we must be poor...'

'But they have no idea where you've come from Sarah, or what we've done or what our family's done... they have no idea. Just because they can't peg us into a social class with our accent...'

Meg's livid, but John just squeezes her arm. 'So what,' he says 'it's not a bad thing cutting our cloth to suit.'

Meg doesn't dare speak.

Later in bed, she raises the topic again.

'Miles was saying at work today that we are going to have to make cut backs. Things are getting tough with the GFC.'

John looks up from the technical manual he's studying.

'But you're so busy!'

'I know, but you know what they say – last one on, first one off.'

He returns to reading. 'You'll be alright,' he says.

Meg closes the laptop lid and settles her head on the pillow. She curls her foot over his foot and moves her body close to his.

'Aren't you going to kiss me goodnight?' she asks.

'Maybe.'

But it is a full twenty minutes later that he turns off the light and in the dark moves closer to her.

Meg wakes at the alarm at 5:30am and groans before remembering that she doesn't have to be in the office until midday because she's visiting the teachers at Sarah and Alex's school. She rolls over and badgers John until he wakes. At first he's grumpy but then ire is replaced by ardour and for a moment they forget the daily duties and pretend they are on honeymoon somewhere warm and wonderful.

Mid-fantasy they're interrupted by eight-year-old Jayne marching into the bedroom and throwing herself on top of John. Meg is horrified.

'Jayne, you can't just come in. Did you knock?'

Jayne nods.

'Yup. Twice. Very loudly! Anyway I know what you're doing. I know all that that.' She points at the bedclothes accusingly.

'Well. All the more reason why you should knock, wait for a moment until you hear us say it's OK and then come in,' John adds.

'Don't you want a baby brother or sister?' Meg says.

Jayne starts to giggle. 'Pah! I know you can't have children. Your body's gone pffft!'

Meg dies with laughter. So that's how Jayne sees the hysterectomy she had several years earlier.

And then Jayne continues. 'I know all about that, but I do have a question: What are you doing together in the shower?'

'Saving water?' Jayne suggests stifling embarrassed giggles.

Mood destroyed, John and Meg wearily get up and start breakfast. Over coffee and in hushed voice Meg asks John 'how the hell do the English procreate in these tiny houses?' Then she mutters darkly 'we need to get a place with thicker walls, or bigger. Yeah. We just need a bigger place.'

She banishes the memory of the five bedroom two-bathroom double story home she sold in Auckland. Would she ever have that large comfortable home back again?

Bugger that. Would she ever have a *home* again? John was fighting with Sarah, Sarah was fighting with Jayne because they shared a bedroom, and Alex just seemed to vanish, not talking to anyone about anything.

'You don't know what you've got till it's gone,' she growled. She slammed her cup down on the kitchen bench and rushed out of the kitchen, falling over her aggrieved Labrador.

'Bugger! Sorry Bailey. Sorry puppy.' The dog replied with a big wet tongue swept across her face. She stroked the Lab's ears and muttered. 'Why can't we just get a house Bails? Eh? Why?'

And then she screamed a low throttled frustrated scream all the way up the stairs.

Chapter 18

White Christmas

THE TELEVISION MOUNTED on the wall opposite
Meg's desk is promising imminent disaster. If not
immediately at least sometime in the next 24 hours
before the wind down to Christmas. In stark visual contrast,
the offices of Faberge Marketing are looking cheerful -
decorated with tasteful decorations. no crappy tinsel garlands
here, and a large traditional Christmas tree. Meg needs to
leave early as Jayne's school are performing *the* nativity play
this evening. Apparently the nativity play is a big deal in
England, something that seems odd for a country that doesn't
seem particularly Christian. Meg had noticed that there was
even a call for the words 'Merry Christmas' to be replaced
with the words 'Happy Holidays'.

Meg had scoffed at the suggestion. But she had also
noticed that there was considerable backlash with the Daily
Mail devotees spewing vitriol about immigrants wanting

to change England. 'They should all go back to their own countries instead of taking our jobs and changing our religion.' they mocked. Meg had shifted nervously in her seat when she saw them on tele. She was one of *them* now. She was an immigrant. And obviously she was solely responsible for England's overloaded healthcare system, the rising unemployment rate and the division of church and state.

The BBC is broadcasting the early evening news and Meg slyly gets up from her desk and wanders through the office, coffee mug in hand as if she was about to make a plunger of coffee. As she walks through the converted barn she glances over at Miles' desk and is relieved to see that his computer is off, his bag gone. Good, he's gone for the day. Miles, wasn't the easiest person to work for - he was demanding at the best of times, but in recent weeks with some undefined problem at home these were far from his best times, and now her boss was insufferable. Rude, argumentative and determined that he get as much work out of his staff as humanly possible. So much for work life balance, Meg thinks ruefully as she slips out to the car.

She favours the accelerator all the way down the M3 and arrives just in time to grab Jayne – appropriately dressed as a shepherd, complete with a teatowel tied around her head dressed in one of John's dressing gowns – her muttering siblings and John, for the short walk to the local junior school.

The school hall is packed with eager parents, whose excited chatter is not subdued by warning to refrain from taking photos of the show or any of the children for fear of breaching privacy regulations. Meg supposes that makes sense in a town where the main employer is the atomic bomb factory. She smiles quickly at a mother she knows from Breakfast Club, as the house lights go down for the show.

The Virgin Mary is a pretty little blonde haired girl with beautiful rounded vowels. She's slightly taller than Joseph, who is a stocky dark haired boy. Meg recognises him as the eager kid who had wanted to be Jayne's boyfriend within the first few weeks of school. Meg was horrified and reminded Jayne that she was eight years old. Way too young to be worrying about what boys thought.

The Angel appears and the shepherds – two boys and Jayne – listen attentively to the Angel's message. And then it is Jayne's big moment.

She boldly faces the audience and says in pure unadulterated Kiwi accent – 'Ewe hurd the angul letz folla the star!' Her Kiwi twang hangs in the air and then the audience erupts in laughter, Jayne looks bemused, and the show goes on.

'A star is born' Meg whispers to John.

Later that night as they are finishing off hot cups of chocolate Jayne shyly sits beside John. 'I've decided,' she starts. 'I don't want to call you John any more. I want to call you Dad.' John responds with a hug and Meg daren't breathe out for fear of dispelling the magic.

Two weeks later

The other company directors are already on holiday leaving Meg and her team of two young women slaving away over hot computers. Outside the converted barn it's -2 degrees celsius and snow is falling like confetti. The squirrels have disappeared from the ancient oak trees, and even the horses are sheltering in winter barns.

Meg is trying to concentrate on her computer screen – she's emailing a client in Israel – but she keeps getting distracted by the news and every time she passes the window she can't help but stop and look.

April's snow seems a long time ago. That was when life in England was a dream, now it is part of her day to day. Then she could play in the snow, marvel at its purity, smile at the icicles on tree branches and laugh at dragon-puffs she made when breathing out. Then, she didn't need to consider driving home on the M3 in the snow, and the chaos that would undoubtedly develop. Then, she wasn't concerned about work pressure and getting new clients 'immediately before we go out of business' as Miles liked to threaten at least five times a day.

Then, it was a dream, a honeymoon, a fantasy. The snow was beautiful then, it wasn't chilling, it didn't turn to sludge on the door step and it didn't make tights and socks soggy. Dreaming of a white Christmas was one thing, living with it was something altogether different.

Andrea, her Accounts Executive appears at her desk looking sheepish. 'Meg it is 3:30pm on Christmas Eve, I've tidied up the notes on the Stoneways' project and I've sent Christmas greetings and hours and stuff to our clients, do you think I could set off now? It's just I've got to get home in time to head up north to Mum's...'

'Did you hear back from Frank Goldberg?'

'At Mobiglo? No, I haven't. Have you heard?'

Meg purses her lips. 'No, not since I sent him the proposal on Monday. '

Andrea looks concerned. She knows that Faberge need that project. The first thing to go in a financial crisis is marketing spend. At least that's what Meg has told her. At only twenty-four years old she's never experienced a recession before, but as Meg had reassured her team, she had experienced at least two recessions.

'Go, Go! Get out there before it gets murderous on the roads. I won't be far behind you. Quick! Go!' Meg waves her off.

Andrea smiles her relief and grabs her coat yelling 'Have a great Christmas' and leaves for Christmas break.

Twenty minutes later Fiona is at her desk repeating the same request, almost word for the word and Meg also waves her off.

The office is quiet now. Only the TV drones on. More banks have toppled. More images of woeful looking young bankers clutching boxes of possessions, standing shell-shocked on a frigid Canary Wharf. Meg winces. She knows she told Andrea and Fiona that it would be OK, that she's weathered at least two recessions previously and all would be OK, but still... that was in New Zealand, things tended to be different in England.

In other news, the runways at Heathrow are being cleared but they're anticipating problems later in the day if the snow settles, the TV informs her. The dark eyed woman is promising chaos on the M4 and suggesting that Londoners leave for their holidays early.

Meg doesn't need telling twice. She logs off her computer, turns off the TV and sets the alarm before heading out to the car. As she drives down the farm road out to the highway she looks back at the dark converted barn offices of Faberge Marketing. The last six months have been a baptism of fire, but she's got there.

It's all working out. Finally. Meg thought, blissfully happy.

It's already dark outside. It was dark when she left for work this morning and these days it's dark at least three hours before she leaves the office. The roads are slick and snow is piling up on the verges. As she drives through the villages Christmas lights wrapped around brick buildings twinkle coloured reflections in the snow.

It is so pretty! It makes perfect sense that Christmas is held in winter.

Meg couldn't help but feel a little sad that the Antipodean, hot Christmas seemed so wrong when compared to a white Christmas. As she drove slowly up the A340 she laughed to herself, at the house that had covered all bases with not only an angel in the front garden but Santa Claus and the latest Disney princess, all lit up in garish pink and white lights. She glances down at the temperature gauge on her dashboard. It reads -4 deg C. but she is warm in the car as the heater works overtime and the windscreen wipers lazily sweep ice and errant snowflakes off her windscreen. She feels a dull ache of exhaustion sweep over her, but determinedly pushes it aside. It's their first white christmas, she will not let anything spoil it.

The moment she walks through the door of the little house the dog bounds up to greet her and John wraps her in his arms and places a large glass of wine in her hand. The ham she prepared early this morning before work is ready to pop into the oven for basting, the kids appear from nowhere and someone finds *Love Actually* on the TV as they settle down to munch on Christmas Eve dinner.

Vicki Jeffels

It's cosy inside the little house with the boiler going full-bore and the curtains pulled tight against the cold outside. Even the cat is unenthusiastic about leaving the warmth and heading out into the garden. She looks up in disgust when Sarah places her unceremoniously outside into the freshly fallen snow.

'If cats could swear', Meg laughs to the kids.

Before too long Meg is undeniably heady with the wine and relieved to be on holiday break for a few days. She snuggles in to John and he places a lazy arm around her shoulders. 'Merry Christmas Ms Sinclair.' 'Merry Christmas Mr Williams.' Meg steals a kiss and then emboldened by the three glasses of wine (or was it four? She can't quite remember) she has a brainwave.

'Let's go to Midnight Mass!'

'What?'

John's confused. Church?

But Meg's adamant. It's a brilliant idea. A white Christmas in church singing carols. 'We have to. We're Christians and it's Christmas. We have to go.'

Before John can even raise a counter argument she's grabbed his coat and scarf and already tidied her own and is standing at the door.

'Kids! Do you wanna come to church with us' she hollers up the stairs.

'Meg it's ten to midnight on Christmas Eve. Shhh!'

'Oh. Sorry.'

And with that she grabs his hand and pulls him out into the snow. Further down the lane where the snow is deep on the ground she forgets the lateness of the hour, but not the occasion, and starts to sing. 'Dashing through the snow, on a one horse open sleigh, o'er the fields we go...

'Huh that song's never made much sense before in Auckland.'

John shakes his head. 'You're impossible' he says, but he can't hide a smile.

They're late to church and as they enter amidst a solemn prayer Meg misses a step and crashes into the back of the last pew. Several parishioners turn around. Meg's sure someone tut-tuts.

'Oh sorry. Sorry.'

There's nothing quite like making an entrance!

The Church of England house of God is stuffy with the exhaled hot air of the parishioners' Christmas chaos. The vicar, dressed in white robes with what appears to be a curtain tie around his waist, is presiding over the front lectern like the conductor leading an orchestra.

He introduces the carol *Hark the Herald Angels Sing* and as the voices round up over the service sheets in chorus Meg realises that for the first time in a very long time she feels calm and happy. Perhaps He didn't care so much about whether she was 'living in sin' with John, or whether she attended church every Sunday? Perhaps, just perhaps, she was exactly where she was meant to be.

Chapter 19

This is the way the world ends

I T'S UNUSUAL FOR the Monday Directors's meeting to be held in the boardroom, and Meg is running late. She rushes in the office door, grabs a coffee that Andrea has made for her and climbs the stairs. The boardroom is in the loft space underneath the thatched roof. It's the only room in the office that has a door that closes; everything else is open plan.

Miles has already started, and looks up, agitated, as Meg sits at the table.

'Nice of you to join us Meg.'

She buries her face in her coffee cup.

'As I was saying,' he continues. '... before Meg so kindly joined us... unfortunately we've not had a good start to the year. Sabico has fallen over.'

Meg's eyes are wide as she moves her hand to play with her mouth. She's aware she's jigging a little under the table.

'*Obviously,* we weren't expecting that. And we're going to take a hit. How much are we down Jeremy?'

The bespectacled accountant traced the circled number on his notepad. 'Fifteen thousand per month.'

No one spoke. No one dared.

Miles stood up and walked over to look out the window. 'Samantha and I have been discussing it, with Jeremy's help of course, and we have to cut costs.'

Meg felt sick.

'All of us in this room are the highest paid staff members,' Miles started. 'I've already decided to let Erin go, but we're all going to lead by example. We have to cut back our remuneration by at least twenty per cent.'

'*Obviously*, it's just for the time being, and it's no reflection on anyone's performance,' Samantha said as she self-consciously fingered the buttons on her crisp, white blouse.

Meg was starting to feel panicky - there didn't seem to be a great deal that was obvious, at all.

'That's right, we expect it will only be for the first quarter,' Miles said. 'After that, and a few more wins, we should be right.'

Everyone nodded consent and the meeting turned to client business and team reports. Meg delivered her team's report – they didn't service the Sabico account, and they had achieved some significant media exposure for their clients – but Meg delivered the report tactfully, mindful that Samantha's team's results would not be as shiny. The other team had serviced Sabico, at least they had done until the Christmas break.

The meeting continued through a refill of coffee from the plunger and a terse reminder to 'drive the teams hard' from Miles before closing at just on ten o'clock. As the others were picking up their papers to leave, Miles asked her to stay behind. Closing the door behind Samantha as she left, he stood tall facing a seated Meg.

'How did you get on with the Mobiglo proposal? Did you close it yet?' He knew she hadn't. If she had, she would have said so in the report.

'No. I haven't heard back from Frank as yet. I'm hoping to hear before the end of the week'.

'Dammit!' Miles thumped the table. Meg jumped.

'What about the others?'

'Nothing, yet.'

'Well you'd better get out there and make it happen. If you don't we'll all be out of work.'

Miles' eyes were hard and his stare was relentless. Meg knew he was under a great deal of strain but surely this was out of order. He looked so desperate, she wasn't sure what he would do. She started to reason with him. To acquiesce her livid boss...

Yes, of course, she would do everything in her power to get new clients on board and close proposals.. she'd cold call prospects, (*ugh!*) she'd call back old clients...she really would do everything she could but...she simply could not make clients buy Faberge's services. If they couldn't afford it, they couldn't afford it...

'I don't bloody care. Just get us more work!'

Oh God if only you knew how much I wish I could.

'Yes Miles, I understand. I will certainly do the very best I can.'

'Just, get it done Megan!' he slammed the table once again in front of her. A white fleck of spit graced her jacket collar. She stumbled for the right platitudes, the correct reasurances, reason, logic, common-sense, all couched in heroically confident tones, but to no avail. He would not calm down. She hastily begged her leave and then with a solid lump in her throat and shaky legs, Meg fled the boardroom and wobbled down the stairs to her desk. Her heart was beating in her ears when she started her computer for the day.Checking her email inbox, the world crashed down around her. It was an email from Murray.

Megan,

As you may know things in the financial world have been crashing over the past few months and the situation is increasingly dire. With that in mind and given that you decided to take the children to the other side of the world I find myself unable to continue providing child support for them.

As you gallivant around the world travelling to the US and Israel, I've had my income cut in half and can no longer afford to pay anything for the children I never see. I will no longer be paying the child support effective immediately. This situation will continue for the foreseeable future.

Regards

Murray

For a moment she cannot move. Panic envelops her. She can feel that she's breathing fast but it's as if she's divorced from her body. She tries to calm down by breathing into her cupped hands. The recycled coffee breath makes her feel sick.

But he was in Germany. He didn't have time for the kids anyway. He said it would be good for them. He was OK with it. It was supposed to be space and time for them all to work out their relationship...

I didn't take them away without his consent...Nine months. Our separation agreement lasted nine months. Now, all the kids' support is on me.

It can't be what he means. It can't be. He's just having a Murray moment. Another email for the Shitty Murray folder. Momentarily buoyed she rereads the email. Nope it isn't just a Murray moment. She buries her head in her hands and then stares into space desperately hoping to see an answer written there.

The work morning passes slowly and Meg struggles to force a smile into her voice when she calls her clients. Frank from Mobiglo is not available to answer her call, so she labours over an email she sends to him requesting he respond to their proposal as soon as possible.

After a quick walk to the Post Office at lunchtime Meg logs into the UK Border Office website and researches the terms of her work visa. It isn't good news. As she's reading and re-reading the words on the screen Miles appears and Meg calls him over.

'I'm really sorry about this but about our meeting this morning... I've checked with the Immigration Office and well, to cut a long story short, I can't accept a pay cut. It's the work visa. I have to be earning more than forty-five thousand,' she whispers. 'Otherwise I lose the it.'

Miles swallows back his fury. 'You've checked this?'

'Yes.'

He moves slowly around the back of her desk and peers at the screen, reading the words over her shoulder.

'Fucking marvellous,' he mutters. His voice is low and carefully enunciated.

There is a reason that all the best Bond villains are English. Fear is pulsing bloodied and desperate in her ear drums and each of Miles' terrifyingly crisp words cuts clean through, like a scalpel.

'Well you'd better pray that Mobiglo jump on board. You'd better get out there and get as much *fucking work* as you possibly can, as I'm pretty sure you'll be on the first flight back to New Zealand if you lose your job,' he hisses into her ear. He is so close to her she can feel the heat of his breath on her neck, and smell the menace through the distinctive scent of Earl Gray tea mixed in with cigarette smoke. She sits completely still. Shocked into paralysis, a rabbit in the vixen's ravenous eye.

Meg struggles through the rest of the afternoon. Glassy-eyed she stares at the screen but cannot read the words. She's lost the ability to read. The words are there but they don't seem to make sense. They hang on the screen like disconnected pictures. She's lost the ability to talk also. She tries to make a couple of cold calls but all she can manage is a croaky apologetic pitch she squeezes out past the gravel in her throat.

By 4:45pm she has sought refuge in the loo and is sitting on the toilet seat quietly tearing up. She panics that the pounding in her chest is signalling a massive fatal heart attack and melodramatically wishes the last ten minutes of her life were not spent in the Faberge Marketing loo with her knickers round her ankles.

At 4:56pm she decides it is safe to leave the loo and pack up her desk. As she's taking her coffee mugs – her dead soldiers – to the kitchen, Miles appears on his way out of the building.

'Well I'll expect to see you in the boardroom at nine o'clock tomorrow morning with news about the business you've closed Megan. And if you haven't closed the business – or any business – by then, I'll give you some training, myself, one-to-one, on how to do so!'

And then he is gone.

Meg chockes down rising bile, slips her personal things into her bag and grabs the one pot coffee plunger she stows in the kitchen and places it into her brief case. No one sees her as she slips out into the dark and makes her way to her car.

It doesn't matter anyway. What would they do about her leaving 30 minutes early? Fire her?

Chapter 20

The loaves and fishes

THE MORNING AFTER, Meg is chided by the doctor. 'I don't even think you're safe to drive to work right now,' she says to a tearful Meg.

'Stress is a killer Megan. You need to take it seriously. And so does your employer. Have you been to the Citizen's Advice Bureau? They might be able to help with some advice about your immigration problems. In the mean-time take these, take two per day when you're feeling you just can't cope. I'll see you back here in a month or so.'

Sighing, the doctor makes a note on her screen and looks up signalling to Meg that she can leave now. As Meg closes the door behind her the doctor sighs heavily. If she had ever known that her eight years of study working twenty hour shifts being screamed at by senior doctors and ignored by worn-out nursing staff would result in prescribing antidepressants all day long for an NHS that really didn't give a shit about

Mental Health, she might not have stuck at her medical degree. But she did, and here she was, in this forlorn little town full of depressed people. Every second consultation resulted in prescribing antidepressants; the GFC, the threat of terrorism, the weather ... all of it contributed to this contagion of miserable malaise.

'What did the doctor say?' John asked Meg, calling on the phone from work.

'She said I was stressed out. Signed me off from work. Gave me a script for happy pills.'

'Oh. How long are you off for?'

'Three weeks.'

'You might feel much better after a break and then you could go back to work' he suggested.

'Mmmm.' She wasn't convinced.

'When did you say Jack and Terri were coming?' he asked.

'Next week.'

'Well that will cheer you up.'

'I guess.'

'They will.'

'What? More mouths to feed. We barely have enough money to feed us all, now.'

'You always look on the dark side of things. You'll enjoy your sister's son coming to stay. You can show them around. It'll do you good.'

'Yeah. I better go now.' She hung up the phone. His positivity was obscene sometimes.

She spent the rest of the day researching how to apply for a visa, filling out the forms and preparing to send them away for evaluation. By the time school pick up came around she was feeling more hopeful. They were a family. Surely she would get a visa based on her relationship with John.

She walked briskly around the corner to the junior school and waited outside the classroom, standing a little apart from the other Mums. They were, in the main, at least ten to fifteen years younger than she was, and most had grown up in the area. They chatted amongst themselves about EastEnders and local gossip. Meg had no idea which was the East Enders talk and which was local - it all seemed to be the same, to her.

Standing there, feeling every bit an outsider, Meg realised that she didn't know anyone in town. She'd been in England for over six months and she hadn't made any friends at all. it was odd. She was an outgoing person. She was! She was the life of the party, the one to organise the Singles' meetups and the mother coffee groups. Oh she had met the neighbours, well one side at least, they seemed nice, and the other side were never there...but she didn't know anyone else. All of a sudden in an alarming rush, she felt overwhelmingly homesick. Not just for her friends, but for the reassuring Greek chorus of people in her New Zealand everyday life. For the smiling Lotto ladies at Eastridge, for the woman at the Post Office who always asked after Bailey. For the pharmacist she knew by name who would lend her an inhaler if she needed it. They never did that here. If she ran out of Ventolin she had to wait until she could see a doctor.

She missed people knowing her too. The teachers at Alex and Sarah's school, the soccer Mums and Dads, the other Mums from ballet and gym and tennis. She missed Friday nights on the beach at Kohimarama eating fish n chips and drinking sneaky glasses of wine, watching the sun set. She missed journalists knowing her name when she rang them and she missed the security that came from having her own home and income. She missed that quiet confidence that came from knowing that she belonged somewhere and was known.

Jayne was delighted to see her Mum waiting for her outside the classroom. She ran over to greet her blushing with pride and together they walked through the gate and across the carpark to home.

Over afternoon tea in the kitchen Meg found a school notice damply curled around Jayne's lunchbox.

'What's this?'

'A notice.'

'Obviously. What does it say?'

'I need Plimsolls for PE. Can I have an apple?'

'Ok,' Meg passes an apple over from the fruit bowl and scans the notice. It is indeed about Plimsolls. They are apparently a vital part of the school uniform. *Underlined!* They must be supplied with the uniform shorts and t-shirt before the end of the week or Social Services will be advised.

Meg can't understand why Social Services would care whether her daughter had Plimsolls. But more importantly than that, Meg doesn't really know what Plimsolls are. After quizzing Jayne and coming up none the wiser, Meg decides to drive to Chineham to visit the shoe store.

Jayne is delighted. This is a bonus. Not only is Mum home after school, but she's taking her to the shopping centre – where, as everyone knows, there will be an urgent need to provide icecream.

The drive through the countryside to Chineham is pretty. Meg's confident driving through the tunnel-like one way lanes now, and the weather has been mercifully dry for the past few days. As they pass the elegant farmhouses and converted barns or 'Kiwi styled houses' as the kids call them, Meg wishes that they had been able to live somewhere like that. The house is crowded with five of them, the dog and cat, and is likely to become even more crowded with her nephew and his girlfriend arriving next week.

God only knows what I'm going to feed us all.

The shoe shop at Chineham is quiet and full of stock. Bright pink sneakers and doll-sized high heeled shoes (who buys them?) and an impressive range of wellies or gumboots as Meg knows them, don the shelves. Meg grabs Jayne's hand

Vicki Jeffels

and they head to the Children's Shoes' department and search in vain for a sign that points to Plimsolls. There isn't one. She picks up a pair of trainers and muses aloud.

'Are these them Jayne?'

'Don't know,' Jayne shakes her head.

You're a great help!

'Well what did the teacher say they were?'

'She didn't.'

Great. Meg moves to the canvas tennis shoes. 'Maybe these?'

'Nope. Don't think so.' Jayne's more interested in a sparkly pair of kiddie heels.

Never in a million years. 'Jayne we need Plimsolls! You need to help me,' Meg begs.

A sales assistant arrives to find a distraught Meg being comforted by her eight-year-old daughter.

'Can I help you?'

'Plimsolls, what the hell are they?' Jayne asks. The sales assistant steps back. *Settle down love. No need to yell.* 'Plimsolls. You know. Plimsolls.'

'I'm from New Zealand and I've only ever read about Plimsolls in *The Famous Five*. I don't know what they are and if we don't get them the school will ring Social Services,' Meg whimpers.

'I see. Plimsolls are inside shoes. You know.'

'But we don't wear shoes inside in New Zealand.' Meg wailed.

The sales assistant took another step back. This was odd.

'In fact we don't wear shoes at all sometimes. People wear bare feet to the shops even and if they're not in bare feet they wear Jandals,' she gabbled.

'When we first arrived here my son got into trouble with the neighbours because he was walking around the street in bare feet. They thought there was something wrong with him. She even asked me if he *had* shoes.'

The Sales Assistant listened. She couldn't understand half of what Meg was talking about (what are Jandals?) but she did know one thing – at the end of the discourse on the merits of bare feet in sunny, warm New Zealand, she would make a £24.00 sale of regulation black Plimsolls. Jayne was just patiently hanging in there for the icecream.

When they returned home Meg picked up a message on the answering machine. It was from Fiona at Faberge. Miles wanted to meet with her the following morning at nine o'clock sharp. The tone of the message was curt. Be there or else, it hissed. Her stomach turned and she fought back the urge to be violently sick. She wearily heads upstairs to her room and as she does so, Alex arrives home.

He breezes in the door, slings his school bag down in the hall and wanders into the kitchen for food.He picks up an apple from the fruit bowl but certain that won't be sufficient to slay the hunger beast growling in his stomach he checks the cupboard for crackers, crisps and other contraband. Mother Hubbard's cupboard is bare. He moves on to to check the fridge, and stands with the door open for a moment, puzzling at the high pitched sound assaulting his ears. It squeals urgently demanding attention. Alex shuts the door sharply. The noise stops. He opens the door tentatively and the electronic buzzing overwhelms his senses once again. He hastily shuts the door.

'Well, don't know what's up with that. Where is all the goddam food?' He swings back from the fridge and peers desperately off into the middle distance, his eyes finally focussing on the perfect snack nestled in just behind the fruit bowl; a loaf of bread.

Gleefully, he grabs the jar of jam from the under bench cupboard and starts preparing the mother of all snacks. Where others would undoubtedly see the week's bread, Alex sees this afternoon's *little snack*.

Just as he is standing at the counter posting jammy bread into his mouth Sarah arrives home from school, throws down her school bag on top of Alex's in the hallway and steps into the kitchen. Her first stop in the search for afternoon tea is the fridge, but no sooner has she opened the fridge door than her ears are assaulted with a high pitched squeal.

'Arrrrrrgh! My ears.' She grabs her ears and scrunches her face in pain. Alex turns around munching. 'It's the fridge. Shut the fridge door!' he yells, his mouth full.

Sarah can't hear over the squealing coming from the fridge and her own screaming.

'SHUT THE DOOR!' Alex bellows and when she is too slow to react he steps past her and hurriedly slams the fridge door shut, and all is mercifully quiet.

Sarah opens her eyes. 'What is it?'

Alex shrugs. 'Dunno. But it's in the fridge.'

Sarah's eyes widen. 'The fridge?' She opens the door once again to check, and swiftly shuts the door.

'What is it?" Sarah screams. 'Why is it in the fridge?' she yelps.

'Drama queen!' Alex mutters as he posts another slab of bread into his mouth.

Hearing the commotion, Meg enters the kitchen. 'Alex you'd better hurry up, don't you have ATC? What's wrong?' She stops when she sees his face .

'Mum, open the fridge door,' he said.

Meg tries to hide a sly smile, as she opens the door, ever so casually. 'What? What's wrong' she asks.

'Arrrrgh! Mum shut it! It hurts my ears,' Sarah wails.

'What does?'

'Can't you hear that Mum?'

'What?'

'That squealing! It really hurts. Alex can hear it too. Shut the door. Shut it! Please' she begs.'

Meg chokes back round chuckles. There were benefits to having a skilled electronics engineer in the house.

'I can't hear anything apart from you screaming!'

'Grrrrr!' Sarah growls as she marches out of the kitchen in disgust. Alex rolls his eyes, finishes his jam sandwich and races up to his room in search of his uniform, and then, safely alone for a moment, Meg allows herself to roar with laughter.

Before too long Alex appears back downstairs looking smart and grown-up in his Air Training Corps uniform.

At least there was that; ATC had been brilliant for him and through it he'd been on trips in helicopters and other military aircraft and away to camps and pow-wows. Celebrate the little wins, she reminds herself. She grabs her keys and says: 'Come on then, I'll take you to ATC.'

*****

Later that night in bed she recounted the story to John.

'But they didn't figure it out?' he asked.

'Alex was close. He knew it was in the fridge, but he didn't know where. It didn't seem to bother him as much as Sarah.'

'Probably because he's just that few years older.'

Meg nodded. 'But it was a great idea to put it in the salad drawer. They didn't think of looking there.'

'I bet they weren't hanging around staring into the fridge long enough to see it anyway,' John laughed.

'No. They weren't. Genius idea! We could sell those you know. To all those Mums who lose the weekly shop in one foul swoop one hungry school afternoon.'

'Do you think anyone would buy them?'

'Yeah! Everyone with teenagers would buy them!'

John grinned in the dark.

'You're a genius you know! I think you're getting this parenting thing down pat.' She brushed his face with a kiss and they snuggled into each other, dozing companionably until lights out.

Meg woke at about 2am. She couldn't sleep. Every time she closed her eyes she felt rising panic at the thought of facing Miles. She could feel his breath on her neck. She could see the malice in his eyes. At 4am she gave up trying to sleep and walked downstairs to draft an email on her laptop which was sitting on the dining room table.

Dear Miles

She started. Then backspaced over it.

Miles

Now what? She really didn't know.

By 7am she had drafted her peace. She was letting the stress and panic go. She clicked send and went back upstairs to take a bath.

She bathed through breakfast, calling out goodbye as John and the kids left the house. Then there was only the sound of the tap dripping hot water into the bath. She lay back in the warm water feeling the peace well up inside her, only to be broken by the shrill tones of the telephone and then soon after, her mobile phone.

He's got the email.

She knew she should feel panicked but instead she felt relieved. He'd pushed but she had preferred to jump. At least when you jump you get to choose where you jump to.

She spent the rest of the morning shopping in Reading for a futon for the visitors. It felt good to be on her own timetable once more. She had worked twelve hour days for months on end and after the stress of the visa application, the divorce settlement and the move to England, she felt surprisingly light and happy to be free to wander around the shops.

She found a futon for the young couple and arranged to have it delivered. There was no room, let alone a spare room, for visitors in their row house so a futon would have to do. John was right; she was looking forward to seeing them. They were a reminder of her family and the Antipodean sea and sun.

The following week she drove to Heathrow and retrieved the tired 21-year-old and his jetlag bedraggled girlfriend off the plane from Sydney. They took to the futon immediately and making the most of the quiet house during the daytime they fell into bed.

As they slept, Meg quietly worked on her laptop on her bed. She had decided to refresh a blog she'd started a few months ago, but hadn't had time to write during the mad times at Faberge. Now, she had all day to write. She revelled in the craft of piecing the blog posts together and learning the HTML code behind it all.

At lunchtime she attacks the visa application. She needs coffee to cope with it. It's confusing and dictatorial and long-winded. After much swearing and rolled eyes she finally seals the envelope ready for the UK Border Agency bureaucrats. There was no clue as to how long that assessment process might take.

Meg quietly boils the jug for coffee whilst the young couple sleep in the lounge. Pouring the water onto the coffee grinds she ponders her predicament. How long could it take them to assess her visa application? She and John had been together for over a year and were living together as a family, of course they would grant her a visa.

It's probably only going to be a month or so without income.

Reassured she returns to her laptop and continues working on her blog.

Chapter 21

Meatloaf and Missing Persons

'Meg, wake up love, I'm heading out and I'm taking Sarah with me.'

'Mmm.' Meg turns over and buries her head under the pillow. Doesn't John know how bloody early it is?

'Meg?'

'Uh huh,' she mutters and then pretends to fall back to the land of nod. He distractedly rifles through the junk on the dresser, inadvertently pricks himself with a fishing hook and yelps.

That'll learn ya, thinks Meg quietly. She's still pretending to be fast asleep. Sleep-ins are precious in the busy household and Saturday morning sleep-in is sacrosanct. It's not merely a practice, it is a religious observance.

A little more frustrated shuffling of papers, and slamming of drawers and cupboard doors and then, mercifully, there is quiet in the bedroom as the anaemic sunshine slides under the curtains. Meg lies quietly under the duvet picking at thoughts that pass through her mind.

The house is a mess. There's fishing hooks on the dresser (fishing hooks! Why?) and four weeks' worth of washing tumbled out from the dryer, now tied around the base of the downstairs' loo. It's probably now so dirty again it needs to go straight back into the washing machine – in the kitchen. Meg was still trying to process that. The washing machine was in the kitchen. There wasn't a laundry. For a moment she wonders how mums with kids in nappies, manage. Do they wash out dirty clothes in the food sink? Ick! At least they don't have babies. God only knows how the carpets would have survived that. The carpets are now grey with dirt – at least she thinks they are grey - it's been a while since she actually saw bare carpet. Seven adults living in a small house has not produced a clean, tidy, nor calm living environment. But at least it's 'a house full of love' John had said when Meg raised the thorny issue of her beautiful big home in Auckland.

The little house in Bottom Hedgeley may well be full of love but it was also full of dog hair, mould, dishes and dirt.

It has been three months since Meg put in her application for a visa and still nothing. Each morning she rushes to the door at the sound of the mail falling through the slot onto the carpet. Every morning she is disappointed with love letters from the banks and the council. Every morning she mutters – 'only bad news comes by mail'. Everything else comes by email.

The Border Agency won't email, nor will they give out a telephone number or a personal contact. She's tried ringing them, but every time she calls she gets a different person with a different view of the complicated immigration regulations. It was enormously frustrating.

Meg scans the ceiling of the little double room. The gentle light is making shadow figures with the oak branches. She should get up, and go for a run. Reluctantly climbing out of bed she slips into long running pants and a long sleeved tee. Her phone tells her it's eight degrees, and after almost ten months in England she no longer considers that cold. Bailey is apoplectic with joy when she spies Meg hunting for the dog lead, and bounces and barks with enthusiasm.

'Shh. Come on girl.' They noisy-quietly shuffle out the front door, through the gate and onto the quiet street. Bailey is already pulling Meg forward as she grabs a breath and starts jogging along the street past the rows of brick houses across the main road and down Church Lane.

Church Lane is quiet. The residents are all still tucked up in bed oblivious to the moody veil of morning mist. Down past the modest two up two down cottages that were built in the 1940s to accommodate the burgeoning workforce for the local airforce base, now the atomic bomb factory. Down the lane, deeper into the bucolic watercolour painting she jogged, down past the detached three-bedroom home with its architecturally on-point sloping roof and its little front garden water feature, and past the old cottage with the thatched roof, until finally only fields lined the lane.

The horses were playfully trotting around the field, lifting their manes and snorting steaming breath into the cool morning air. Meg often stops to pat the horses on her run. She loves living so close to them, it reminds her of the Auckland of her childhood and the paddocks in front of her house and the Howick Pony Club. She had wanted to try horse riding when she first arrived in England, but there had never really been the time. Now she had all the time in the world, and not enough money.

She jogs onwards. Feet crunching on the gravel. She can feel the cool air winding its way down her nose and throat, curling down into the tight reaches of her chest. She stops and reaches into her jacket pocket for her inhaler and as she does Bailey stops also but then turns and stares, dead still.

They were being watched.

A few feet away a small fox is standing in the middle of the lane. Its fur is a russet exclamation mark against the grey still spring morning. Meg quietly gasps, not knowing whether to run or stand still 'like a tree'. Would it attack like a wild dog?

She gingerly reaches into her pocket to grab her phone but when she looks up again and positions the camera to take the shot, the animal had sauntered away into the scraggly hedgerows.

She jogs solidly out to the fence opposite the ancient church, and grabs a breath whilst looking out over the mist covered fields. She can see rabbits scurrying in the distance and reminds herself that she is only ten miles or so from Watership Downs. She had read that when she was a child in her home in Howick, never expecting that one day she would be living here. After gathering her breath and retying her shoe laces she heads back along the lane towards home.

All of a sudden she can hear the approaching thud-thud-thud of a two dark Chinook helicopters. With the lane deserted and the morning still and cool they sounded eerily close. No doubt they were heading down to Bramley, a training ground for the RAF but as they thundered almost directly above her, Meg is thrilled by their unexpected presence. 'Well that's different. You don't get that in Auckland'. In Auckland a helicopter was more likely rescuing someone from an accident at sea or spotlight-chasing crims through suburban streets. She laughs to herself and continues jogging on round the loop towards home.

400 metres or so from the main road they pass an elderly man with flat cap and jacket walking his Yorkie. Meg breezily calls out 'Good morning' and flashes a generous smile. He

catches her eyes for a moment and then purposefully looks away without acknowledging her. Bemused, Meg shakes her head. It's not just early morning RAF Chinooks that are different about living here.

As she enters the little house she scoops up from the doormat a letter with the UK Border Agency stamp on it. She rips it open. It advises that her Work Visa has been cancelled after leaving Faberge and as she is now without a current work visa so she is banned from working in the UK whilst her new visa application is being assessed. There is no indication how long that would take or what it might involve but she is warned three times within the three-page letter to not leave the country (or risk being unable to re-enter) and to not seek employment. Meg panics a little and her stomach flips. How much longer would it be until she knew?

She walks into the kitchen where Jack is making coffee and pouring milk over Weetabix. It was Weet-a-bix in England not Weetbix as it was at home.

'Morning. You're up early,' she says.

Jack smiles and his dreadlocks jangle as he enthusiastically wipes the spilt milk up from the bench. 'Yeah. Thought I'd go into Basingstoke and look for a job.'

'Good plan. Where are you going to go?'

'Going to head all around Fesitival Place and go into that bar.'

'Grilled to Thrill? That's a great idea. I can drop you in if you like.'

'That would be brilliant, Meg, thanks. I'll just have brekkie, give this to Terri and smarten up.'

Meg looked over his earnest face. She hoped like mad that there were some tolerant employers in Basingstoke who didn't take a hard line on alternative appearance. Somehow she suspected it could be a problem. Basingstoke, was not known for its alternative lifestyle. Basingstoke was so conservative the sushi bar had to close within three months of opening, because no one would eat raw fish. The only place that served decent coffee was a small café in the bookshop, the second hand clothes stores did a roaring trade and every second shop on the high street was a loan shop. Basingstoke was a long way from the leafy slopes of Auckland's Eastern Suburbs, and every now and again the excitement of Meg's adventure was wearing off and she felt displaced. Lost.

She was a missing person.

Jack and Terri took more than an hour to get ready and it was already eleven thirty and the day half over before Meg had successfully driven them into Basingstoke and was looking around the local market that popped up in the Bottom Hedgeley sports field car park every weekend.

She had grown used to the rag-tag bunch of caravans and traders who sold cheap French cheese and - importantly for Meg's new found enthusiasm for stretching the budget

{273}

– cheap meat. The cheery trader knew her now and would smile heartily whenever she approached the caravan. But this time she didn't buy a side of rump, lug it home and hand butcher it into steaks. This time, she was hunting for sausage meat and mince. The butcher threw in a few extra sausies for free and Meg was grateful. He didn't volunteer where the meat was from, and she didn't ask.

Ask me no questions, I tell you no lies.

Thrilled at the butcher's kindness, she stumbles back to the car laden down with bags of fresh veges and meat. Thank God! This should feed us all for a few days. Throw in a can of lentils and chickpeas and we'll be right. Enormously relieved that she could stretch the food to feed all seven of them, she drove home humming to music on the car radio.

Alex and Jayne were happily watching TV in the lounge when Meg returned from the market.

'Any sign of Sarah and Dad?' Meg asks Jayne.

'Nope.' Jayne doesn't turn her head from the TV.

Meg reaches for her phone and dials as she puts the vegetables into the fridge, carefully portions the meat and slips it into the freezer. The phone rings through to the answering machine. 'Hi hun, just wondering where you are and when you'll be back. Give me a call.' She rings off and climbs the stairs to her room.

She falls fast asleep sitting bolt upright and wakes in a panic at 4:30pm. The kids are still sitting in front of the TV as she wanders into the kitchen for a drink of water.

'Why don't you go outside for a walk?' She asks them.

'Nowhere to go,' Alex said, biting his lip as he waved the PS3 controller wildly and thumbed the buttons.

'The park? Go for a walk down Church Lane or...' Meg trailed off. Alex ignored her. Jayne looked up and smiled.

'We could go to Sainsburys for you if you want' she says hopefully.

'Pffft.' Meg brushes her off.

They used to be such outdoorsy kids. They used to disappear around the neighbourhood with the local kids for hours, when they lived in St Heliers. And now they were becoming Playstation champions.

It wasn't supposed to be like this. They were supposed to be travelling around Europe seeing the world...they were supposed to be having adventures as a family. Spending time together, learning more about the world, pulling together...

With a sigh, Meg pulled out the mince from the fridge and started de-skinning a sausage. Meatloaf for dinner. That's a very long way from steak.

She reaches into the fridge and finds the bottle of £3 Australian chardonnay that she'd found at Lidl. The shopping-at-Waitrose phase hadn't lasted longer than a week or two at the most.

As she pours the second glass of wine, Sarah bursts through the front door with John not far behind her.

'Mum we've had a brilliant time.' Sarah rushes into the kitchen tripping over her words with her excitement.

'We went on a drive and we had lunch at a pub and ...'

'Wait. Where did you go? You've been ages!' Meg asks. Sarah looked at John and firmly pursed her lips frowning a little as she did so. Meg glanced at John quickly. He just smiled broadly.

Bastard! Not releasing the littlest clue.

'I had wedges Mum and it was brilliant!' Sarah continued.

'Uh huh.' Meg looked sharply at her beaming daughter and smiling boyfriend. Somehow, she knew they were keeping a secret.

Meg hated secrets.

Chapter 22

So Bloody Unromantic

WE NEED TO have a talk. A serious talk. About romance!

Meg opened and shut her mouth, like a guppy, but couldn't get the words out. When John had revealed on Wednesday that he'd organised a weekend away for just the two of them, Meg had been delighted. She didn't know where they were going, John told her firmly that it 'was a surprise'. But, no matter - a weekend, away. Just the two of them!

At first the mystery was sweet, and she wistfully imagined far-away places, air tickets, beaches, bikinis and sunshine. Though obviously they wouldn't be leaving the country anytime soon, the UK Border Agency had put paid to that idea, and there was little sunshine in the UK in early April.

But most of all a weekend away meant one precious thing - uninterrupted time alone together.

It had been fun showing her nephew and girlfriend around Reading and Basingstoke and even driving over to Highclere Castle where Downton Abbey was filmed but after a month or so, seven people living in the three bedroomed house, was stifling! She needed a break, from the kids, the cleaning, the cooking and the house.

At first Meg was excited. Time alone would be fantastic! But when John arrived home from work to find her in tears, on the day of their departure, he was alarmed and then confused. She didn't know what to pack...

'Pack something warm,' he said.

'For the warm?' she asked.

Pina coladas, and sunshine and topless sunbathing and swimming in the sea...

'No, like mountain gear'.

We're going to the mountains? She daren't ask.

Meg finished throwing in clothes and toiletries and then with a snif she grabbed her ski jacket and gloves and trudged the gear out to the car whilst John gave instructions to the nephew about what to do with the kids and where they could reach them, in an emergency.

'You can contact us on this number, at my parents!' he told them. Meg seethed when she overheard.

GRRR! A weekend away, the first in ages, and we'll spend it not-making-love in the twin single beds of his boyhood! GRRRRRRR! This was too much! How bloody unromantic!

She fumed up the motorway as John pushed the car north.

Yes, Mister, we really need to talk about romance!

But five hours later as they arrive in North Yorkshire, Meg had come to terms with the disappointment. It *was* nice to see his parents, and they were too tired after the drive and the stress of the past few months to get up to anything much anyway, so she settled into a chaste sleep between the floral sheets quite willingly.

The next day they woke late and after a full breakfast and decent pot of plunger coffee they drove north across the Moors to the coast.

'I thought we'd drive over to Robin Hood's Bay' John tells her. 'I used to go there as a kid.'

Meg nods. 'What's there?'

'It's a real old fishing village. It's known as the smugglers central around here,' John says.

He drives to the edge of the moors, parks the car on what appears to be a sheer cliff and ushers Meg towards the path that winds down the cliff face.

'Down there?' Meg asks. The path is almost straight down. 'Yup. Straight down,' John laughs. 'That's where the village is.'

They while away a lovely morning exploring the coves, in the drizzle and the whistling wind, around Robin Hood's Bay and as it starts to spit with rain John leads Meg towards an old stone pub built so close to the sea she could lick sea spray off her nose.

'Why is it called Robin Hood's bay?' Meg asks John.

'I'm not too sure. Some people say that Robin Hood stopped French pirates who had raided the local fishing boats. Apparently, he fought off the pirates and returned the riches to the poor in the village.'

'*The* Robin Hood?'

'The same. And then other people say Robin Hood was never in the area and the name comes from the legend of the local woodland spirit, or elf, also called Robin Goodfellow. I guess that's more feasible... but I know which story I prefer!'

'Me too,' Meg said.

'Nobody disputes that this place is ancient though. The first record goes back about 3000 years, so it's proper old. Not New Zealand old. The other thing everyone agrees on is that it's smugglers' paradise.'

'It's like something out of the Famous Five' Meg interrupts.

John laughs. 'Yeah I guess it is. Underneath the houses there are all these interconnecting tunnels that lead down to the sea. All of the villagers were involved – the good the rough, the clergy. It was the local enterprise! They used to brag that a bale of silk could enter at the bottom of the bay and exit at the top of the hill, without ever leaving the houses. And Bay women knew how to manage the excise men; they'd just pour pots of boiling water over them, straight out of the bedroom window onto the men passing below.'

'And this is where you're from? That explains quite a lot...' Meg laughs.

'Not too far from here, yeah.'

'Let's go and look at the shops as we walk back up the hill.' He takes her hand and they walk out of the cosy fire warmed pub lounge and into the sideways rain.

The village is set into the hill and the lanes are impossibly steep, though quaint, in their winding, narrow way. Meg could well imagine stoushes between smugglers, pirates and the excise men. They stopped to admire antiques and curios at the stores as they breathlessly climbed their way up the hill. Meg tried to hide the evidence that her heart was exploding and her lungs were rigid with the struggle for air. Whenever he looked over at her she held her breath and smiled, trying to swallow down a hideous stitch.

When they reach the car parked at the top of the hill she was red-cheeked and glowing and hoped that John assumed the moisture on her forehead was rain. John didn't seem to notice. He was too busy master-minding his grand tour of his God's Own, North Yorkshire.

'What's next, driver?' Meg asks.

'Inland. Back across the Moors,' he said elongating the vowels so it sounded to Meg as if he was saying moo-ers. She noticed he'd picked up an accent within an hour or so of arriving in North Yorkshire.

'We'll drive inland across the moors to the ruins of Rievaulx Abbey.'

Clueless about where they were anyway, Meg just smiled and nodded. John wasn't waiting for feedback, he had been plannning this for some time. He turned the car onto the highway and headed south. As they drove along the Moors, John pointing out the various rock formations ('they date back to the Jurassic period') and the heather that bloomed purple in the Autumn, Meg could hear the fondness in his tone of voice for *his England*.

'You'd love the heather...' his voice trailed off.

'I think we'll go to Reivaulx Abbey first and then pop into Helmsley afterwards,' he said.

'Sounds good.' Meg had no idea where either place was. John summoned up Google Maps on his phone, nodded authoritively at the phone's advice and shifted the car into gear, urging the Astra down a narrow road that wound down the side of tall wooded hills.

They drove for ten minutes or so and as they descended into the valley, Meg could feel the energy change. An almost imperceptible change, a half-tone off the note - a sharp or a flat - or a touch of the piano pedal. Visually, it would have been the equivalent of an aura - white light with purple edges and a bleached serenity.

Nestled there, on the valley floor amongst the serenity of cattle grazing and ancient woodland covered hills, was an extraordinary sight -the ruins of the Cistercian Reivaulx Abbey. There at the bottom of the valley surrounded entirely by hills, the ruins stood. White stone arched buildings still standing tall, dating from 1132. White stone window arches - a fragile lattice in stone, Grecian columns of the temples (added in the 1700's) and the black-smudged white stone of stairs and plinths.

Meg is mesmorised. Quietly, for that seemed the most appropriate reaction to the Abbey, they wandered through the ruins reading about the monks who lived here, how they retired at dark and rose twice in the night - once post-midnight and once in the dark of the early morning - to pray before their God.

'I can't get over how beautiful it is here' Meg tells John quietly. John nods and they walk hand-in-hand to the refectory building.

'Look at this Meg,' John points out an information panel. It illustrates the furnace the monks operated.

'It was way before their time,' John tells her excitedly 'it says here it was every bit as good as a modern blast furnace'.

Meg had no idea what that meant.

'Amazing, love,' she says.

As he wanders off to find out more and to examine the remains of the furnace Meg sits still, drinking in the far-off sounds of birds in the surrounding woods and the calming mooing of the cows grazing in the Abbey's grounds. She let her mind slip back in time to a quiet, pious life. A melodic chant in the new born dawn. Silence as meals were taken and solemn gentle vows given.

Time stopped.

Later, as they drive together into the market town of Helmsley she asks John: 'Did you feel it?'

He studies her face. 'the peace?'

She nods. 'Something so very spiritual about that place. I feel really moved,' she whispers. No further conversation was required. They had both felt it.

Then as quickly as they had gone back in time, they re-entered the 21st century. They drove into the pretty market town of Helmsley, found a park for the car in the shadow of the castle on a back street by Castlegate and walked into the town square, hand in hand. The stone walls are lined with spring flowers - tulips and daffodils - and the town is buzzing with market day visitors.

Meg window - shops happily through the towns high street dragging John into this shop and that. An upmarket store selling elegant dresses catches her eye and she badgers him to go inside with her. She wistfully flicks through the racks. They are all gorgeous. Any one of them would make a perfect wedding dress... not that she was getting married any time soon... she was never getting married again...but if she were, well one of them, the light blue one? ...that would be perfect.

Yes, she loved him dearly. Yes, she'd sold up and moved to England to live with him to see *if* they could live together. It had worked, they were happy. The kids were happy, and settled and everything was going well. Mostly. She didn't have a job, she was running out of money and still unable to work or leave the country or even identify as a resident of the UK. But otherwise, things were pretty good.

'Are you hungry?' John asked her as they walked through the cobbled streets of Helmsley.

'I am a bit.'

'Let's grab something to eat. This looks nice,' he said. John led her into a small delicatessan. It wasn't a large space and almost all of the shop was taken up with a gigantic glass cabinet full of food. There were cheeses of every shape size and description, sausage rolls, Cornish pasties, scotch eggs, cornichons, picked onions, and pickled eggs. Slices of pink ham piled up on white serving plates and bowls of olives and caperberries. 'What's that?' Meg pointed out a round pastry shaped like a chef's hat.

'That's a pork pie. Do you want one?' John asked. She nodded and stood patiently waiting for service. As they waited a young deli assistant come over to them with a tasting plate.

'It's our special today. *Stinky Bishop*. Do you like blue cheese?' she asked them.

'Not for me thanks,' John said quickly.

'Absolutely, I love blue cheese.' Meg was in.

Meg considered all those days of eating specialty cheeses at Annabel Langbein's cookery school and gulping down anchovy dip at Sabato. She had a reputation to maintain, and that reputation squarely rested on her ability as an adventurous (and able) home cook and gourmand. She reached over, grabbed a toothpick and speared a small piece of white rind and confidently placed the cheese into her mouth.

Almost instantly, to her horror, she started to retch.

John looked over bemused as Meg desperately searched for a paper napkin. The Stinky Bishop tasted like vomit trickling down her throat. She retched a little, in her mouth. 'Arrrghhh ick hick bleurgh...'

John translated. 'I think she needs a napkin.' He couldn't contain his laughter as the alarmed deli assistant passed over paper relief.

Meg quietly turns away and releases her mouth from rancid hell and then laughs roundly, desperate to save face.

'So, I'm not as keen on blue cheese as I might have thought' she laughed self-deprecatingly.

'That'll learn ya,' John roared with laughter.

She wraps the napkin around the offending morsel and hands it over shamefacedly to the shop assistant. She daren't catch her eye. John approaches the counter once more and makes his request.

'Hi, yes I'd like one of those pork pies please. Would you like one love?' he asks.

Meg shakes her head vehemently and John simply grins.

*****

The following day Meg and John drive up to Northallerton to meet some of John's old college friends. It's fun meeting some of his oldest friends, and through them Meg can see the fun, easy-going guy he'd been in college days.

Not that he's not easy-going now, Meg thinks to herself as they drive back along the country roads, across gorgeous green James Herriot country. Who else would have put up with her, the dog, the cat, the kids....not to mention the Aussie cuzzies... She just wondered if that easygoing tolerance had a use by date, and whether, with the stress of the visa, her work and now immigration hell, whether they were fast approaching that date.

And inheriting a half-grown family! That can't have been easy.

Vicki Jeffels

Meg looks out the window at the lush green pastures of the Yorkshire Dales. James Herriot had been a favourite read when she was a young teenager. Back then, she would never have believed that she would ever be driving through Herriot country let alone, with the man she loves.

The countryside is undeniably beautiful, but she has no idea where they are. The drive back to his parents' house seems to be taking longer than she expected. The thought passes. She doesn't need to know where she is. She can, just let go, just for once. There's a companionable silence in the car and she feels light and happy. It's dusk when she really starts to wonder where they are. Surely they should be back by now.

Are we lost? John doesn't have the most reliable sense of direction...

The roads are deserted, and the faceless wind turbines lining the fields claw at the leaden skies. She hadn't seen the wind turbines before, on the way up to Northallerton. She would have noticed them; they were massive. The road starts to wind up into the hills.

Was it this hilly before?

They pass a road sign pointing directions to the M6. *Isn't the M6 on the western side of the country?*

She must be tired and confused. But then a few miles later, the giveaway signpost.

From Pavlova to Pork Pies

WELCOME TO THE LAKES DISTRICT

John pushes the car down through the hills along the dark lake front and by the time they park up in the carpark of a gracious Ambleside hotel Meg's eyes are popping out of her head.

'You do!' she says.

'I do?'

'Yes, you do know something about romance!' she laughs. 'Huh,' he shakes his head and they settle in for a very romantic evening.

'Hear that?' Meg asks as they sit quietly reading intertwined on the plush queen bed. John's head is in her lap as he reads. Her hand is tracing through his hair.

'What?'

'Listen,' Meg says again.

'There's nothing there.'

'Yup. That's right. No murmured voices in the background, no dog crying to be let out, or kids turning on the TV at 6am to watch cartoons while they devour all edible substances in the cupboards and fridge.'

John laughs. 'Nobody to disturb us,' he says as he pulls himself up and kisses her plumb on the mouth.

'Hey,' Meg interrupts. 'I'm sorry'.

'What for?'

'All those things I thought about you on the way up.'

'Were they very rude?' he asks.

'They were really. I'm quite good with words. All sorts of words. Even some choice Old English.'

He doesn't reply in words, but his lips still do a great deal of talking.

Meg wakes at about 8am the next morning. Through the little lace curtains of the hotel window she can see a stretch of verdant green and a flash of steel blue lake. John rouses gently. As he does, she lies back on the pillow and thinks about everything that has happened in the past year. Paris, Las Vegas, Israel. Trips to Ruapehu and the Bay of Islands. Summer holidays swimming with sharks, drinks at The Pineapple pub down the road from Bottom Hedgeley and Phantom of the Opera in London on her birthday. She's moved four times in the previous year alone. She's travelled between the UK and NZ on that bum numbing 30-hour trip three times in one year.

We've done so much together.

'How about a little walk today?' he sleepily asks her.

'Ok. That sounds nice. Where?'

Meg envisages a country picnic by the lake. Cosy. Very English. There'll be little sandwiches and maybe even a pork pie or two. After lunch they'd explore the local towns, maybe grab a proper coffee somewhere deliciously quaint and a sneaky bacon roll, or two.

'I'd like to climb Helvellyn.' John murders the fantasy.

'Oh.' It's all Meg can manage to squeak.

Not a little walk in the country then. Nope we're going to climb a mountain.

After a full English (got to get the energy up!) they prepare themselves and drive to the start of the route. Past the waters of Lake Windermere and up to a non-descript gate in a non-descript field with sheep grazing peacefully and squirrels darting in the trees. Behind the immediate hill, Helvellyn rose, needling the sky. Helvellyn, England's third highest peak, standing an impressive 950m high above the Lake District.

So today's going to be one of those days. Meg swallows. This, is the problem with loving Action Man.

But I'm scared of heights. I'm too unfit (and fat) for this.

She didn't dare say anything. John was looking keen and amped.

Girls can do anything! Meg reminds herself nervously as she takes a deep breath and walks through the gate and they start to climb Helvellyn.

At first, the route is quite easy, meandering over undulating farmland, but it doesn't take long for the track to really start climbing. In fact, Meg soon becomes convinced the track is indeed, straight up. They make height quickly and despite plumbing her depths for resolve, she starts to tire. The backs of her calves are throbbing with lactic acid and her face is the colour of a burst tomato.

But this is so romantic!

They stop to take a swig of water from the bottles and to pull on beanies and gloves. John tries to gee up her spirits and admires the view.

'Isn't it beautiful?' he says pointing to the lake waters way down below.

'It is. But we could of course have flown up here in a helicopter to see the views,' she tartly replies. He tsks tsks. They continue to climb. The path starts to wind its way around boulders and there is loose scree under-foot. Meg tries to keep a brave face, but feels certain the climb is, indeed, killing her.

'Remind me. Why are we doing this again?' she asks.

'Special reasons.' He smiles briefly and continues climbing.

She promises herself she won't say another word until they reach the top. Instead, she just keeps putting one foot in front of the other, climbing steadily, trying to not stress at the beads of sweat forming on her forehead and the aching pull in her calf muscles. They are close to the top (at least they must be, surely!) and Meg can feel an icy breeze through her jacket collar.

'Not long now,' he calls back to her.

You'd better hope so Mister.

With a few more steps, up and around a rocky buttress she could see the cairn of rocks marking the summit. John is there waiting patiently for her at the top of the ridge, where the path levels out.

'Whew. Made it,' she says.

'Well done love. I'm so proud of you. Look, isn't it beautiful,' he says as he points out over the ridge to the slick of snow - the last vestiges of the season – an icing on the mustard mottled landscape, and down the other side to the large body of water. The wind is blowing a gale, and it is very cold. But the views are incredible and the sense of achievement immense.

Meg wipes her forehead with her bandanna and starts to slug from the water bottle, but distracted, John rushes forward to investigate something over at the cairn. Meg drinks some more, pushes down the lid of the bottle and then follows his urgent beckoning. She doesn't really want to walk another step. Not one more. But she does.

'Is there something interesting there?' Meg walks over to him to see. 'Probably a rare spotted wanderlust duck or something', she mutters.

'I think so,' John says.

She can barely hear his soft voice in the wind. She walks over to the cairn, not seeing the reason for the fuss, at first.

Then, there it is.

More lovely, than a rare spotted wanderlust duck. More lovely than a bubble bath and a bottle of champers (both of which she definitely deserved right now!) She had to look twice. Just to be sure.

On the top of the cairn of rocks, lies a white gold ring iced with a glistening solitaire diamond. Meg is speechless, then she stumbles over the words.

'Is that for me?' *Does everyone who climbs the hill get one?*

'I'm sorry I can't quite get down on my knees,' he's saying excitedly 'it's a bit rocky...but Meg, love, would you do me the honour of being my wife?'

Tears as she mumbles yes and the small crowd of climbers clap. For the briefest of moments that feels like a lifetime together, there is no visa issue, no work hassles, no money problems and nothing and no-one else. Just them, the grey shale, the mustard grey mountainsides, the cry of a mountain bird, the snow, the mountains and the whole world at their feet.

Chapter 23

I Pledge Thee My Troth

They took the long way home winding back down the country through Kendal and Lancaster, skirting Manchester and Birmingham, down the M40 past Bicester, before slipping onto the A34 skimming the outskirts of Oxford – somewhere over there beyond the fields - then past the familiar M4 and the turn off at Newbury onto the A339.

Meg couldn't stop herself from sneaking regular peeks at her ring with its beautiful diamond and involuntarily smiling all the way home and John seemed more relaxed than he had been in weeks.

'How long have you been keeping that a secret?' She asks.

'Quite a while. I hid it in my locker at work.'

'Safest place for it I guess.'

'Sarah helped me pick it at a little jeweller in Guildford.'

'That day you went missing?'

He nodded.

Meg joined in the nodding and added a smile. 'Good thinking, treating her to being part of it.'

It was a hot afternoon and the traffic was slow and by the time they reached the little house in Bottom Hedgeley, the sun had set.

Jack and Terri greeted them at the door and Sarah came racing out of the front door. 'Do you like it?'

'I love it!' Meg grinned.

'I chose it. I *mean* I helped John choose it,' she corrected herself.

'You did a wonderful job, it's absolutely beautiful.'

John strides purposefully to the kettle and switches it on. It was undoubtedly tea time. Meg disagrees. She grabs a bottle of wine from the fridge.

'Any news?' John asked Jack and the young man handed over a pile of letters including a very large envelope with the UK Border Agency stamp, addressed to Meg.

Avoiding his eyes, Meg rips the envelope open and starts to read. As she does, her face drops and morphs into horror.

'What does it say? Have you got it?' John asks.

'They turned us down.'

'So you'll try again,' he says carefully.

Meg shakes her head.

'No. It's worse than that. They've given us 28 days to leave and go back to New Zealand, or face confinement in an immigration centre and deportation. What do we do now?' Meg slumps defeated on the couch. John's face darkens.

'We'll appeal it,' he blusters.

'That won't help. They want us to go back to New Zealand – all of us, Me, Alex, Sarah and Jayne – and then apply for a visa from there. Where are we going to stay? How do I pay for that and what do I...'

'Hang on. Calm down love. Maybe you could go to the New Zealand embassy in France or somewhere and apply from there. That's New Zealand isn't it? For all intents and purposes....'

Meg's face brightens for a moment. 'Maybe... it would be a hell of a lot cheaper than paying for three adult and one child's fares back home. Pass over my laptop.'

Meg swiftly finds the UK Border Agency website and clicks through to the Family and Partners section. Jack appears with cups of tea and John gratefully gulps it down. Meg waves it away, gulps down her wine and continues to search frantically for answers.

For a while the only noise in the room is the TV in the background. It is, like all of the other furniture, too big for the room. Meg had bought it when she had money, back when she was one of the power players at Faberge.

Now, on the verge of being homeless the flat screen TV screams excess.

Meg is trying to read through the thumping headache behind her eyes. The words are confusing. One minute she thinks it says that it would work, if she could get to Paris, she could apply for a visa from the NZ Embassy there, and the next minute, her hopes are dashed.

'No. It's not going to work. We can't apply from anywhere else except our home country. How am I going to afford that? I don't have a job, or a home or anywhere to go in NZ. I don't even have any family there anymore.'

Meg starts to cry. John eases himself on the couch arm and puts his arm around her shoulders. Instinctively she pulls her face into his chest and releases a tortured howl.

Jack, Terri, Sarah, Alex and Jayne all try to be as small as possible, until finally when invisibility appears unachievable, Jack decides to slide back into the kitchen.

'I'll just make us some dinner. Terri? Wanna help?' You really do, his face suggests.

Terri nods solemnly and the kids evaporate from the room. John starts soothing Meg's distress.

'Come on love. We should be celebrating not crying. We can fix this. Why don't we see if we can get an immigration lawyer tomorrow? Then we can see what's what.'

That, sounded a sensible plan. Meg nods meekly.

'It doesn't seem right. I'm sure there's been a mistake. You haven't done anything wrong. What about all those other immigrants? They seem to get through and stay. See if you can search for a lawyer in Reading or Basingstoke,' he says.

The rest of the night Meg and John search for a lawyer and scoff down the macaroni cheese that Jack has kindly made. All thoughts of engagement rings and *happy ever after* long forgotten. Bedtime comes but sleep is scarce. Meg lies in night's womb jumping at every sound in the darkness.

Ibrahim Kasana's office is tucked down the back of a run-down building in eastern Reading. It had taken Meg forty minutes to find the office and though she had left plenty of time when she left the house that morning, now she is running late. She checks the name-plate on the white nondescript wall and rushes up the stairs, panting a little as she bursts into the reception.

The older woman behind the desk is on the phone and she absent-mindedly points to a clipboard perched on the counter.

Meg nods. She knows the drill. She grabs the clipboard and fills in her details. It doesn't take long and when she is finished she pops it back onto the counter, with a nervous smile.

'Mr Kasana is running about twenty minutes behind schedule I'm afraid. Would you like a cup of tea or a glass of water?'

'A glass of water would be great, thanks.'

Meg walks back to her seat on the red leather lounge and thanks the receptionist for the water when it arrives, moments later.

The waiting room is busy. An Indian woman in a bright cobalt blue sari holding the hand of an immaculately dressed little boy - about three or four years old - is waiting in the corner. The little boy is starting to fidget. Meg looks around. *Are there any other solicitors?*

Time passes very slowly and Meg has downed two glasses of water and debated having a third by the time another woman arrives back in the reception, offloads her client to the receptionist and greets the Indian woman. Meg breathes a sigh of relief. Surely not too much longer.

But why am I so nervous? What am I? A criminal?

She crosses her legs and then her arms and just as she is contemplating rearranging her arms, a tall dark Pakistani man greets her.

His voice is warm and he smiles kindly at her. 'Sorry, been absolutely snowed under today. Whew! I'm Ibrahim, you must be Megan Sinclair. Come on through.'

Meg picks up her handbag and the huge folder of documents that details everything about her life - her birth, her degree, testimonials from friends and NZ powers-that-be (not that it will necessarily help) and a detailed history of her immigration story.

She is reduced to this: a big manilla folder full of letters that say 'Megan is..' 'Megan has..' 'Megan does...'

Ibrahim Kasana's office is bigger than it appears but it is cluttered with piles of files and books; big sturdy text books. Meg can't help wondering whether the British legal profession had heard of that modern wizardry; the Internet.

But she's a book lover herself and after the first ten minutes or so of talking with him she is more than satisfied that Ibrahim Asana really knows his sauce. He's an urbane man. She can imagine him at home surrounded by a young family. Perhaps he's a squash player or a jogger, she ponders.

The time seems to pass quickly. Meg is articulate and thorough but it isn't until Ibrahim starts suggesting ways in which they could fight the deportation order, does she consciously draw breath.

'Well the first thing is we need is to get you married,' he says. Ibrahim leans forward. 'When are you getting married?'

'We haven't picked a date yet...' Meg is taken aback.

'Well that's the first step. You're obviously living together with the children as a family, and wish to get married,' he said pointing at her engagement ring.

'So, it would be in your best interest and in the interest of your case if you get married as soon as is practical. Oh, and in a church.'

Meg hadn't yet had time to talk with John about the ceremony. 'We're both Christians so it would be in a church,' Meg said slowly.

'Church of England?'

'Oh. I guess it could be. John's family goes to a Church of England church. I've been a bit of a church collector in my time – Presbyterian, Baptist, Pentecostal...'

She has no idea why Ibrahim Kasana, her immigration lawyer, needs to know this influx of information. Ibrahim nods solemnly, picks up a large text book and thumbs through the pages.

'Yes, see here... if you are married in the Church of England then it's seen as a religious rite and carries with it a special dispensation.' He rereads the text book out loud to her.

'If a foreign national marries in the Church of England they do not have to gain a Home Office certificate of approval prior to the marriage.'

'Really? But if we don't, we need to apply to the Home Office to be allowed to marry? Wow!' Meg shook her head. She had never even considered that she might need to ask the state's permission to get married.

'So we should go and see the vicar?'

'Ideally yes. Then if you were to get married say sometime in May then you could appeal the Border Agency's decision as a person married to a UK national. To disallow your marriage would deprive you of your human rights.'

Meg was following carefully. 'So we need to set a date, sometime in May. That's six weeks. That's not a lot of time.'

'No it isn't, but I think it's your best chance of winning the appeal. In the meantime, I'll put in an application for them to put aside the deportation order whilst we wait for the Immigration Tribunal case to be called."

Ibrahim glanced at his watch. 'Unfortunately Ms Sinclair, that's us. Come back and see me in a month or so, after the wedding. Sandra will help you make an appointment.'

Rising from her seat, Meg offers her hand to the lawyer. 'Thank you so much! I really appreciate all your help.'

He nods kindly and waves her through the door, and out into the reception area. Sandra, the receptionist, looks up as Meg approached the counter. 'Did Mr Kasana need you to make another appointment?'

'Yes, about the end of May beginning of June.'

Sandra glances at the computer screen. 'How about 15th June at 10:30am?'

'That's fine.' I can squeeze that in. Meg didn't want to admit it, but she didn't have much on. It wasn't as if she had work or anything. She quietly panicked. Would they need payment right now? There wasn't enough in her account to cover the bill, she needed John to pay it or move some money into her account. She waited for the crucifying embarrassment but the receptionist said goodbye and returned to her computer screen.

Well, that's another love letter for the mail.

When she gets back to the house she rings through to the local Anglican church where they had spent Christmas Eve. The church secretary answers and promises that she would get the vicar to call her, 'right back'.

It wasn't until much later in the afternoon when the vicar calls. He is bombastic on the phone and as he speaks, Meg's heart sinks.

'So you're telling me that not only have you been married before, but your partner has too?' he said.

This didn't sound good.

'And you're both residing at the same address?'

Bugger.

'I'm very sorry Ms Sinclair but I won't be able to help you.' He had a reedy voice. Meg's imagination lit up with images of a donkey.

'Because we're divorced?' she asks.

'Well the Bible is very clear about that matter.'

Bullshit.

'But I thought the Church of England remarried people, after divorce.'

'Some vicars do, but the church allows us to make a decision based on conscience...'

Seriously? The church wants to stop people who love each other, getting married?

'.... And in my opinion, marriage is entered into so very unwisely these days. People seem to think they can get married and divorced, willy-nilly.'

15 years. Three kids. 18 stretchmarks, financial ruin, two dogs, two cats, and, and...Willy nilly?

Meg is seething.

'And it's not consistent with what I believe are God's wishes for us. It does say very clearly in the Bible that marriage should be a commitment that's kept, not one that's discarded when things get tough. No, I'm sorry you're going to have to find someone else.'

Meg's anger blisters under the rays of shame. She wants to argue. She wants to please. She wants to just get off the call as quickly as possible before she said something she might regret. She mustered as much icy politeness as she could to end the call and then sat on her bed, ironically calling out to the very God whose wise, dutiful servant had just told her to get lost.

And then, out of nowhere, John's mother called. She is also indignant when she hears the vicar's pronouncements but she reassures Meg that she would speak to their own church vicar, in North Yorkshire.

A couple of anxious coffees later, and John's mother calls back. It is all arranged. They would be married by the vicar in the family church in North Yorkshire. But first the banns would have to be read in Meg's local church.

Meg had never heard of banns.

Apparently reading out the wedding banns was an old English tradition.

For centuries, couples had their wedding banns read out in their local church on three Sundays before the wedding, to give any dissenters time to register their vote against the union. Apparently, it was still a legal requirement in the Church of England.

Meg dispensed of her pride once again and rang the local vicarage. After much cajoling, the vicar agreed to read the banns, albeit somewhat begrudgingly.

By the time John returned from work she was sitting contentedly on the couch waiting for the Beef Bourgeon to cook. He was excited to hear that the wedding would take place at home after all, though he was embarrassed that the local vicar had refused to marry them.

'He actually said that? He won't marry us? How Christian is that?'

'Not very', Meg nodded.

It didn't matter. They would get married and they would get the visa and lawyers and bureaucrats would sod off and leave them alone. The kids were settling in, they all had friends and activities.

See, it was all working out. Maybe someday she would get another job and then they could buy a house in a friendlier town – one with a church that was nice and people who kind of got her. But first she had six weeks to plan a wedding. What could possibly go wrong?

Chapter 24

Till Death Do Us Part

THE AMERICAN GUY had been insistent. Drunk, but insistent. He wouldn't let anything happen to John. Not. A. Thing.

So why wasn't John home?

That had been last night, whilst Meg agonised until early morning printing out service sheets on her Canon printer and fussing over flowers. Their little house looked as if it had been flower bombed. Calla lilies and roses in shades of white and maroon bundled into cellophane wrappers were drinking in buckets, all over the lounge floor.

Since yesterday morning, John had (mistakenly) ironed his face, driven into London, been out on the town with a bunch of army guys (doing God knows what! Best not ask!) rung through with drunken vows of love and adoration and then subsequently disappeared off the face of the earth.

It was 10:30am.

Time to leave for North Yorkshire, and no John. Where is he?

Meg rang and left another message on his mobile, as Alex marched through the lounge on a quest for a Nintendo and promptly stood heavy footed onto a mirror tile – she was using them to dress the tables at the hotel - breaking it into a thousand shards.

Meg groaned. *Seven years' bad luck. Happy, happy, joy, joy.*

She hadn't worried about John's stag night on the town. She'd had a small gathering a few weeks ago, but as she still didn't really know anyone in England, it had been quiet.

If only we were getting married in Auckland. There'd be lots of friends, and family...

She banished the thought. Her sister and her family were arriving from Australia today and would be making their way up the country to the North Yorkshire church, this afternoon. They would be the only ones representing Meg's family and friends at the wedding.

At one point during the past three weeks her mother and her father had both been coming, but then her mother had backed out when she'd heard her father was coming, and then not knowing her mother had backed out and he wouldn't bump into his ex at his daughter's wedding, her father had backed out. That was the problem with weddings – they brought up family issues. *Lovely!*

Meg walks into the kitchen, and turns on the kettle for coffee. She doubts the coffee will settle the churning in her stomach, but it will help keep her eyes wide open for the trip up north. When John did arrive home she would need to be alert.

Sarah comes bounding down the stairs dressed in her wedding outfit and yelps as she places her foot squarely on a piece of glass.

'Owwwww! There's glass all over the floor!' she wails at top volume.

'Alex managed to step on one of the mirror tiles and break it...Sarah, don't be such a drama queen, you haven't cut your foot off! And don't get blood on your dress!'

I really don't need this right now.

'Where's the bandaids?' Sarah cried.

'You don't need bandaids, it's a wee scratch. It'll stop bleeding soon. And go and take that dress off. You don't want to ruin it for tomorrow.'

'But I like it. Don't you think it looks pretty?' She did a turn, swaying her skirts.

The dress was strapless and featured a beautiful flower pattern in a deep maroon colour. It matched the lilies Meg had ordered in directly from Amsterdam. They had arrived last night along with big bunches of roses and white calla lilies which she was using in the bouquets.

'Yes, it is beautiful. But you'll ruin it before the day. Go and put it on a hanger and put it in the car.'

Sarah hurrumphed and flounced back up the stairs to slip back into her jeans. Meg couldn't help laughing; she could count on one hand the number of times her eldest daughter had worn a formal dress, and now she won't get out of it!

Meg pours the boiling water into the plunger and Jayne appears dressed in her white bridesmaid's dress. It had a plain flat bodice and a big white tutu skirt and though Meg had picked it up ready-to-wear from Debenhams, it hadn't been cheap. She'd worry about the cost of it all when the day was a wrap.

'Not you too!' Meg groaned. 'Take it off honey, you'll get it all dirty.'

'But it's pretty,' Jayne says.

'Yes, yes I know. But. No, don't go in there, there's glass all over the floor. Alex grab the vacuum cleaner. Sarah, that's better! Seriously. Jayne, take it off!'

Just as she was loudly giving directions to all three children, John sheepishly walks in the front door.

'Dad!' Jayne races to hug him. 'Pooh! You smell.' She wriggles out of his arms as he turns, ashen faced, to Meg.

'You're late,' she told him sternly.

'No, not really.'

'And you smell like a brewery.'

'Well, only a little. I had a couple...'

'A couple? Is there any beer left in London?'

'Nawww, Meg darling don't be mad. Come 'ere.'

He grabs her and pulls her into a hug. She melts. Despite drinking London dry he was in a remarkably chipper mood. *Is he still drunk?*

'I'm glad you had a great time. I'm just a bit stressed. And we're meeting the vicar at 3:00pm and at this rate we'll never get there.'

'We will. It doesn't take that long,' John dismisses the thought with a lofty wave, turns to the sink, fills his glass and greedily gulps down a glass of water, and then another and another, in quick succession.

'It takes at least 6 hours, love!' Meg insists. She's marrying him tomorrow. She doesn't want to fight.

'Nah, we'll get there.' He continues to glug down water.

'We need to get going. I'll drive.' Meg's tone is urgent. She is worried about her fiancé's colour. It is puce. In a dress it would have been a perfect tonal match for the flowers, but in the face of her bridegroom? No, she would drive.

And it takes at least 7 hours.

John put down his empty glass and dashes to the loo before ferrying clothes, kids, flowers into the car. He squeezes them in alongside yet more bunches of flowers, dresses, a wedding gown, mirror tiles, six glass vases and a carton of champagne. With much muttering and a bit of quiet retching John slips into the passenger seat. Meg grabs her sunglasses, (you never know it could be sunny. It was summer, after all) adjusts the mirror and turns the ignition.

T minus 20 hours. And counting.

They were on the road in half an hour, and six hours later were by-passing Birmingham. They had made steady progress up country and would have been feeling relaxed if they hadn't been expected at the vicarage at that precise moment. Meg was grateful she was driving, as it gave her something to do other than stress about the wedding plans. She hadn't eaten much all day and she had to struggle to keep her concentration for driving. They had stopped at a Little Chef at the Services some time back but she had found it difficult to eat. John didn't each much either. The fish is off, he'd proclaimed darkly and then raced off to the loo. Meg suspected he was still evacuating all that he'd consumed over the past twenty-four hours.

The drive hadn't been eventful. John had spent most of it fast asleep under his dark sunnies like some kind of errant rock star, but now he was on the phone talking to his mother who was trying to negotiate with the vicar.

'Oh. OK. But we're only about two hours away. There's really heavy traffic around Birmingham. Can't he do it at 5:00pm?'

Meg can't hear the reply but John called off and sighed.

'No good?' she asks.

'No. The vicar says we've missed the rehearsal so too bad' His words. We'll just have to turn up and follow the cues.'

'He won't meet us later?' Meg was incredulous.

'No. Must conflict with his evening sherry.'

On two of the previous three meetings the vicar had been decidedly worse for wear.

'But he wouldn't ... really?.... It's our wedding rehearsal!' Meg was in a state of shock.

'Watch out!' John drew her attention to the speed camera sign. 'It'll be OK. Just one less thing to have to do tonight.'

'Was your Mum annoyed?'Meg asks.

'Not really. More flustered.'

Meg could well imagine.

For a moment there's stunned silence in the car, and then Meg asks: 'By the way, I meant to ask you: how did you manage to iron your face?'

John chuckled. 'Well, yesterday morning I was trying to iron my shirt for London and the iron didn't appear to be working. I tapped it and shook it and turned it off and on. Still, nothing. So I put it up closer to my ear to see if I could hear if it was working. At first I couldn't hear anything so I moved it closer... yeah, I heard it eventually. It made a nice sizzle, as it ironed my cheek!'

'So let me get this straight... you, a highly qualified specialist design electronics engineer, who should really know better, put an iron to his ear to hear if it was on? And then, when you still couldn't hear it, you moved it closer? So close, it slipped onto your face?'

Meg laughed so hard she almost drove straight off the road.

By the time they reached the little village of Stainton John's mood was effervescent.

Every time. Meg smiled to herself. He'd live here if he could.

She could see why. It was a pretty spot. The sun was setting far off over the plains – the remnants of an Ice Age lake – over the gaudy patchwork yellow of rapeseed and the beige lines of country tracks. Even though it was late in the day it wouldn't be dark for a few hours yet. The sun was casting long shadows over the tarseal of the A64 and Meg couldn't help but smile as she eased the car into the village. John, was smiling too, as the car rattled down the narrow lanes to his parent's home.

This was his home. And soon England would be *their* home.

Meg didn't allow herself to think about her heart's home all those tens of thousands of miles away – that green land in a Pacific sea. After all, home isn't a place, it's the people you want to be with, she reminded herself.

And tomorrow she would be Mrs Williams.

They spent the evening with family, re-telling the stories about the ironed face, the London shenanigans and the ropeable vicar. After dinner, Meg drove with the girls north of the town through the dark Forge Valley Woods to Everton Park House, where they would stay the night and tomorrow hold their wedding reception. She could barely see the way and she drove half asleep, listening faithfully to the sat nav and praying quietly that they'd get there safely and that no-one – especially not a claw fingered stranger – would stop the car and murder them all. Such dramatic events were always a possibilty with 'Hurricane Meg'.

Before long, they reached the two storied hotel. It was a small, charming old stone building. Only ten rooms, a country bar and a large lounge room that looked out over verdant green lawns and down to the River Derwent.

Meg had loved the hotel at first sight and John had been secretly pleased that his special spot would be the venue for their first night and day as husband and wife.

Meg checks into the hotel and followed by the girls ferrys dresses and flowers from the car, up the spiral staircase to their room.

'Is that all of them?' Meg asks Sarah.

'Yup. Thank God.' Sarah lies back on the bed. 'I'm exhausted.'

'Come on hun, no sleep for the wicked.' Meg prods her and when she doesn't budge Meg brought out the big guns.

'I've got chocolate....'

Rubbing their eyes, the girls sat on the edge of the bed as Meg revived their flagging energy levels with the chocolate she'd squirrelled away, just for this purpose. And then they started to work. Meg organised the flowers into appropriate bunches and then showed the girls how to tie them into buttonholes.

'How many do we have to do?' Sarah asked as Meg was fussing with the champagne coloured roses she was twisting into her bridal bouquet.

'John said all the men need one. Not just the men in the bridal party, but all of them. So about 30 I think.'

Sarah's eyes opened wide. 'All of them?'

'I know it seems odd but that's what they do here.'

Sarah shrugged, - whatever - and reached for the white roses and taking one she pricked it into position. With her little sister's help they tied the button holes as Meg worked on the girls' bouquets. They weren't finished tying bouquets and the button holes until 2am when they collapsed, all three of them, into the plush queen bed.

It was dark, cool and 4:30am when Meg eased past Jayne's sleeping body and tiptoed to the bathroom.

She'd barely slept. Her stomach was curdled with anxiety and she'd lain there in the pre-dawn darkness listening to the girls' rhythmic breathing, panicking about the flower arrangements, the speech she hadn't written yet and the timing of everything on the wedding day. For a brief moment, she wondered what she would do if he didn't turn up at the church.

Is there such a thing as a runaway groom?

She carefully edged past the bouquets of flowers which she and the girls had finished hand-tying only a few hours before and sat down gingerly on the toilet. Her stomach was full of hell-fire. Her head was thumping. She felt like death warmed up.

Something wasn't right.

It had been stressful. She shrugged to herself. When was marriage not? Let alone the immigration problems and the anxiety about reshaping a new family. This week she was getting married, but in a few weeks' time? Then it could be all over and she could be thrown into an immigration centre and deported, with all three children.

She glanced down at her watch. It would be dawn in an hour and they would need to be up early to prepare all the tables in the hotel's lounge. She had organised the table decorations herself and prepared the seating plans. All the tables were named after James Bond films, and each one would feature a mirror tile with an elegant vase containing a simple pure white calla lily, surrounded by tea lights. She lifted herself off the loo and reached to press the flush, but stopped short, something compelling her to gaze into the toilet bowl.

The white bowl was stained, deep crimson.

Meg didn't have time to react as Sarah unexpectedly appeared at the door of the bathroom. Meg hurriedly flushed the toilet.

'Morning darling, are you OK?' Meg asked her. Sarah nodded sleepily and placed herself on the toilet while Meg stumbled back to bed. She couldn't sleep and when the light signaled the dawn she opened the curtain to inspect the sky.

Red in the morning, shepherd's warning.

She'd figure it out, she'd see a doctor, it was probably nothing, just a minor stomach upset or something - but first she would get married. She reached down to the bedside table and picked up her phone. Her phone's screen was covered in messages.

I wish you all the best for a brilliant day and a long, happy life together. Tom x

OMG Today's the day! I wish we were there. Have the most wonderful day and give my love to the kids and John! Ally, Elliot and kids xxx

Go get 'em Hurricane Meg. Did you get the champagne I sent you? I wish you all the best. Mike x

As she was laughing over the messages the phone in the hotel room rings. She picks it up. Her Mum's voice is steady. 'Oh darling, I just wanted to catch you before you got into the day. How are you feeling?'

'Hi Mum, I'm really excited. I think we've got everything organised, and if we haven't.... well it doesn't really matter...'

'I'm sure you have. You always were so good at organising things. How's the dress? Does it fit? And is Michelle there, yet?'

'They arrived late last night. They drove up from Heathrow yesterday. I don't know how they did it. And yes Mum, the dress fits fine.'

'It's great they're there... Michelle was really worried about getting there.... I so wanted to be there with you. I always knew you'd get married again.'

Meg stifled a laugh. *Did you really?*

'Thank you Mum. I really wish you were here too. Do you want to speak to Sarah? Love you...'

She passed the phone over to her daughter and briskly walks into the bathroom to grab a tissue.

Mothers!

She wished more than anything she'd been able to shout her mother the trip to England for her wedding, but, it just wasn't to be. Maybe they'd have another wedding, on the beach at Whangapoua in the summer and they'd invite all their family and friends. They could get married standing barefoot in the sand, the only accompaniment would be the sound of the surf – nature's music – crashing onto the shore behind them.

But a wedding in a quaint Yorkshire church, that was John's family's church, well, that would be great too. Hell, she'd elope and travel to Honduras if they needed to. Not that she was allowed to leave the country, right now. Sarah passed the phone back to her. 'Grandma wants to say goodbye.'

'Oh hi, Mum? Yes, I love you too Mum. I know. It's just too expensive. It's OK, we'll come back sometime soon. Bye. Love you. Bye.'

She sniffed as she put the phone back into its cradle and was pleasantly surprised by a knock on the door. It was John's Mum, here to take her to her only concession to bridal fuss – a proper blow wave.

The hairstylist delighted Meg with her skill and by the time she had finished and returned to the hotel room, her sister had arrived with Meg's niece and youngest nephew. Her nephew, not a very tall teen, appeared to have been swallowed by trousers.

'I didn't have time to cuff them. We'll just roll them up, they'll be OK,' Michelle said. Meg laughed. Yup, they'd be fine. Michelle started fussing about with the flowers, as she prepared to decorate the wedding cake.

'I bought it at Marks & Spencers,' Meg told her. 'It's perfectly nice and with some fresh flowers on top it will look brilliant.'

'Hmm. I hope I don't stuff it up for you' Michelle said.

'You won't. You're good at this. That's why I asked you to decorate the cake. Are you still going to do the reading at the church?'

'Yes. 13th chapter of first Corinthians right – the school verse?'

'Yeah. I've always loved it. I thought it would be appropriate. Faith, hope, love...'

'these three...' Michelle contributed.

'but the greatest of these is love,' they finished together. Laughing, Michelle rounded on her. 'But you hated school!' her sister said.

'Yeah, but that doesn't make it a bad sentiment. What time is it Jayne?'

'Ten to twelve.'

'Really? Arrrgh. We better start getting ready. I'll have a quick bath if you can help Jayne and Sarah with the curling tongs,' Meg instructed pointing to her niece.

'I'd better hurry with the cake and get it downstairs,' Michelle said as Meg closed the bathroom door behind her.

Just six hours previously this bath had been full of flowers... and now it's full of me!

Meg swirled some bubbles under the tap and eased into the water.

She did this when she was tense. If she was *really* tense she would wash her hair too, but this time she would only be able to bathe and whilst there perhaps she would remember how to breathe. It seemed as if only ten minutes had passed before Michelle was knocking on the door.

'Come on beautiful bride time to get your dress on.'

Breathe. Just breathe, Meg reminded herself. She continued the quiet refrain as she climbed into her wedding underwear and then stood with her arms high above her head, as her sister slipped the gown over her head and started to address the lacing.

Meg had chosen a chiffon gown confettied with delicate diamantes, topped with a fitted laced corset and matched with a little chiffon bolero they made out of the gown's original train. She had no need of a train. Trains were for first time brides and ingénues – she was neither. No, she would use the bolero to cover her shoulders if it were cold. Secretly she'd told herself the bolero would cover any misplaced flabby bits. Oh the joys of being an older bride!

'The dressmaker said you start at the bottom, and not to be afraid to pull it really tight. It won't break.'

Michelle started and deftly started winding the laces through the eyelets until she reached the top.

'Oh hang on, that's not right.' she said.

Meg spun around to catch a glimpse of her sister's handiwork in the mirror. The elegant lacing panel appeared to have prouted a muffin top and there was half a lace still undone, hanging limply down her back.

'Oh my God, it doesn't fit! But I dropped another half stone in the stress of last week!'

'It will,' her sister soothed. Michelle dragged the laces back out and started again. When she got to the small of Meg's back, Meg couldn't help but pitch in with advice.

'The dressmaker said you really have to pull it.'

Michelle pulled sharply on the laces.

'*No*, harder than that! Really stick the boot in,' Meg pleaded.

Was it possible that she could have put on weight in the two days since her last fitting? She'd barely eaten anything. She pondered quietly over her swollen stomach. She didn't want to say anything, just yet.

Michelle tried again. 'It's not fitting Meg,' she said.

'It will,' Meg said firmly.

In the midst of the panic there was a knock at the door and Sarah opened it to see her cousin there.

'The driver's here.'

Meg yelped. 'Please Michelle, stick the boot in really, really hard.'

Michelle did and with a relief she lightly patted her sister on the back. 'You're all done. You look amazing. Now, go! Just remember Meg... breathe!'

Meg ran her hands down her dress, admiringly tracing the cinch of her waist and the curvature of her hips, before agreeing that it was ok. 'I'm ready. As I'll ever be,' she said.

She applied the last coat of her lipstick, slipped her shoes on and started to gently walk down the hall and then down the old semi-circular staircase. The stair boards creaked as she walked down the red-carpeted hallway past the bar where a couple of locals were enjoying a Saturday afternoon pint. They gawped as she passed and she quipped 'oh, just popping out to get married, back soon.'

She continued the refrain – breathe, just breathe – as the Aston failed to start and the driver had to hold his tongue this way or that way and pull this or that and then finally in frustration rang the car's owner in nearby Scarborough.

She was breathing still as the car slipped past John's parents' street and down the old road to the church at the end of the lane.

The sixteenth century stone church stands at the end of the old lane surrounded by large green lawns, a collection of jauntily placed headstones and an ancient wooden gate. It has a stone turret, beautiful stained glass windows and is encircled by an ash grey dry stone wall. It reminded Meg of the dry stone walls in Cornwall Park in Auckland. This was almost as far from Auckland as she could get. Nothing could have told her that one day she would be here in North Yorkshire getting married. Let alone getting married again. She smiled. But then nothing about the past two years could have been predicted.

The 1930s Aston carrying Meg and her daughters - that John had insisted he order for their wedding, surprising her with his romantic display - came to a stop just outside the church and they stepped out to excited giggles and gasps from the gathered villagers. Standing just outside the church door, dressed in white vestments was the waiting vicar.

His face was murderous.

'You're thirty minutes late!' the vicar hissed at her as she stepped out of the car. Meg ignored him and reached down to smooth out the skirt of her wedding gown.

It's the bride's prerogative to be late. And there was a bit of a hitch with the car and the laces...

Now, as she stepped away from the vintage car she could see a trailing corset lace slipping along on the ground behind her.

Damn! I guess Michelle missed that one.

The vicar was hurrying her. She ignored him and instead turned to one of the watching villagers. 'Hey, can you do me a favour? Can you please just pop that tie down the back of my dress.'

Though surprised, the woman obliged. And then, after taking in a deep half-breath half-prayer, Meg took her tall, dark haired son's waiting arm and walked up the church path and into the church.

The church was only half full with John's family, a few friends, and Meg's sister and her family, but it was warm and intimate. John's mother had tied flower bouquets from flowers picked from her own garden onto the end of each old wooden pew and placed a bunch in a large vase on the table in the vestibule - where they would sign the register later with her new name - a bunch of country flowers.

She hadn't intended on changing her name as she'd only just reclaimed her maiden name. But then, she had argued with herself, she hadn't intended on getting married again, either. When John had realised that she wasn't intending on changing her name he was visibly upset.

'I wanted to feel that you were with me. Under my wing.' She had seen tenderness in his face and even though she'd told him he was a 'soppy old git' she decided that a name was something she could concede, even if it was as far from the feminist ideals of the past few years that she could possibly get.

Nothing is as amusing as a complete and utter change of direction, she reminded herself now as she prepared to walk down the aisle. Her head full of memories of the past two years. So much had changed. She wasn't even the same person she had been only two years ago.

John, Alex and John's brother and partner had spent last night at the men's childhood home and Meg and John hadn't seen each other, as per the tradition, until now.

And now, there they all were. There he was, standing smart if a little serious, at the altar.

From Pavlova to Pork Pies

The ancient stained glass windows shone colored light and the old organ wheezed into action spluttering out the familiar refrain. John's brother who was wielding a video camera whispered encouragement to her: 'You look beautiful', he said, and smiling her thanks she started her walk down the aisle.

The aisle was at least three miles long.

Just look straight ahead. You've done this before. What are you worried about? What about that telecoms presentation to two hundred people? You weren't worried then. Just smile. Not too much, he's not marrying the Cheshire cat. Don't be so self-conscious. Be poised. Can they see the tie? Or is it safely down my bum?

Oh Lord, please don't let me look fat....

John sneaked a look and then swallowed, hard.

What if he doesn't like the dress? Or me? I should have run further and lost more weight. Huh there's the vicar. All smiles now, eh vicar? Had your lunchtime sherry now, eh?

The vicar did indeed have his game face on.

As she arrived at John's shoulder he leant over and with a look of joy he told her quietly: 'You look stunning love'.

After the greeting, the congregation sang together one of the hymns Meg had chosen from her Presbyterian church days.

It's all the same anyway – Presbyterian, Catholic, Church of England, non-church-going-but-often-praying-Christian.

It's still the same God. My wedding gown isn't stuck in the back of my knickers, is it?

Meg listened in to the vicar. He was saying something about her being the valley to John's hill. It didn't seem entirely appropriate.

'And a river runs through it...' She stifled a giggle.

More hymns, a reading, and a prayer and then it was vows' time. The vicar reached for their hands and thinking that he wanted them to hold each other's hands, Meg reached forward and grabbed John's hands. The vicar shook his head and grunted. John released his left hand and Meg followed his lead.

'The other hand,' the vicar barked.

Meg offered her left hand and John put forward his right. John's best man coughed nervously into his elbow.

Do the hokey pokey and turnaround and that's what it's all about...yeah!

Meg started to laugh properly now. John soon joined in as they swapped hands tried version four of the hands-together thing and the vicar snarled instructions. 'No, not like that.'

They offered their hands again (version five) as the vicar reached for his white scarf to bind them together. His face was apoplectic. The congregation was oblivious. All they could see was a lag in proceedings and something going on at the altar, but as Meg and John gave in to full-blown laughter, the vicar leaned in and in a very low voice he hissed quite plainly:

'Stop fucking around!'

Who knew that vicars could drop the f-bomb?

Are they even allowed?

Meg blinked in surprise and daren't catch John's eye. He'd heard it too. She knew he had. If he giggled or even breathed funny, or made the slightest acknowledgment of mirth, she'd be gone. She half expected to see Father Ted sitting in the back pew. The moment passed and they did indeed stop 'fucking around'. She even teared up as she said her vows, as did he.

to have and to hold

from this day forward;for better, for worse,

for richer, for poorer,in sickness and in health,

to love and to cherish, till death us do part...

The rest of the ceremony went off without a hitch, save for the vicar growling at the girls to bring ye boukees to the registry table. Neither girl could understand his accent and in the end the good-natured best man reached forward and placed the flower bouquets in the girls' hands so they could obediently bring them to rest on the registry stand. Meg didn't notice, she was concentrating hard on not giggling. She wanted to laugh and dance and sing and yell. She was fizzing with joy and nothing and nobody could dampen her spirits.

Then finally, the solemn part was over and there was a triumphant walk down the aisle (which seemed to Meg significantly shorter than on the way up it!) and out into the church garden with the old church bells peeling and smiles and confetti raining down.

They drank champagne in each other's arms as they were driven in the Aston over the rolling hills through the ancient Forge Valley - deep green decorated with Forget-me-knots, bluebells and primroses, scented with wild garlic and dotted with the last of the daffodils, as if for that very occasion – to their reception at the grand old Everton Park.

On the edge of the North York Moors, these woods were another of John's favourite haunts, enchanted woodland decades away from London and the grim reality of immigration persona non grata.

For one day, Meg felt relieved, relaxed and secure. She truly did feel under his wing and the children seemed happy and having fun. It didn't rain, she didn't forget her speech, and he hadn't scarpered from the altar.

There had only been minor mishaps – the flowers started to wilt prematurely, they couldn't corral the guests into the best spot for photos ('as organised as a piss-up in a brewery' one of the army mates muttered) the best man inadvertently set his speech notes on fire with the tea lights on the wedding table and Jayne managed to dribble food on her white dress – but these were minor things in the scheme of things.

As Meg settled into bed that night with her husband by her side, she couldn't help feeling the tough bits were behind her.

Chapter 25

Go Home

Three weeks later

'CAN YOU JUST listen for a minute?' Meg's eyes flashed as she turned to confront her daughter.

'You can't write that!'

'Why? It's how I feel. I hate it here!'

'So what Sarah? So *what?* So, things are a bit tough, we'll get through it but not if you keep writing that stuff to your father.'

Meg felt sick. She turned to the kitchen sink and the greasy dishwashing water. Last night's dishes. Or pots as John liked to call them, even though they weren't bloody pots – big, grey pans in which you cooked stuff – there were plates, and knives and forks and even a few tea mugs some with tea bags still clinging on.

Why nobody else (like John!) could do the dishes, Meg didn't know.

Sarah was still ranting. Meg could hear the words burning with rage. The pinched faced woman from down the path walked past and put her head down when she heard the yelling.

Meg hated that people could walk past, or look in. She hated that their tiny little shit-box house and everyone in it was on display all the bloody time. There was no privacy. Sarah had complained about them in their own bedroom only a few weeks ago and Meg had wondered whether they were in breach of some kind of good parenting code.

Thou shalt not make love with thy husband.

Or, no sex please we're English.

What if she'd told Murray?

'...but you don't care. Every time Jayne gets up in the middle of the night to go to the loo she knocks my bed and wakes me up.' Sarah lamented, loudly.

No, she didn't care. There were much bigger things to care about. Like Sarah telling Murray she was miserable. Like a court appearance.

She gulped and glanced at Sarah. She was still yelling. The people in Basingstoke 10 miles down the road could hear. Meg wondered idly whether the UK Border Agency had spies listening in.

'I hate it here! I HATE IT! I told Dad that. *He* listens to me...' she roared, her face crimson. Eyes wide with rage come desperation. She was a cat knocked down by a car and standing up on broken limbs hissing and growling at the offending vehicle.

'You told him? What? On Skype?' Meg demanded. *Does the UKBA listen in on personal Skype calls?*

'Yes. How else am I going to talk to Dad? You don't listen to me. You DON'T. You just don't CARE!'

Meg could feel the anger rising. It started as a warm feeling in her fingers, at first she'd written it off to dishwashing water, but that was lukewarm at best. Now the feeling took over her arms, it blasted through her veins, her skin crawled with itch and then the seething rage beat hard down and subdued her shoulders, neck and head. At the same time a sharp piercing pain ripped through her lower belly and through her backside. The pain caught her breath. She closed her eyes to gather herself, but breath was writhing under the weight of pain.

It was too late. She could not stop it. The words came...

'You just don't get it do you? You selfish, silly little girl. Tomorrow I'm going to stand up in court, COURT, me, who's never done anything wrong in her life. Like a bloody criminal.' She spat the words out. 'It's cost me tens of thousands of pounds to just be able to be there and stand up and say - I want to stay; we want to stay. But you don't. And then all we need is for one of the neighbors to testify that we're all unhappy and fighting all day and we will be kicked out. You might not like sharing a room with your sister, but boy, how are you going to feel about sharing a cell at the bloody immigration detention centre?'

It was too far.

Sarah was sobbing now, terrified. 'I just want to go home and see Dad and my friends,' she sobbed.

'Well you will then, won't you! But we won't be going back to that comfortable house in St Heliers and that expensive school. That's all gone. As if it never existed. I have no money left to pay for anything like that.'

Sarah's eyes were wide open wild and her anger dissolved into desperate, snotty sobs.

'I hate you. I hate you and this horrible place. But most of all I hate him!' Sarah pointed to the figure walking through the door.

'Him? That man has kept you from starving for the past six months. He has tried to provide a warm loving home for you and Alex and Jayne and all you've done is be a right bitch!'

Meg followed Sarah as she stomped up the stairs.

'Don't you storm off madam...'

There was no stopping her. Sarah slammed the door at the top of the stairs and Meg slunk back downstairs staring helplessly into John's wide eyes.

'What the....?' he asked.

But before he could finish his sentence Meg rushed past him, up the stairs to the sanctity of her room. She couldn't speak to him right now. She couldn't speak, at all.

John breathed out, he hadn't realised he'd been holding his breath, and walked into the kitchen to make a cup of tea. He boiled the kettle and grabbed a mug from the cupboard and walked over to the fridge to get the milk. There was only a dribble of milk left in the bottle. Too much for the bottle to be called empty, but too little to do anything but taint the tea.

He sighed deeply.

It had been a busy day and he was beyond tired and right now all he wanted was to come home to an empty, quiet house, and sleep. And yet, he'd come back to this. The kitchen was a bombsite. Dishes from the past three meals were still oozing oil and bubbles on the counter top. where they had been left to marinate in dishwashing liquid. The lino floor was peeling in the corner and in its edges dirt had built up and was now crowned with wads of thick brown dog hair and someone had left bowls with residual cereal concreted to the bottom of them on the bench.

We'll never get that Weetabix off!

He grabbed his cup of tea, shaking his head sadly at the brown liquid in the lipstick stained mug and walked through to the living room where he collapsed onto the leather couch. It smelt. Of spilt coffee and wine bottle dregs and even long-forgotten asylum-seeking chili beans.

Three weeks ago, they'd posed and smiled in the sunshine and Meg had looked radiant with happiness... three weeks ago they'd stood in the church where he'd once served as an altar boy with the old vicar, the one who'd grabbed him by the shoulders and told him that he could be anything he wanted, such was his talent. They'd stood there in front of his Mum and Dad in the sight of God and everyone that mattered and said they were building a family.

Who knew that families could be this loud?

His grandmother had come up to him in the late afternoon sunshine on his wedding day and said; 'you're taking a lot on you know.' He'd smiled and been polite, but really, did he know?

He placed his tea down on the couch arm, and turned his attention to the carcass of the mountain bike that was balancing on its seat, upside down, on the cream carpet, in front of the flat screen TV. The brakes need adjusting. He started to work and focused on the task at hand, soon losing all sense of time.

As the shadows lengthened Alex and Jayne arrived home from school, dropped their bags in the hall blocking the entrance way and wandered into the kitchen. Soon after, John heard the fridge door open and shut and Jayne appeared at the door of the lounge.

'Dad what's for dinner?'

John looked up. Jayne's face was flushed with the cool of the afternoon and there were dark smudges under her eyes.

'Not too sure. You'll have to ask Mum.'

Jayne nodded and left the room and John continued working on the bike.

'How the HELL would I know?'

His wife's voice was loud enough for the Royal Shakespeare Company. And wait for it, he murmured quietly to himself, and then after several heavy footsteps (why does everyone in this house walk so loudly?) the loud voice had sprung down the stairs and was in the room with a whining nine-year-old hard on her heels.

'I don't know what to make for dinner.' Meg looked over helplessly at John. 'Could you help?'

John frowned and reached into his pockets for change.

'What happened to the money I gave you yesterday?' he asked Meg.

'We spent it! And it wasn't yesterday it was on Sunday. It's now Wednesday. A family of five can't live on £80 week. I can't do it.'

'But there's no milk...' John stammered. Or bread. Best not say that.

Meg rounded on him.

'No milk, no bread, no coffee, no fruit, no meat...' she snarled.

'and no wine...' John muttered.

She scowled at him. 'We can't live like this. I need more money to feed us all.'

'Where's your money?'

He knew the moment the words had left his mouth that he'd prepared the device. There was no making it safe. This device would operate; it would not fail and despite his skill and years of experience, this time, there was nothing he could do to stop it.

Meg's eyes narrowed. 'My money? My money? I've spent ALL of my bloody money getting here, being here and trying to bloody stay here! I don't have anything left. I don't even have enough to leave. And tomorrow, I have to stand up in court and tell them everything's wonderful and I love it here and I want to stay. And you know what John? I don't. I hate not having enough money. I hate your bloody bike in the middle of the lounge – what are we students? I hate being stuck in this crappy little house whilst you come and go on your boy's own adventures. I'm lonely and miserable and bleeding... I just want to go *home*.'

Wait. Bleeding?

But before John could ask, she was gone. Out the door, across the road and down Church Lane. At first she could barely see through flooded eyes. Bitter salt on her tongue and the familiar tension in her lungs choking her breath. She was breathing in needles and each one scraped the side of her chest.

She marched on. Past the house with the thatched roof. Past the architectural Kiwi house, the one she thought she was coming to England to live in. And the alternate vision – the one with the pond and the old fashioned kitchen no doubt complete with aga. Back then, her vision of life in England had been drawn from a Penny Vincenzi novel. She was going to live in the country and write aga sagas and together they would raise their family and holiday on the continent. Maybe they'd head back Down Under for some sunshine and bragging rights about their beautiful, exciting expat English life. Friends and family would be impressed with them, a golden couple. Her books would publish and she'd get an agent from Bloomsbury and the blog would become so popular she would finally once again be that woman – the successful one.

Ouch, that hurt.

The road had turned to gravel and Meg slipped, kicking her toe through the hole in her trainers.

But the novel hadn't leapt off the page and into her personal life. Instead, she was here in this sad town with no job, no money and a huge date in court, tomorrow.

Tomorrow. She gulped.

Out over the fields she could see rabbits darting from hole to hole. All beady eyes, button tails and quivering they were constantly on high alert and would scatter at the merest touch of a vixen's paw on sod, half a mile away. Meg couldn't help but feel for them. Behind them, far off in the distance an anaemic sun was sliding down the horizon, its weak rays only faintly lightening the steel skies.

'It's all just so bloody sad God. I hate my life.'

All this way just to be turfed out.

She'd tried so hard, and yet here she was... She wanted the happy ever after, but it didn't seem to be... And the kids...

'...they're miserable. And I don't know what to do,' she cried out loud to the wind. There was no reply from the heavens, only the sound of the wind whistling through the trees.

If we lose tomorrow will they immediately take us into custody?

Surely not.

But she wasn't sure. Her heart quickened and she sucked back the rising feeling of terror. She hadn't expected that the UK Border Agency would want to break up a family, either... but it appeared they would... Panic gripped her and the needles dug in once more.

Where would they go? Would John just let them go? Or would he come too? How would they get the dog and cat back? The UK Border Agency would hardly deport them too. It cost thousands to get them here in the first place. Now there was nothing left of her savings. Nothing left of the earnings from frigid dawns working between breastfeeds, or the struggle being Mum and Dad...nothing left of the precious hours with new babies sacrificed on the altar of work and progress. It was all gone. All of it. It was all worthless. As if it never happened.

No one had told her that she would be stuck on the other side of the world with no income. She'd signed the divorce settlement in good faith. She'd come all this way to take up a job that had seemed so good. And she'd worked so hard. God, she'd worked hard. Even, when she should have been here at home with her poor kids, helping them to settle in... No one had told her that Murray would let her down, let the kids down so utterly. And then work had ended, after only six months. Six months! No one had warned her that she would be banned from working on pain of arrest for almost a year. The poor kids had never eaten so much mince and sausages in their lives.

A car pulled up and parked in the cemetery carpark and a well-dressed elderly man clinging onto the arm of a plump middle aged woman stumbled towards a fresh grave. Meg looked away, to give them privacy and then quickly walked across the lane from the stile, fields, and cemetery, to the garden of the seventeenth century church.

St Peter's was worse for wear and though the sign out front advertised services here at 6:00pm on Summer Sunday nights, Meg had never seen the church opened up. Maybe they had trouble deciding if it was summery enough. Ever. She wondered uncharitably as she walked past the dilapidated sign. Or maybe no one cared enough.

It occurred to Meg that the church itself was the headstone for a dead faith. There was a heaviness in Bottom Hedgeley, a dark force choked the town. The kids in their black trackies huddled around the car park at Sainsburys, the solo mums with their translucent skinned babies in chocolate smeared prams, and the listless youth with their downward stares, they all knew it.

There was no radiation in the area. They'd been advised by leaflets dropped by the local youth group. There was nothing to fear. There was nothing to see behind the wire, or in the bottomless vents that spat steam into the country air, or even in the dark cavalcade of lorries that slithered through the town in the godless hours of frozen mornings, on their way to Scotland. There was nothing to fear from the protestors at the fenced gates or from the sirens that blew from time to time - their shrill screeches reverberating around the town, calling attention to problems no-one outside the wire would ever know - but there was this; an ambivalence. It permeated the town with hopelessness; a dark, damp nothingness.

That was the town's radiation. The physical wire outside the site wasn't the only grim barrier, just outside the gates, the real barrier was this dark, hopelessness, and it encircled the entire town and all of its inhabitants. You were either behind the wire, or you weren't. And if you weren't, you were nothing, and if you were, well, you were nothing still.

If only they'd settled in Newbury or Bramley or Chineham even Reading, Meg thought to herself. Maybe there would be more village life there. She had wanted that life so very much. She had wanted the bunting and the summer fairs and the Parish Council meetings and the local pub where everyone knew you...She knew there were villages like that within a short drive but this town wasn't like that.

'It's a commuter town Meg,' John had told her. 'People live here and drive into Basingstoke or Reading to catch the train to London.'

She knew. She just wished it wasn't true.

Meg wandered around the back of the church eyeing the long grass suspiciously. She feared the adder she couldn't see. She stood transfixed looking out to the elderberry bushes and beyond to the little copse...

She would tell them she didn't want to go back, she wanted to stay here. But did she?

'If I get the visa and I can work again, I can fix this,' she told the grass moving gently in the breeze. 'Please God, can I have a chance to fix this?'

As she watched, drinking in the stillness, an owl swooped down to perch on the branches of the black-green tree in front of her. It watched her watching him, with round yellow eyes.

What does it want?

It didn't say.

Meg had read that in the middle ages, the Northerners had hung dead owls to their barns to ward off evil spirits and the scream of the barn owl was often a portent of doom. But this owl didn't screech, it just preened its feathers, undisturbed by her presence. It didn't seem evil at all. In fact, as it sat there she felt a wave of calm.

Wise old owl.

Owl's eyes can see through the dark...

She didn't need to know what would happen. All she had to do was have hope and faith that she could get through it.

That was all.

The night was falling quickly and without warning the owl flew off into the dusk. Meg took it as a sign that it was time to head back to the house. She walked the full way round, down the narrow lane lined with trees and past the green, leafy woods, stopping only to watch a deer grazing between the trees.

It was beautiful. For all its difficulty and stress, life could be beautiful here. She quietly walked on. Just past the one lane bridge there was a sign nailed to a post. Though she had walked or run this route many times before, she had never stopped before to read it. It said: CAUTION. HORSES.

Her head was full of pictures of rapid, wild horses coming to get her. What could they possibly do? Sit on her? Neigh furiously? What was the danger? Were they were-horses? She started to laugh.

'What else can you do?' She asked out loud.

'If the judge says leave I'll go, but if he says stay, then I will make it home. Here, with the were-horses.'

She walked the rest of the way home, breathing in time with her steps. Across the main road and back into the estate, she walked. Past the guy peering under the hood of a car on the side of the road and his joking friends, each one laughing as they considered the mechanical disaster before them. Past the anaemic looking girls standing smoking and gossiping on the street corner, and past the young Mum desperately walking her baby 'Go ta sleep will yer' she begged as the baby bawled tirelessely.

As Meg walked through the gate and up the path to the house she could hear cheerful chatter and then smell cooking. She opened the front door and stepped into the hallway.

The school bags had been cleared away, the bike was gone from the lounge and Jayne was in the kitchen, hands purposefully holding the electric beater, which was shrouded in egg white. Meg glanced at the oven but couldn't see through the sepia-dirtied glass.

'What are you cooking?'

'Dad took me up to Sainsburys and I'm making Five Spice Chicken for dinner. And guess what Mum? I'm making Pavlova.'

Meg planted a soft kiss on top of Jayne's head and smiled relief. 'What a great time to eat Pavlova!'

There was never a bad time to eat Pavlova. In Auckland they'd served up Pavlova to celebrate Christmas and birthdays, special days and feel-better days.

Meg had a theory about Pavlova; it was magic food. It was impossible to continue to feeling down when licking the spoon clean of that white magic. How something so light and sweet and joyful could emerge from mundane mucousy egg whites? She didn't understand. Something so simple – egg whites, sugar, cornflour, a dash of vinegar perhaps a spot of vanilla – and yet that simple something rose into heavenly cake. And that cake was nothing short of magic.

Jayne turned back to enthusiastically beating the mixture and Sarah appeared behind her quietly grabbing the milk from the fridge.

'Sarah...' Meg said.

'Yes Mum?' She answered quietly. Her long dark hair curled around her ears, her eyes still glistening and cheeks still wet, she met her mother's gaze.

'I am so very sorry darling. I shouldn't have said all that. I shouldn't have...' Sarah threw herself into her mother's arms, crying and nodding.

'But will we go to a detention centre Mum?'

'No, of course not. I was just being an absolute cow. I am so sorry darling girl. We should be OK. God willing and the planets being in alignment.'

Sarah nodded again and breathed in her mother's hug.

'Whatever happens we will be OK. I promise. I promise,' she whispered into her daughter's vanilla scented hair.

After a restorative shower, Meg gathered with her family, in the lounge, the hot sweet chicken on their plates, and the news on the TV. The ads came on and the Italian opera singer guy character urged them to 'Go compare, go compare' and then another ad featuring Jaime Oliver and Sainsburys flashed across the screen and then an ad with women cavorting in white jeans and smiling alarmingly at the freedom of it all. Freedom to do what? Meg wondered. Jayne's voice interrupted her thoughts: 'Mum, what's a tampon?'

'Well that lightened the mood!' Alex laughed as Sarah melted with embarrassment into her dinner, John decided that now was a good time for a cup of tea and Meg rushed to explain.

Dinner was delicious but desert was the highlight of the Last Supper, as Meg had laughingly dubbed the evening. The Pavlova was perfection; its snow white magic stole the show and in every sweet intoxicating mouthful, Meg could taste heaven.

After the dishes had been returned to the kitchen benches, the kids settled in front of the TV – Alex absentmindedly patting Stella the cat who was sitting on his knee, Sarah gently stroking Bailey's head and Jayne wrapped up in her Nintendo. Meg wandered into the kitchen to sort out the dishes and started wiping down the sink as John slipped into the kitchen behind her. He slung his arms over her shoulders and drew her close.

'You ok love?'

'Getting there,' she said. Her face set.

'Really?'

'No.'

She crumpled into his arms.

'You're under my wing Mrs Williams. If they say you go, then I go too.'

Chapter 26

Home Office Secretary vs Mrs Megan Williams

IT WAS HER name on the papers. She was the appellant. She was the one bringing the appeal against the decision of the Secretary of State to cancel their visa, and yet, Meg felt like the defendant. She was in the gun. It wasn't John's name beside hers. She was on her own. It was there in black and white.

John was there, of course, sitting in the seats at the back of the room. He was a witness for her case and as such he didn't need to sit in the hot seat. She swallowed back the desert in her throat. She was the one pleading for justice. For someone who had never been in trouble with the law and had only ever had one speeding ticket in her entire life, (Yes one. Only one!

She'd confirmed with Mr Kasana) the past year had been full of lawyers and case documents and accounts for legal fees. First the legal stoush around the divorce and now: this.

Meg shuddered. *All that money gone. Which play was it that said first, kill all the lawyers?*

She couldn't remember the early morning drive up to London to the Asylum and Immigration Tribunal rooms in Hatton Cross. John had driven so wildly she had wondered if the hearing might need to cancelled, on account of their sudden demise!

The hearing room was like any other meeting room in the corporate world, sans boardroom table and inspirational art. It was plainly painted and dog-eared. The cloth stackable chairs were spotted with scuffs, marks and splodges and they were laid out in a u-shape with the judge was sitting at the front of the room, Meg and her lawyer sitting on one side and the Home Office representative sitting on her own facing Meg and her counsel.

How very adversarial, Meg thought.

Judge Wozniack was speaking. Did she accept the evidence-in-chief? She glanced down at the 60 pages of documents that outlined her argument. Yes, she did. She agreed that she'd arrived in the UK on a work permit and that yes her work permit had expired as she had left her job.

Been forced to leave. She could still smell stale Earl Grey tea feel his hot breath on her neck and the sharp cutting pain in her lower stomach.

But her situation had changed and as she was now a partner of a UK citizen she was appealing against the UK Home Office's decision to curtail her leave.

Meg smiled nervously at her lawyer sitting next to her. The dark eyed woman briefly returned her smile.

The judge was confirming that the appeal was to be heard in light of the provision of Article 8, in-so-much-as requiring her to leave the country with her children and return to New Zealand to file an application for a spousal visa, was a breach of Article 8 of EU law; her Human Right to an uninterrupted Family Life.

Prudence De Beer had been thorough in her counsel. She looked capable and calm now, in her dark skirt and formal cream blouse topped with a navy jacket. Her dark eyes shone with intelligence and her olive skinned face was brushed with the merest hint of makeup and smudge of lipstick. Meg wondered how many other cases in immigration court Ms De Beer had on today.

There had been crowds of people milling around in the waiting reception area when they arrived at the grim, grubby offices this morning. Meg clocked dark skinned Africans and olive skinned Indians and a small group of Asians. It was a desperate United Nations. Each group clutching onto their supporters, speaking quietly but quickly in their own language and each one sporting the same panicked expression. Meg wondered idly where the other Australasians were. In fact, she noted that there were very few other litigants with a European appearance.

Typical. Trust me to be flying the flag for the colonies at the Immigration Tribunal.

Judge Wozniack nodded his approval of her acceptance of her statement. Now, it was the Home Office Representing Officer's turn to speak to the Secretary of State's decision.

Sybil Shand looks about thirty, wears thin-framed spectacles - the kind on perma-sale at Specsavers - and a plain pair of black trousers with sensible shoes. She stands to make her statement to the judge, but in her head, she is miles away, thinking only about her Siamese cat. Sigmund hasn't been well, his coughing kept her awake half the night and this morning she had found him lying in a lethargic ball under the bed. Sybil lived for Sigmund. He was her significant other, the only male in her life, and now, though her words were present and accounted for in the courtroom, all her thoughts were diverted to Sigmund's health.

In fact, she had been so concerned she'd considered not coming into work today and had lain snuggled under the bedclothes with her poorly cat, stealing an extra half an hour with him. What would she do if she were to lose Sigmund? She'd missed the first train from Finsbury Park station and the second one had whizzed past too full to stop. By the time she'd arrived at Hatton Cross she was woefully late. On her way in to court she'd had a quick look through the appellant's statement. It was cut and dried. The Kiwi woman had come to the UK on a work visa, she'd left the job, lost the visa and should go home. It wasn't rocket science.

All of this irritation was plainly registered on Sybil Shand's face as she started to present the prosecution's case and then cross examine.

'So you say,' she paused to check the document on the table in front of her, 'Mrs Williams, that when you moved to the UK on a work permit that you intended to stay permanently?'

Meg nodded.

'Could you speak up for the court records please,' the judge opined.

'Yes. I arrived on a work permit for Faberge Marketing and even moved my cat and dog from NZ so definite was I about staying.'

Sybil's eyebrow raised slightly. She wondered how poor Sigmund was. Meg gulped; she was not feeling terribly eloquent.

'Yet, despite these *intentions* you lasted less than six months at your job.'

Meg looked down. 'Yes.'

'Why did you throw in the towel at your job?' Sybil demanded.

Meg bristled. 'I didn't just give it up. With the GFC, sorry, the Global Financial Crisis, we lost a major client and they came to me and asked me to accept a pay cut. I was unable to do so as I would need to seek a new work permit from the UK Border Agency and it was unlikely that I would get one at that lower salary.'

'So you left.'

Stupid woman. Sybil could do with earning £45,000 per year.

'It wasn't quite like that.'

Prudence rose to her feet. 'Your Honour, as stated in our evidence Mrs Williams was unable to accept a new position at Faberge Marketing due to the restraints of her work permit status which required that she maintain a full-time position at or above the remuneration level of £45,000 per year. Unfortunately, when the company were advised of this limitation, they increased the pressure on Mrs Wiliams, causing not insignificant work related stress. You will see in the documents evidence from her GP outlining the devastating effect this had on Mrs Williams's health.'

As the judge rifled through the papers, everyone in the room stopped to watch. Finally, the judge nodded to Ms Shand. 'Please continue,' he said.

'Mrs Williams, as you had left your employment, your work permit leave was curtailed and the Secretary of State required you and your dependents to return to New Zealand.

Yet now, you say you want to stay. Is there any reason why you cannot return to New Zealand? Would it be unsafe for you and the children to return?'

'No' Meg stammered.

'No reason why you would need seek asylum in the UK, from New Zealand?' Sybil stifled a snigger. 'No civil unrest, terrorism, or natural disaster to flee from?'

'No,' Meg replied quietly.

'So why don't you just leave Mrs Williams? Go back to New Zealand and apply for the appropriate visa?'

Like everyone else?

Meg wondered: why doesn't she leave. Why?

'Because I wish to remain living in the UK with my UK born husband,' she said.

'Well, why doesn't Mr Williams return to New Zealand with you and the children?'

'He was born here and his family are here and he couldn't replace his job in New Zealand.'

'What does he do?' Sybil asked.

'We'll leave those questions for the witness, Mr Williams, thank you Ms Shand' the judge interrupted.

Sybil Shand nodded.

'Mrs Williams - is it true that you married your partner in haste as soon as you realised your immigration status was in jeopardy?'

‘No. That is not correct.’ Meg spoke firmly. ‘We married at the right time for us. The children were having time visiting with their father in May which allowed us time to honeymoon in Scotland. My husband had already made plans to propose and purchased the ring a few months before we found out about the Home Office decision. The receipt indicating the purchase date, of the ring, is in the documents.’

‘Did you fabricate a wedding for the sake of remaining in the United Kingdom?’ Sybil went on.

‘No. I did not. In fact, as you can see from the pictures we included, we married with our family and friends in attendance, in a church wedding in my husband’s home town.’

Meg turned to plead wordlessly with the judge. Nodding, he rifled through the copied pictures of the girls in their wedding finery, Meg and John kissing in front of the wedding car, and Michelle and family gathered in the garden of the Everton Park.

Sybil changed her tack. ‘If you are not requesting asylum from New Zealand in the UK, why then are you unable to return to New Zealand to apply for a spousal visa?’

‘As stated in my evidence, it would cost well over £8000 for all of us to return to New Zealand, and then there’s the problem that I no longer have a home in New Zealand, my family all live in Australia and the kids are only just getting settled in the UK. It’s cost me, us, well over £30,000 so far

{360}

to get here and to pay for legal costs. My son is doing GCSE and returning to NZ at this point would seriously impact on his school exams...'

'You say there's no family in NZ, but the children's father lives in Auckland doesn't he?' Sybil asked, her eyes hard and narrowed.

'Yes. He does.' Meg reddens.

All of a sudden, the judge speaks up from the front of the room. His voice, nasally and thin. He looked over-tired and he absent-mindedly brushed flecks of white off his shoulders, as he spoke. 'Mrs Williams, I have a few questions I'd like you to answer for me please. Firstly, did the children choose to come to the UK with you even though doing so would mean leaving their father?'

'Yes that's correct. I put it to them and they were all keen to come. Their father is very busy and didn't have a great deal of time for them. It seemed like a good solution. In fact, he was working over in Germany when we first arrived in the UK. We even paid for them to fly over to Germany to see their father for a few days...'

'I see. Did their father agree in writing that the children could travel to the UK to live with you and your partner, er, husband?'

'Yes he did. I have a letter indicating his consent in the document package.'

'Page 57 Your Honour,' Prudence piped up, rising briefly from her seat.

'Very good,' the judge nodded. 'I see. Here. Mrs Williams, do the children like living here?

Sarah's voice rang out too loudly in her head: I hate it here... and I hate him...

'They've taken a while to settle, but they are finally starting to make friends and to feel happier. My son has been doing Air Training Corps and really enjoying it and the girls are doing drama once again. They are all slowly making friends but they are finding the insecurity of not knowing whether they are going to have to leave at a moment's notice very difficult. We all are.'

The judge nodded. 'One last question for you Mrs Williams – did you not think that moving the children to England might be unsettling for the children?'

Meg's blush deepened. She had thought of them. She had.

'I had hoped, Your Honour, that the children would have a brilliant expat experience as I had as a child. I lived in Fiji as a child and I feel that experience helped me to see myself as a global citizen. I had hoped that we would all be here a great deal longer than nine months. I also thought that we would have an opportunity to bond together as a family and we are doing so. All three children were a key part of our wedding and when my husband recently went away for work they missed him. Especially Jayne. She calls him Dad now.

Of course she calls her father Dad too, when she's speaking to him....' Meg was babbling now.

'Yes, I see.' the judge shuffled the papers impatiently.

'Well that's all the questions I have for you Mrs Williams. Ms Shand, have you completed your cross-examination?'

Sybil rose to her feet. 'Yes, Your Honour.'

'May I suggest then, that you ask Mr Willliams to come forward and to give his witness statement. As he does so, Mrs Williams, could you step out into the waiting room please. Your counsel will come out to get you when we are ready for you.'

Meg's heart stopped. Was this the green card moment where they asked John what kind of toothpaste she liked and what her favourite perfume was? Meg started to perspire heavily. John wouldn't know. Her favourite perfume changed, frequently. For the moment it was the cheap perfume oil you found at *The Body Shop*. He'd say *Versace* wouldn't he?

Mentally, she tried to send John a message: it's *Body Shop* oil and *Colgate Fresh Mint*. And then feeling helpless she left the hearing room.

Meg was shaking as she sat down in the crowded waiting room. Sitting opposite Meg, a dark-eyed curly haired toddler shrieked and giggled while a sad eyed dark skinned woman – her hair tied up in a colourful head scarf – tried to restrain him. Meg shot a sympathetic smile across. The woman returned the briefest smile come grimace. Behind her, an

Indian family were loudly talking. She couldn't understand what they were saying but their tone was urgent, laced with panic. Their young, grey-suited counsel came in and urged them to remain calm with a strangled voice. He looked about twelve and Meg wondered what chance they had.

Meg wasn't sure if she was still breathing. Would John remember how they met and how it had all happened? She shook her head as if to loosen the fear and drop it onto the juice stained, threadbare carpet.

'When are you going in?' she asked the Nigerian woman.

'After you.'

'Oh.' Meg felt guilty. How long would they be? 'Is it an Immigration case?'

Of course it was. They were at an Immigration Tribunal court house.

But the woman was generous. 'Yes. I was born in Nigeria and left there ten years ago to come to England with my husband. He was a doctor, but he was a cruel man. He beat me. He beat the children. I went to jail for cutting him with my knife, but when I came out the Government came and said I had to go back to Nigeria. But I want to stay here with my children.'

So many questions, but Meg couldn't think of one appropriate one. Instead she weakly said 'It shouldn't be too long.'

Then she retreated into silence, sitting opposite the abused woman, the domestic violence victim who was now being deported because she stood up to her abuser. There she was: Meg Williams - the quintessential good girl whose only mistake had been to fall in love with an Englishman in Paris.

She closed her eyes. She hadn't slept much last night, and what little sleep she'd had was marred by night terrors. It would be over soon, she reassured herself. Then they would drive back to Bottom Hedgeley and wait for the Judge's decision. How long would that take?

No bloody idea.

Behind her closed eyelids she melted into the red-black dark. Her body was shaking. Her stomach was on fire and she felt as if she was sitting on a knife's blade. She tried to focus in on the sound of her breathing and in so doing lost track of time.

It was half an hour later when Meg felt a hand on her shoulder and opened her eyes to Prudence De Beer gently motioning that she was needed back in the hearing room.

'How was he?' she squeaked.

'Good. He did very well.'

'Did he say Versace?' Meg asked her counsel. Prudence shot her a confused look. Meg hung her head and waved her own question away. It didn't matter. And then they walked back into the courtroom only to be dismissed by the judge ten minutes later, and released out into the sunless London sky.

At least they weren't to be escorted to Heathrow, yet, Meg though to herself quietly as they drove helter-skelter back through the city and countryside to Bottom Hedgeley. They were safe for the time being.

Chapter 27

The Good Doctor

I T WASN'T THE best week in her life, Meg admitted. Court on Wednesday and now here she was on Friday at the doctor's surgery with a tube up her bum.

If it wasn't so painful she'd laugh. Maybe there was something in what they said: Hurricane Meg. But every time she moved to cough or breathe, pain ripped right through her, and naturally, as was her luck, Meg had succumbed to a hacking cough that would likely turn into bronchitis, on Wednesday afternoon.

Which would probably get serious and then I'll have an asthma attack and probably die and all that money we spent on staying here would be a complete waste....

'OW!'

'Sorry. Just need to move the sigmoidoscope a little' the doctor said.

Was it her warped imagination or was the doc taking undue pride in his thorough examination?

'It's an easy procedure,' her own GP had assured her blithely a few weeks ago. 'Doesn't take long. The worst bit is taking the pills beforehand and sitting on the toilet all night.'

Meg grimaced.

'Ow. Ow. Ow.'

Nope, taking the pills WAS NOT the worst bit.

Meg's doctor chuckles lightly. 'Sorry about that. Just trying to get a good look behind this bend. We want to get a good picture of what's going on in here so we don't have to have another examination.'

Another exam? '*Eff off.* Meg bites her lip instead of crying out. The doctor starts to chat attempting to take her mind off the discomfort. He's pointing out the landscape of her innards on the monitor as enthusiastically as a real estate agent might point out the features of his prized property or a radiographer might highlight the baby's heartbeat.

'It's like getting a baby scan, just without the glowy moments.' Meg says to no one in particular.

'And you don't get to take the scan home and put it on the mantelpiece either,' the dark haired nurse pipes up.

Meg smiles wryly. Nope, she can't imagine you would put this up on the mantelpiece to show off to your family and friends.

And here it is, the very first scan of my jacksee...so proud...

There's only the specialist and his nurse assistant in the room with her and the mood is surprisingly light. The portly doctor is engrossed in the image on the monitor but laughs belatedly at the thought of taking home the results of the sigmoidoscopy.

'Now, Mrs Williams, could you just take in a deep breath and hold it for me... ahhh... that's it... just around the back here...'

He points to a dark red blotch on the screen, and Meg wonders how many bums the good doctor and his nurse investigate in a working day. Or in a week. Or a year.

Man, that must be a hell of a lot of arses.

'Have you been under any stress at all lately?' the doctor asks.

Meg giggles self-consciously. 'Mmmm. Yeah. You could say that. I moved here with my three kids from New Zealand last year and then lost my visa and was scheduled to be deported. I married my partner three weeks ago and was in an Immigration Tribunal Court hearing on Wednesday.'

'So, quite a lot of stress!' the doctor whistled softly. 'And how's your diet been?'

Fine. If you're keen on sausages, mince and the occasional pork pie.

'Lots of fibre? Eating enough fruit and veges?' he asked.

'When I can.' *When the kids haven't eaten everything in the fruit bowl.* 'It's been a struggle. Quite a change in diet... in lifestyle ...'

'Oh you poor thing, it must have been very hard,' the nurse suggests.

Don't be nice to me, I'll cry.

'It has been. I used to cook in New Zealand, friends' parties and things, but these days money's just too tight. It's been a struggle to...' She trails off.

'I see from your notes that you've had problems with IBS... Ah yes there. That's it. Yes. You have a number of nasty looking internal hemorrhoids. No sign of polyps as far as I can see.'

'That's a good thing?' Meg asks.

'That is a very good thing,' the doctor replies. 'Polyps can indicate cancerous cells. We could schedule you for surgery to remove these hemorrhoids but it could be a fairly big event. I think the first thing we should do is to get you medication and see if it sorts itself out without further intervention. Then if you have any more trouble we can go down that surgical route.'

'But no cancer?' Meg asks.

'No. Not that I can see.'

No cancer.

And with that pronouncement, the doctor completes his examination and leaves his nurse to clean Meg up, see her out the door and ready the room for the next patient.

'Are you OK?' the nurse asks her as she helps Meg to get back into her clothes.

'Relieved. Incredibly relieved.'

'I can imagine. You really have been through a tough time,' she said. Meg sniffs a little and nods.

'Why did you move here from New Zealand?' the nurse asks.

'I met my husband in Paris and a year later I moved here with dog, cat and kids to be with him.'

'But from there to here? Why didn't he move to New Zealand? You'd think that would have been the best idea.'

Meg nodded thoughtfully. 'Yes, but he works up the road and really didn't want to lose his job. And he had a house here and I thought it would do us all good to get out of the drama of the divorce from my first husband. And England offered so much opportunity...' she adds.

The nurse smiles briefly and changes the subject. 'I think it might be best if you go home and get some rest,' she said. 'You might be a bit sore for the next few days, so just set yourself up on the couch in front of the TV. Let the family run around after you. Just lie back, relax, and avoid as much stress as you can.'

Yeah, right. Like that'll happen. Meg smiled her thanks and shuffled out the door and into her car.

When she arrives home the place is deserted. She eases up onto the leather lounge and lies down closing her eyes to the bilious waves of pain. Bailey padded alongside her and with a generous tongue starts licking her face. Meg reaches forward and buries her head in the dog's brown fuzz, ruffling her silky ears.

'It wasn't cancer Bails' she quietly says. 'Thank God.'

Jayne is the first one home. She wandered into the kitchen and found some crackers and a banana and gently sat down beside her Mum on the couch. 'Are you OK Mum?' Her eyes were wide with concern.

'I'm OK. I had a wee operation today. I just need some rest now and then I'll be really good. How was your day at school?'

'It was good. Anthony asked if I could go over to his place tomorrow after school.'

'Whose Anthony?'

'A boy. In my class.'

'Well, I gathered that!' Meg laughs. 'Did he give you his Mum's number?'

'Yup.' Jayne walks into the hall and grabs the scruffy piece of paper on which she scrawled the telephone number.

'He said his Mum gets home at six.'

'Ok. I'll call then. Why don't you go upstairs and get out of your school uniform.'

'Yeah, but Mum....'

'Mmmm.'

'Did you hear yet?'

'No. We won't hear back for ages yet, probably best to just forget it.'

'Forget what?' John interrupts, as he walks through the door.

'You're home early. I was just telling Jayne she probably should not worry about the judge.'

'True. We will be OK, no matter what happens,' he says. Jayne considers it carefully and then looks up and asks: 'Dad, Mum's had an operation and isn't feeling very well so maybe we should get dinner from Sainsburys tonight.'

'Good idea! What do you feel like?' he asks Meg.

'What about one of those Thai curry meal box thingies.'

'A meal box thingy?' John raised his eyebrow.

'You know...it has two or three curries in it...'

'Oh...I know what you mean. Go and get changed Jayne and we'll go up to the shops.'

As Jayne left the room John quietly kisses her forehead. 'You ok love? What did the doc say?' She nods and blurts out: 'No cancer.'

'No?'

Vicki Jeffels

'Nup. I just need some rest for these haemmorroids' Relieved, he kisses her again.

Yeah things are OK, Meg thinks as the kids go with John up to Sainsburys to grab dinner in a box.

Thank God for Sainsbury's dinner boxes, and England's love of instant meals, Meg thinks to herself as she dozed in front of the TV.

Now all she had to do was get through the next few weeks waiting for Judgement Day.

Chapter 28

Judgement Day

THE BLACK SKY cracked into shards of colour. A screech and boom accompanied the colour burst and then light petals fell to earth or dissolved into the fiery tongues of the pyre.

'Ohhhh, how beautiful.' Sarah gasps as she points out the cascade shower to the group of girls standing with her - a collection of friends from school. A tall blonde haired girl and her sister, and a dark haired elfin teen dressed in black, eyelids licked with dark liner – nodded, chatting excitedly. John good-naturedly teased Alex as they lit sparklers, and handed them to Jayne and her friends who drew loops and bows with them, in the dark.Meg felt full to the brim with happiness.

She was standing a few feet away watching Jayne, the boys, Sarah and her friends and occasionally looking up to admire the fireworks as they whizzed into the night sky and burst into large flowers of light, wowing the small crowd of locals in the field. This was a tradition – Guy Fawkes night fireworks at the field on the corner of Harts Lane, just down from the farm selling Christmas trees at the gate.

Meg was pleased she'd talked John into bringing the kids. They still celebrated Guy Fawkes in New Zealand, but not like this. Back there, it was usually a public display of fireworks, all tickets and assigned places to stand and sit, not this vaguely reckless assembly of townspeople selling tickets at the gate and waving people on to stand in the searing heat of the massive bonfire. The field was dotted with stalls selling chestnuts, hot dogs and sticky toffee apples. All rugged up against the cold with scarves and hats and gloves, people stood around watching the flames devour the Guy only turning away to watch the fireworks' display.

After watching the last sparkler die and transform to grey, John and Alex were dispatched to buy hot dogs and they soon returned with white rolls smeared with sauce, each bread sleeve cradling a sausage.

'Mmmm. Yum!' Meg enthusiastically bit into her hot dog.

'I thought you didn't approve of sausages!' John jokingly hassled her.

'Well, there's a time and place. BBQ's, campfires and of course Guy Fawkes Night are of course the perfect time and place.'

John laughed and started devouring his hot dog also.

They all leaned in closer to the roped off area around the bonfire.

'Are you warm enough Alex?' Meg asked her son.

'Yeah.'

Meg frowned. Hardly likely. What was it about teenagers and their coats? It was freezing – literally – and yet he still wouldn't wear his coat. 'Stand closer to the fire, warm yourself up' she urged him.

'That fire is huge!' Alex said.

'I guess they can have it as big as they want. It's not going to burn anything after all, the ground is frozen.'

'You couldn't do this in Auckland,' Alex said.

'No. You couldn't,' Meg agreed quietly.

John started chatting to a bald haired man who was walking past them. 'Dan! How are you?'

'Great thanks. And you?'

'OK. Keeping on the straight and narrow,' John replied. 'Dan this is my family – my wife Meg, and there's our Alex, Sarah and Jayne.' He pointed each family member out as his friend smiled his hellos.

'Dan works with me,' John told Meg. She knew better than to ask what Dan did.

Instead, she left the men chatting together and turned to survey the scene. There weren't many stars and it was bitterly cold, but it didn't matter. The starless night simply made the fireworks more stunning and the hot dogs and hot chocolate were the perfect antidote to the cold air. There was a jolly atmosphere in the field as kids played and parents relaxed and everyone stopped their conversation to exclaim 'wow' 'gosh' 'OMG' as the fireworks lit up the skies.

The display was over before she was ready for it to stop, and then the family walked home over the fields, down the lane till they reached the outskirts of the estate and then across the street to their little house.

'Cup of tea, hun?' John asks as he makes a beeline for the kettle.

'Why not! After a perfectly English evening, I think a cup of tea would be the perfectly English thing to do.' Meg laughs.

Before long, he places a warm cup in her hand and they sit down together in the lounge, quietened by the ritual of the tea.

Mock the Week was on the TV and distractedly John and Meg watched until realising with a gulp that it was long past time to get the kids into bed. They bundled the girls into their lilac room amidst the complaints.

'I'll just read for a while. Just a bit,' Sarah said.

Meg turned out the bedroom light.

'Muuum! It's not fair!'

'Life never is darling, but that's OK. It makes us strong.'

'Oh Muuum GRRRRRR! You're impossible.'

Alex turned in to bed more easily, though Meg knew he was going to hang out online before sleep subdued him in the wee hours of the morning. How he was growing so tall without sleep, was a mystery to her.

Meg washed her face and brushed her teeth before piling into the double bed. As she dozed off to sleep she thought she could hear the owl calling in the oak tree outside her window.

*****

A week later, the windows rattle intensely and Meg can feel the thumpitythump thumpthump thumpitythump outside the house. She swings open the lounge glass door and races out into the garden, just in time to catch sight of a dark RAF helicopter lurch down behind the fence line. Her face burns with pride.

'That's picking up my man!'

There is no one there to share her pride; the kids are at school and John is at work waiting to be whisked away on work business. Ever the daredevil, he had excitedly announced that his transport was a helicopter this time. Meg couldn't help but grin. Her wiry man off on exercise with those strapping built-like-a-brick-shithouse army blokes. They called him Danger Mouse and she'd even found him a DM t-shirt at a shop in Basingstoke. He loved it and had placed the t-shirt carefully in the drawer with the other t-shirt treasures – the Top Gun tee and the Felix Fund tee from the Bomb Disposal Charity.

The helicopter had disappeared from view, but she could still hear the blades cutting through the air. They'd be getting on board, now, and she would be on her own for the next day and a bit.

Which is a very, good thing.

She didn't admit it often, but at times she missed time on her own. When she'd first separated from Murray there were times – albeit not regular enough – but times nonetheless when she had whole weekends to sleep, and mooch about the house. She'd eat steak sandwiches and salads and wouldn't have to put the dishwasher on all weekend. Bailey would accompany her on runs and she'd watch TV, read, write and disappear into a fantasy world. And then there were all the other perks – the whole bed to herself, sitting around in her PJ's, heading off to the shops for no reason at all, except to window shop. Bliss!

Solitude was good medicine.

The thumpitythumping turned into windows rattling and Meg knew that John and his mates were on their way. She wasn't entirely sure where, somewhere north of London he'd vaguely told her last night, as he was packing his black kit. She didn't really need to know anymore. He did this. Sometimes he went away, she wasn't entirely sure what he did or where he went but she trusted that he would be OK. He would come back.

She grabbed her handbag, coat and scarf and headed out to her car. Putting the Vauxhall into reverse she pulls out of the shared car park and up the lane towards Sainsburys. As she passed the rows of yellow and red brick homes she smiled remembering back to when they had all looked the same to her, and each home had seemed like half a house.

Jeez that was a long time ago.

Now she could agree with John that their house was larger than most, for the style. Not in New Zealand terms of course, but in UK terms. He'd once said that their house wasn't big but it was filled with love and she'd rolled her eyes in response.

But now, yeah, it was. She got it.

She drove the car into the supermarket car park and entered into the shop. The Christmas decorations were up and the shelves were groaning with Christmas merchandise. Meg placed a cinnamon candle in her trolley, then found some packaged Indian meals and tossed them in also. She grabbed a pot of prawns, from somewhere in the world (who knew where?), then stopped at the Deli counter where she grabbed a pork pie (on special), for John's lunch later in the week.

The carol music boomed out and Meg found herself singing along to 'dashing through the snow, on a one-horse open sleigh...' It would be hot in Auckland now, she murmured to herself. She smiled. She'd said Auckland, not home.

At least this year I will be able to enjoy Christmas, not like last year when I was working every hour God sends.

'Oh hi, how are you?' She calls out to a small red-haired woman she knows from Jayne's school, who is walking past.

'Hi, I'm OK,' she flashes a smile, stops her trolley and turns to chat with Meg.

'But not brilliant?' Meg asks gently. The woman looked surprised.

'No, well still having a few problems with my ex. Money, seeing the kids, you know how it is..'

Meg nodded. 'It can take a long time. You think it's going to be OK, well at least civil, but for quite some time you burn with rage.'

The woman nodded. 'What happed with you and your ex?' she asked Meg.

'Oh it turned out OK, eventually. The government caught up with him and he's been dutifully paying child support.'

'Wow. That must be a huge relief.'

'It is. It's nowhere near the private agreement we made and by the time we've converted NZ dollars into pounds a month's support doesn't even pay for a week's expenses, but hey, it's something. But what's even more important is that he's making a real effort to see them. When John and I got married in May he took them off on a tiki tour around

England and Wales. Made a huge difference! They all came back so much happier and settled.'

'That's incredible. I can't see that happening to us. My ex is still begging off having the kids and with my work schedule it's getting really difficult.'

'It must be really hard,' Meg said.

'It's just when I have to work nights, I can't leave them at home and then if I don't work nights – I'm not doing them at the moment – I just don't have enough money to make ends meet.'

'It just takes some time. I think they have to get over the indignity of it all, especially if you were the one to instigate the separation....'

'But I wasn't! It was him. *He* was the one who decided the Italian girl in the office was far more interesting...'

'Mmm. What an arse,' Meg said. Rachel nodded.

'Hey, what are you doing on Friday night? Would you like to come over to ours?' Meg asked. 'Bring the kids, they'll love it. They can all play *Little Big Planet* and we can sit at the table, drink wine and moan about our noxious exes,' she said.

Rachel's face brightened. 'Oh that would be great. Wait till I tell Anthony and Simon. Can I bring anything?'

'Maybe some desert? Even some icecream and fruit salad would be good.'

'I could make a pumpkin pie, I've got a great recipe from when I was living in Canada,' Rachel said.

'Yum. That sounds amazing. Bring it, it will be brilliant. All sorted.'

'Oh, I meant to ask: Did you hear yet about your immigration thingy?'

'No.'

'No news is good news. Right?' Rachel asks.

'I suppose so. I'm just not thinking about it. Trying to make the most of living here. Day to day. Blogging a bit and running and home-making.' Meg laughs suddenly. 'I never thought I would be willingly *home-making!* Oh dear, my inner feminist dies a little more each day.'

'Probably a good thing.' Rachel giggles. 'Well I'd best get on as I need to get back for Anthony's school pick-up.'

'Yeah, living next to the school is brilliant. Jayne just comes home by herself.'

'So pleased I bumped into you. See you Friday,' Rachel hurried off to the counter and Meg placed milk and bread into her trolley before following suit.

The checkout operator has served her at least fifty times since Meg arrived in Bottom Hedgeley, but each time Meg appears at the counter the checkout operator thinks this is the first meeting.

'How are you today?'

'Fine thanks,' Meg replies.

'Is that a South African accent?' the checkout operator asks.

'New Zealand.' (Same accent as last week.)

'Oh. Are you on holiday?'

'No, I live here now.'

'Oh.' She seems surprised. She always is. Meg wonders if she has short term memory loss.

'How long have you been here?' the operator asks.

'Over a year now,' Meg says.

'New Zealand. I always wanted to go there and see the kangaroos.'

'Er, that's Australia. But New Zealand's right next to it, just off the coast of Australia.'

'But it's hot and sunny too?' It seems important that it is, at least to the checkout operator.

Meg furrows her brow. 'Mainly.' She pushes visions of an August rain-sodden Auckland, to the back of her mind.

'Why on earth would you move from there to here? Do you have a Sainsburys's card?'

'Yes.' Meg passed the card over. 'I get asked that a lot! Well I met my English husband in Paris and moved here with my kids and dog and cat and everything.'

The woman brushed an oily strand of hair out of her eyes. 'You moved here for him? You must love him. That's £40 please.'

'I do. And I quite like it here too.

Meg placed her card into the EFT machine, then packed the groceries into the bags as the operator grabbed the receipt and gave it to her. 'Thanks a lot,' she said to the operator. 'And I do like it,' she reminded herself as she pushed the trolley to her car.

The weather is threatening. Cloud is hanging low and the north wind is biting at the exposed flesh on her neck. She quickly piles the shopping into the car, returns the trolley and then drives the car down the back road towards the little house.

After putting the shopping away and devouring the prawns for lunch, it was time for coffee and a good book. She made her cup using the flash coffee machine that Ally had sent as a wedding present, and headed back upstairs to her room with the dog padding faithfully behind her and slumping into a snoring mound of brown hair, beside her bed. The coffee machine had been a god-send. Ally must have realised that Meg was desperate for great coffee, out in the English countryside – a lifetime away from the café culture of London and a world away from good Kiwi coffee. There had been times when she would have gleefully sold one of the children for a decent cappucino.

It had been four months since her procedure at the doctor and she had spent the time doing exactly what the doctor had instructed. She'd read some, walked quietly when she was able, and blogged most days. She even had a few initial friendships budding online and the blog had won a couple of awards. Funny how things worked out. If she hadn't been told she couldn't work, she would never have prioritised the blog or found her online tribe. And as the doctor had promised, after a few weeks of lying on the couch dosed up with pain medication and simply resting, giving her body some time to heal, her pain disappeared.

'I'm all fixed! I could even go horse-riding now,' she told John, and then she'd added softly '... if we had the money...'

Jack and Terri moved out to their own flat but still came by for the odd dinner. It was fun having them just down the road in Basingstoke where Jack was perfecting the art of cocktail-making at the local Grilled to Thrill.

The kids started getting involved in their school work and activities. Jayne had signed up to be the dog in the local production of Annie, and they'd all gone to watch her performance, grinning wildly at her swagger on stage and at Sarah's dancing in the chorus.

Meg leant back onto the pillows and glanced out the window at the old oak tree. The tree was completely denuded of leaves and the squirrels were racing over its branches stashing nuts for the fast-approaching winter. The old oak tore the sky tissue with bark fingers. The Nor'easter was icy, but inside the little house the boiler was doing its best to pretend it was Auckland in early summer.

She reflected a little on her conversation with Rachel at the supermarket. The tribunal had been considering her case for over four months now and while she waited she had

Vicki Jeffels

finally accepted that there was nothing more that she could do. Not caring, was a huge relief, and slowly, the tension had lifted. If they had to go, then that wouldn't be so bad. John would come too.

For better for worse
For richer for poorer.

She grabbed a swig of coffee and reached over to pick up her journal from the bedside table. As she wrote her eyelids became heavier and heavier until inevitably they closed and she fell asleep.

She didn't hear the thud of the mail through the slot in the door. She was oblivious to the sleet showers that iced the ground and stone path, but she did wake to the sound of the front door being slammed shut. Blearily, she opened her eyes and listened for further sounds. She relaxed as soon as she heard the familiar humming up the stairs. It was Jayne, home from school. She burst into Meg's room and tossed a large envelope onto her mother's bed.

'Mail for you.'

'Oh? How are you hun? Good day?'

'Yes. They told us who was in the nativity play. I'm the Innkeeper's wife.'

'Oh. Well done. You'll steal the show like you did last year.'

A whole year ago. Amazing. Time flies when you're having fun.

'What's for afternoon tea Mum?'

'Food.'

She was almost certain there was something left in the cupboards and fridge that looked like afternoon tea.

'Muuuum!'

'Go and see. There is food there. Vegemite on toast. I think there's a few apples left. Go and see.'

Jayne wandered off downstairs leaving Meg to sift through the mail. Meg flipped over the large white envelope. It was addressed to her, and on the top left hand corner was the insignia of the UK Border Agency.

Her blood bleached white hot. Her fingers trembled and the back of her neck prickled. After shooting off an arrow prayer, she rips open the envelope as if she was ripping off a bandaid.

Nothing hurts more than the terrible, horrible things I can imagine might have happened. I'd prefer to know so I know what I must deal with.

The first page contains the case details. There it was, her name – and only her name – in the details section. She remembered back to when she was desperate to leave and suspected that John wouldn't come.

He'd leave now though, wouldn't he?

The case is outlined in detail. She winces as she re-reads the judge's questioning especially; 'do the children like it here?'

Much more now, than then, she admits.

Why doesn't Mr Williams go back to New Zealand with you? she reads. It takes her some time to read the seven-page decision, and reread it – just to make sure – and then her mouth falls open.

'That's it? After all that?'

And quite suddenly she starts to cry.

All of that fight. The stress, the fear, the money wasted on legal fees and visas, it all came down to this. She reads the decision for the second time and as she reads she finally understands what the judge had ordered.

She sat there quietly, sitting with that knowledge in the waning light, watching the naked branches of the oak tree turn skeletal in the moonlight. No words. No feelings. Just numbness. She watched the neighbours in the posh detached house over the fence behind the oak tree come home from school, practice piano and prepare dinner. She heard the kids shrieking over the PS3 downstairs and the muffled sounds of the couple next door making their dinner, sharing their day's news.

She should tell John. She grabs her mobile and texts a simple message.

It's in. The Judge's decision. Can you call me please! It's urgent.
Xxx

Chapter 29

Christmas in Croydon

'Mum watch out there's a car coming straight for us!' Alex yells.

'Arrrrgh!' Meg slides the car into a car parking space on the side of the road, in the nick of time just allowing the on-coming car to slip past her Vauxhall.

How did that happen?

She knew she wasn't concentrating – she had a lot on her mind – but did they need to almost die on a narrow street in Croydon because of it?

Stress is a killer, but really?

'It's a one-way Mum,' Sarah advises authoritatively.

Bugger! Bloody sat nag.

She waits until the street was empty and then drives the car carefully to the end of the street and turns back onto the right side of the road. She'd warned the children that this trip to London wouldn't be easy, but she hadn't intended to kill them all.

'There might be lots of waiting around,' she warned Jayne on the drive up the M4. 'It will be fairly boring and then we'll have to do what they tell us, without arguing, and hopefully it will be all over. Afterwards, we'll meet Dad in London and go and see the lights.'

'What lights?' Sarah asked.

'In Oxford street. The Christmas lights, they're meant to be amazing. We can't come all this way to England and leave without seeing them.'

But right now, they were at the boring bit, and she was desperately seeking a car park in a building that looked as if it was a gang headquarters. Finally, she spied one and after parking, the kids all jumped out of the back seat and into the cold damp. The stairwells smell like pee, and pot. Meg grimaces. She loves London, but not this bit. Not this dark, dank, depressing underbelly. She much preferred London, when the city had her glad-rags on.

Like, when the women had their Ascot hats on and the men their tophats and tails... She smiled at the recollection.

They raced down the carpark building stairs and out onto the Croydon streets and on to the UK Border Agency building. There was already a queue of people; all shapes, sizes and colors of unwashed humanity winding down the street waiting for the office to open. Meg and the children joined the queue and pulled their jacket collars up around their chins. It was freezing, but it could have been a tropical day in Hawaii and Meg would still have felt chilled to the core.

After an hour of queuing they finally entered the building where in Reception they were greeted and passports were checked and then taken. In return Meg was given a number. 155.

I would have preferred to keep my passport.

They sidled through into the large waiting room, or Hell's bus station as it would be forever known, in their memory. The room is grey-green and depressing; wall-papered with grief and carpeted with fear. And here they stay - too frightened to leave and get food from the Tesco across the road - for five hours.

Finally, the balding man behind the counter callsout '155' and Meg and the children present themselves for inspection. They were taken to a windowless room, questioned by an unsmiling woman with a double chin and cigarette yellowed teeth, and then, one by one they were photographed and finger-printed.

It is depressingly dehumanising. Meg can't help thinking that at nine years old Jayne was way too young to have a fingerprint record.

By the time the authorities are done with them it is dark in wintery London and city workers are storming the streets and spilling down into the tube. Meg grabsJayne's hand and tells her to hold on for dear life. They race through the throng to the nearest tube station with the older children sticking close behind them. The tube is frantic. Everyone has their rush-hour armour on; hiding behind sullen expressions. Everyone, except Meg's children. They were reveling in it.

Despite the commuter weariness, there is a lively energy, a vibrant, cosmopolitan buzz and the children lap it up. They are mesmerised by the sheer amount of people, and so many cultures and nationalities. They stop to watch a young Santa busking admirably in the tunnels, indifferent to the tut-tuts of the commuters, and smile at tourists desperately clutching their smartphones, consulting the oracle (Google Maps) impatiently waiting for the train to deliver them to the next stop on their London whistle-stop tour.

'but where do we need to get off for Big Ben?' Someone close-by drawls.

When the train whooshes alongside the platform, Meg and the children are swept along with the herd, spilling into the jam-packed carriage.

Alex is struggling to look cool hanging off the roof straps of the train carriage. His face is flushed with the heat of hundreds of people crammed into the carriage, and his knuckles are white. He is holding on to that strap with every ounce of strength remaining in his lanky teenage body. Meg smiled at her tall dark haired son. He would get there. They all would. Wouldn't they?

The train continued on the line, whipping through the tube. A small Asian uni student sneezes loudly next to Sarah. The student doesn't cover her mouth with her hand, and Sarah wrinkles her nose in disgust. A sweating businessman seated on the seat opposite is glaring at his papers, as if by sheer stare power alone he can reduce the words written there to ash. Meg can't help thinking: I'd love to have that superpower.

The train wheezes to a stop and even more people board until they were standing face-flat against the closing carriage doors. Meg sucks back the stench. The man in front of her has marinated in garlic at lunch and the one beside them is ripe too; the stench of BO wafts over them in sickening waves. She smiles sympathetically at another woman who is holding firmly onto the hand of a little girl dressed in her best clothes and her broadest smile. They appear to be heading out to see a show – a London Christmas treat, perhaps?. Maybe a panto – an English tradition Meg hasn't yet embraced. The little girl is almost bursting with excitement and Meg couldn't help smiling some more at her joy.

'The next station is Oxford Circus' the disembodied voice advised.

Meg nudges her girls, sitting on either side of her, and nods to Alex and they make their way to the carriage doors. The train slides to a stop, the green button lights up and they spilled out with the masses onto the platform, into an ocean of strangers.

Meg loses sight of Sarah for a moment and panics. But then she spies her, standing waiting by the door that leads out from the platform, just waiting calmly. She looks so independent and self-assured. Meg is conflicted – proud of Sarah's independence but frightened by the potential danger. Meg grabs her hand, a little briskly, and they are swept along with the tide of people out onto the tiled floor and then up the escalators.

'Alex move over!' Meg instructs her son, sharply. 'People want to get by.'

Alex looks bemused and moves to stand on the right side of the escalator. *Just like a proper Englishman.* Meg smiles. He'd started to mature this past year. Having his older cousin stay and having an interested father figure in John, had really helped him grow up.

England has been good for him.

It had been good for all of them. One way or another. Meg noticed in herself, a growing tolerance, and dare she admit it, a greater patience. It didn't matter if the house was big, if her car was a glorified Holden (as her ex had teased) or if people were guarded. They had worked hard to bring the family together and build budding friendships. And they *were* closer, the five of them. If nothing else, she would be forever grateful for that.

Spilling out of the cavernous white tube, Meg and the children are greeted by lights everywhere. Large blue nets of lights are hung across the road and in their centres are gold sparkling stars. As they shuffle with the crowds down Oxford Street they can't help gasping and pointing.

'Ooooh wow. Look Mum, there's an umbrella!'

Meg wasn't entirely sure why there were blue umbrellas created out of thousands of LEDs suspended over Oxford Street, but it *was* England in winter. Didn't everyone need a brolly?

It is magical though.

In the face of thousands of twinkling lights, the nightmares of the day and the past twelve months, melted away into the cool winter's night.

They walk further down the road past the curtains of lights hanging down the side of *John Lewis* and down to *Zebra* where they find a table and wait. There was no fuss in waiting. They laughed amongst themselves, and people-watched as they waited.

He was always late. She knew that now. She knew too that he would, from time to time, disappear off on his boy's own adventures...he would never call a plate anything but a pot and he would often lose fish hooks and bike tools on their dressing table. But then, just as importantly, he would always be a kind-hearted Englishman, no matter where they ended up.

My Englishman.

The kids chatted amongst themselves as they waited. She wasn't really listening to their conversation; she was too tired by the events of the day. Her brain was fried.

She didn't see John enter the restaurant, she was too busy laughing at something Alex had said. Alex, who had apparently grown a foot since this morning. Standing taller, sitting up straight and strong. He was all over-sized limbs now and on his lip there was a dark foreshadow of the man Alex would grow into being.

Meg just suddenly looked up and there, John was, magically materialised, right in front of her. His eyes were wary and his chin wobbled a little with conflicted emotion. His face questions his right to smile. She collapses into his arms and then can't hold it in any longer. She pulls back and in answer to the question in his eyes, she shakes her head.

'Computer says no.'

His face drops.

Obviously the confusing, illogical, ridiculous UK Border Agency website was right.

'But, judge says YES! We won,' she says quietly.

'We won?'

'Yup!'

She was half-smiling, half-crying now.

'How long for?' he asks.

'Two years, but then we can apply for Permanent Residency.'

He groans. 'More visa hassles?'

'Yeah, but it should be ok. We'll cross that bridge when we come to it. The judge agreed that for us to go back to New Zealand to sign a bloody form was illegal under Article 8, our right to an uninterrupted family life. And oh, ridiculous! He said the Secretary of State made the wrong decision to deport us. We have our visas back. And, soon we'll get our passports back.'

'They fingerprinted me, Dad!' Jayne interrupts.

John takes his seat at the table and leans forward to listen to Jayne's explanations about the immigration process.

She chatters fast and loudly and each sentence is laced with wide-eyed wonder.

I hope she always remembers it as just a a big adventure.

'There was this woman crying in the corner,' she informs him as he nods patiently.

'She was really upset. I think they said she had to go home.'

Jayne was matter-of-fact; more interested in the story, than the emotion behind the day.

Maybe, she will get there.

'And a baby with only one sock who kept on disappearing', Sarah adds.

'The judge probably thought it was stupid', Alex chips in.

Meg sits back and listens, letting the kids have the floor. She has no energy left to contribute to the tale. She is done. She sits there beaming at her crazy, reconstituted family.

They are up-cycled people, a little beaten and scuffed about the edges but reshaped into something wonderful. And funny! Oh, so very funny.

Crazy, shiny, funny people.

After dinner they all walk back out onto Oxford Street to gaze at the Christmas lights. They ooh and ahh over stars shining in silver and gold and waterfalls of blue lights and more umbrellas and then hanging boxes of gift-wrapped presents. Further down the road there are huge oversized Christmas baubles shining in the store windows and hanging from invisible wires, large warm-white snowflakes.

Everything is magical and the streets are filled with Christmas shoppers each walking purposefully to the next shop, the next café, the next Tube station, ticking off a mental to-do list.

Meg beams at them all. Now, she is just like them.

She has a place here, too.

'Look love,' John taps her on the arm and points skywards to the fragile flakes that fall like confetti from the heavens.

'It's snowing.'

Everything made new.

Meg pulls him close and squeezes him hard and arm-in-arm they stand still, watching the snowflakes fall, listening to the kids shrieking with excitement.

'Snow day tomorrow! Wooohoo!' Alex whoops.

'I love you,' she whispers to John.

'You too,' he replies. 'All of you,' he motions to the kids around them, and then kisses her.

The kids roll their eyes and groan loudly.

'Hey, what did you mean by computer says no" John asks her.

'I meant that the court found that the Secretary of State, in her infinite wisdom, had the right to curtail my leave as I'd lost my work visa *but* they didn't have the right to require me to return to New Zealand to get a spousal visa.'

'So you don't need to go home?' John asks her gently.

'No. Not at all. But then, we're *here* with you. Where the heart is, and all that. *We are home.*' She gestures towards the kids, 'all of us.'

Wherever they were - these four - that was where she belonged. That was home. It wasn't bricks and mortar built, it was built with every challenge. It was earnt and learnt. Bound with laughs and adventures, sometimes stirred by loud arguments but all set rock-hard on a foundation of love. All that time she thought she was running away - and she had definitely been running, hard breaths and tears of frustration and the ache of the race across the world, from Auckland to

Paris, to Auckland, to Bottom Hedgeley, – she hadn't been running away at all.

She'd been running towards home.

'I'm absolutely knacked. Let's go home' she suggested. And so, they did.

The End

THE BEST PAVLOVA

Try this recipe from my friend UtterlyScrummy's blog. It's bound to help you appropriately celebrate the good times and commiserate the bad times. This recipe makes one pavlova 25cm/10 inches in diameter

220g/1cup caster sugar
2 tsp cornflour
1/4 tsp salt
1 tsp wine vinegar
1/2 tsp vanilla bean paste
3 large or 4 medium free range egg whites

I use my stand mixer to make a pav, sometimes I use my hand held electric beaters but find it much easier in the stand mixer. Make sure the bowl and beater are completely spotless because any trace of grease will stop the eggs from beating and aerating well.

Measure the caster sugar, cornflour, salt, vinegar and vanilla in to the bowl and then add the egg whites. Make sure there is absolutely no yolk at all in the mixture as this will stop the egg whites from beating up well.

Beat all the ingredients at high speed for about 15 minutes, until a thick meringue forms. Make sure the mixture is not gritty and that all the sugar has dissolved. When you lift out the beater blades, the meringue should form peaks that stand up stiffly.

Draw a circle 25cm/10 inches in diameter on a piece of non-stick baking paper large enough to line your oven tray. Turn the baking paper over and secure it to the tray using a little meringue dotted under each corner. Pile the mixture onto the circle on the baking paper and smooth the surface. If you have the time or inclination you could pipe the mixture into the circle.

Bake in a preheated oven at 100C/90C Fan for 60 - 70 minutes, then turn the oven off and leave the meringue in the oven for another half an hour. Take the pavlova out of the oven. Leave for an hour then top and fill as you wish.

Read more on.... utterlyscrummy.blogspot.com/

Vicki Jeffels has lived in four countries, both hemispheres and has travelled around the world only to end up back where she started, in Auckland, New Zealand.

She lives by the sea with her husband and youngest daughter, a crazy Lab puppy and two smart alec cats, and is visited frequently by her two adult children - most often when they need a good feed and a good yak.

Vicki has been writing commercially for over 27 years and has worked in Digital Marketing and PR for a number of well known global brands in New Zealand, Australia, and the United Kingdom. She has also worked in advertising, as a radio copywriter, and as a freelance writer.

Starting her blog in 2007 was her introduction into writing 'proper', telling stories about people not things. The blog has been very successful over the years, amassed a large following and received a number of awards for its entertaining storytelling about recycled families and expat family life.

Vicki has a droll sense of humour and loves travel, chocolate, food and wine. Preferably, all at once!

From Pavlova to Pork Pies is the first novel she's written *and published* and she is currently working on her second novel.

You can read more from Vicki on her websites or sign up to her newsletter via the links below.:

www.vegemitevix.com

www.writerscat.com

www.facebook.com/VickiJeffelsAuthor

ACKNOWLEDGEMENTS

It's surreal sitting here writing the acknowledgements as this book has taken over eight years to write and publish, and over that time so many people have helped, inspired, and supported me. If this book was a baby, all these people have been its amazing midwives!

First to Mark, Oliver, Hilary, and Felicity, thank you so much for allowing me to tell this story and to use some of our experiences. Mark, the gnashing of teeth and writer mardiness should stop now, or at least until I start writing the next book. But seriously, you are an absolute hero for 'taking on me and the kids'. Thank-you for all your love and support - I honestly couldn't have done it without you.

To Mum, Dad, Kim, Reub, Jo, Amelia, and Ally, thank-you for always supporting me even when you no doubt dispaired of me, at times. I said I'd publish a book...and hey, I did!

To Rob, Chris, Allan, Jane, Ros, Maf, Clare, Paul and so many other friends and family, thank-you for inspiring me.

To Sarah and Steve, Ellie and Harry, without you guys there wouldn't be a story (or marriage) to write about!

As you'll no doubt realise, no one character is written based on a person - they are all composites of people I've met over the years. Naturally, some names, dates, chracterisations, events and organisations, have been purposefully created expressly for this work of fiction.

To Sarah and Dan, thank you for your beautiful quiet home to write in.

To the orginal Vegemitevixens - Sabina, Rachael, Hannah, and Heather and my blogging friends - I am so grateful to you all for picking up this lost, displaced Kiwi and showing me the real England, full of spirit and laughter and fun. I don't think Reading will ever be quite the same again! I think it's highly telling that of the five of us, three of us are now published authors.

To Ros, Jill, Cheryl, Rebecca, thank you for showing me where to pick the elderberries, and where to find beautiful jewellery and candles, and for putting up with me when I was homesick and pouty. You provided friendship to a very prickly Kiwi who was going through an extraordinarily hard time, I'll never forget your kindness. Mi casa, tu casa.

Thank you Angela Lees for the magnificent cover, Cathy for pushing me over the edge ('just do it girl!') Katrina, Kim and Cara for reading and proofing, thank you all so very much. Mwah!

During my travelling years I've realised something quite remarkable - what we learnt as kids, by rote, is actually true.

Faith, hope, love, these three, will get you through. But oh, love...love is the greatest of all.

Vicki x